W9-ASM-001

ALSO BY ARTHUR A. COHEN

*Fiction*

Acts of Theft        (1980)
A Hero in His Time        (1976)
In the Days of Simon Stern        (1973)
The Carpenter Years        (1967)

*Nonfiction*

The Tremendum: A Theological Interpretation of the Holocaust
Osip Emilevich Mandelstam: An Essay in Antiphon
Sonia Delaunay
If Not Now, When?
*(with Mordecai M. Kaplan)*
A People Apart: Hasidic Life in America
*(with Philip Garvin)*
The Myth of the Judeo-Christian Tradition
The Natural and the Supernatural Jew
Martin Buber

*Editor*

The Jew: Essays from Buber's Journal *Der Jude*
The New Art of Color: The Writings of Robert & Sonia Delaunay
Arguments and Doctrines: A Reader of Jewish Thinking
in the Aftermath of the Holocaust
Humanistic Education and Western Civilization

# AN
# ADMIRABLE
# WOMAN

# AN
# ADMIRABLE
# WOMAN

A NOVEL BY

ARTHUR A. COHEN

DAVID R. GODINE · PUBLISHER · BOSTON

First published in 1983 by
David R. Godine, Publisher, Inc.
306 Dartmouth Street
Boston, Massachusetts  02116

Copyright © 1983 by Arthur A. Cohen

All rights reserved. No part of this book may be used or reproduced
in any manner whatsoever, except in the case of brief quotations
embodied in critical articles or reviews.

*Library of Congress Cataloging in Publication Data*

Cohen, Arthur Allen, 1928-
   An admirable woman.

   I. Title.
   PS3553.0418A66    1983      813'.54      82-49342
   ISBN 0-87923-474-1

Two small sections of *An Admirable Woman* were published in *Fiction* (Volume 6, Number 3) in 1981 under the title "Points of Origin: Where My Mind Comes From." Another section, "Uncle Salomon's Slap," appeared in *Forthcoming* (Volume 1, Number 1) during 1982. "A Last Word from Berlin" was published by *Present Tense* during August, 1983.

First edition

PRINTED IN THE UNITED STATES OF AMERICA

Characters and events in this novel may evoke reminiscences of real characters and events. Despite accidental resemblances, they are derived wholly from the imagination. Reality suggests, to be sure, but no reference to persons living or dead should be inferred.

# AN
# ADMIRABLE
# WOMAN

I am not wholly admirable.

I admit this without embarrassment, even though the Chancellor of my university, reporting what he had told his trustees when I was appointed, had said I was "wholly admirable." In this country hyperbole is a way of life. The truth is that in some respects I am admirable and for the rest quite unexceptional. But what was Dr. Brightman to tell his trustees? Only exaggeration seemed likely to carry the day. Nobody really wanted me appointed. I was an itinerant (some called me a vagabond) intellectual. Less openly, I know they muttered that I was a woman, a foreigner, possibly even a Jew, not really a historian, perhaps a sociologist, a philosopher without credentials; argumentative, impatient, proud (all of these); polemical, vain, sly (none of these). Most of all, they couldn't bear the fact that I was famous, that my books had achieved such notoriety as to be consistently misunderstood in the popular press, and that I had accomplished all this on my own, out in the cold, so to speak, without back-scratching and sycophantry. Most of all, they hated my fame, but this they wouldn't admit. And so finally they couldn't block me. The more they sniped, the more insignificant their objections became, until finally, with Dr. Brightman's proclamation of my unqualified excellence, their opposition collapsed and I was appointed.

Whatever my personality – its stubbornness, its pleasure in combat, its intolerance of stupidity – it is my *brain*, not my

3

personality, that is unconditionally admired. It is treated like an organ in formaldehyde, stripped of the animate life of affections and passions which, after all, charge the brain and impel its course. Those who would treat my brain as though it were not party to my passions lie about me more deeply than those who deny I have a brain at all.

It is for this reason more than for any other that I have written this memoir: to set straight from where I come and what my life has been. I am indifferent whether this account is credited with being whole truth or merely partisan rendition. There is enough I tell to make clear that I have suffered as much as I have achieved, but I refuse to elaborate these — the suffering or the achievement — more than is necessary for affectionate readers to recognize that understatement is a better warrant of authenticity than any amount of gnashing or thrashing.

# PART ONE

# EUROPE

I was late leaving Berlin. Not as late as others, but much too late for my kind of intellectual historian.

I began to pack on April 7, 1933, the day the boycott against the Jews was announced. Martens had returned from his café as he always did about five and had brought me the news. He passed his afternoons in the café, reading newspapers, holding his slides to the light, playing chess, and smiling at old friends whose words he was none too certain of being able to understand. He was growing more and more deaf. His deafness accelerated after Hindenburg's seven-year term of office expired in 1932. Hindenburg was then eighty-four. Martens, nineteen years older than myself, was forty-five. By then, he could hardly understand the radio which was always on in those days.

The announcement had come late in the day. The Reichskanzeler didn't make the announcement himself. Someone else spoke. Martens couldn't make out who it was. Goebbels? Rosenberg? Streicher? He had tried to concentrate on the voice, but admitted it was an indecipherable jumble of sound. (It was several years before I persuaded him to buy an aid. In those days a hearing device was a cumbersome apparatus and, since he no longer lectured at the University, he thought it unnecessary to hear. He read my lips; when I said something that particularly delighted him, he sometimes kissed me in gratitude – that gesture nearly brought me to tears the first time.)

When Martens came home, he told me there had been an

announcement on the radio. Arnold Grunstein, who owned a secondhand bookstore, had broken out in a sweat and nearly fainted when he heard it. I turned on the radio and caught the evening news. A gritty, mean voice was declaiming against the Jews. It was, I understood, the first formal move. The civil service and universities were to be cleansed. Starting the following day, Jewish shops were to be boycotted. Aryans were warned to pass by Jew-stores, to force them out of business, to break their stranglehold on the German economy. I repeated the words of the announcer. Martens read my lips. He looked at me with such pain. Martens was Aryan or rather Christian or more precisely the son of a railway conductor from the Ruhr; he had worked his way through University and, until the onset of his deafness following a botched mastoid operation, had lectured on the history of art. His specialty was the French rococo – Fragonard, Watteau, Chardin and the rest.

Before Martens disappeared into the kitchen to fix our tea, he motioned wearily to the telephone. He knew I would be calling my parents in Charlottenburg (where they lived in an ample bourgeois house) to interpret the day's news. I had gotten into the habit several months earlier. My father invited my reading of events. Invariably, our conversation began as history and ended with civics and patriotism. I would explain the news – the election campaigns, the street riots, the assassinations, the roving gangs of Nazis and Communists, the whys and wherefores of the hopelessly divided and cowardly center parties – and as my exegesis became more grim and relentless, father would begin to temporize, always ending with reassurances to himself that all would be well. "Germany is Germany, after all," he would conclude, as though that promised optimism.

Papa was a printer whose principal accomplishment was his design of a particularly elegant version of Unger's *Fraktur* that was much in demand for the wedding and funeral announcements of the rich, but he made his money, his not inconsiderable money, from printing advertisements and throwaways for department stores in Berlin, hundreds upon hundreds of thousands of flyers delivered in a fleet of vans identified by immense letters, *Hertz und Sohn, Druckerei*. Since papa's presses rolled at night, all the major stores in Berlin had their handbills by opening time in the morning. He was moderately successful and we were moderately rich.

The phone rang several times before papa answered. Mother was already crying. She cried very easily. Everything seemed to agitate her. It was all a conspiracy against her fragility. Papa, on the other hand, was enraged. He was trying to call someone in the Department of Labor to find out more. His workers were mostly Aryans; he didn't understand the boycott at all. He wouldn't let me explain. He asked that I ring off so his friend in the Department of Labor could get through to him after official hours. He told me he would call back. I left the radio on. Martens stayed in the kitchen fixing our tea. He hated my news conversations with my parents.

I had become a University *Dozent*, a rather low-level lecturer, two years earlier. Students sought me out and, when I had enough, I set up shop and taught. It was my turn to teach Heinrich Heine and Ludwig Börne. I didn't get much beyond my introductory lectures. Young Nazi students from the *Nationalsozialistischer Deutscher Studentenbund* were already picketing my classroom and a month later – on May 8th to be exact – I'd be dismissed. My last lecture would be delivered to an audience of two Jews.

I went into the bedroom. The suitcase we had used for a week's holiday at Travemünde a month before was still in the corner near the closet. I opened it and swept everything that stood on the night table near our bed into the suitcase: a travelling edition of St. Augustine that I had once had bound in limp blue morocco, my writing notebook, a hairbrush and a small Meissen dish covered with painted roses, where I put my hairpins every night. In those days I had long hair which I braided and wound about my head. "Erika's Gretchen-look," Martens called it.

The open suitcase wasn't closed, however, for another two years. Each time I had had enough, I added something to the suitcase, but somehow failed to close it. There was always an excuse, an evasion. Not the kind that generally prevailed. I had no illusions. Martens had many more. He kept trying to explain to me that it wouldn't last. I knew better. It was my body that delayed me. It took me months to recover from pneumonia. And after that sheer weariness held me up. I knew. I understood. How, you ask, when so many, so many others didn't know and understand? Don't think the study of history prepared me. (Anyone who thinks history *prepares* is a fool.) No. It wasn't my knowledge of history that warned me. Not even my admirable mind was that serviceable. The business of packing and flight was no intellectual conclusion.

I was more ready to leave – I now believe – because I had learned something when I was a young girl that I never forgot. And even that episode was not a lesson. It was a kind of theater, constructed and staged as such. And as theater, it mimed the rottenness in which our history consists.

During my childhood (before the house in Charlottenburg was built) my mother's uncle, his name was Salomon Klarsicht, lived with us in our apartment in Berlin.

Papa wasn't especially successful in those early days; he had yet to set his business on a solid basis and restricted himself to doing job printing of no particular distinction. He made a living; he employed workers; he delivered his orders once a week on a horse-drawn van he leased from a livery. He was, however, meticulously clean and upright; he wore a cutaway to the office which he removed when he arrived and replaced with a grey alpaca jacket. He was formal, grave, and estimably bourgeois. One would hardly have known he was a Jew. He seemed proud of that invisibility.

It is easy to understand why the arrival of my great-uncle Salomon unsettled him. Uncle Salomon had become religious. He was the only Jew in our family of whom it might be said that he was profoundly, even happily, Jewish. He came to live with us when I was four years old, that is in the fall of 1911, after the Jewish New Year was over. His wife of thirty years had died of a cerebral stroke and he was alone. They had had no children and uncle Salomon, a stamp dealer near the railway station, had modest needs. Uncle Salomon's room, down the hall from mine, was cleared of packing cases and old clothes and he moved in.

My mother found her uncle as unsettling as did my father. Uncle Salomon had turned religious after his wife's death. "Not a good reason," he would say, "but any reason for coming home is a good one." His name had been Guenther, but he rejected it when he came home to Judaism and began to use the Hebrew name he had been given at his circumcision. Uncle Salomon was quite alone; he was quiet, neat, trim, despite the assertiveness of his white beard and the black homburg he kept clapped to his head at all times except at home where he exchanged it for a small black cap. He renounced meat when he joined our household so that he could eat with relative impunity at our unobservant table, restricting his diet to bread, fruit, vegetables, and boiled eggs. He was circumspect around my parents, keeping his conversation to matters of general curiosity, never insisting that my parents join him in his custom nor criticizing them for their indifference to his observance.

To me, however, uncle Salomon was an endless delight, and I adored him. He presented me with a stamp album on my birthday and taught me geography by giving me each Sabbath a dozen or so stamps from various countries, attaching to each a history of its situation, climate, population and customs. His affection, however, was more than pedagogic – it was loving. He respected me even as a child; he bowed to me on occasion; he held doors open for me; he often took his cake from the table to his room, explaining to my parents with some embarrassment that he wished to eat it before bedtime and then, surreptitiously, after my lights had been extinguished, made his way to my room and presented it to me with a whispered "Sweet daughter." Once, several years after his arrival, he discovered me examining by flashlight a map book beneath my blankets. He lay down beside me, conspiratorily joining my cause by holding the flashlight, and we did Melanesia and Micronesia together, his white beard, redolent with pipe tobacco, lying like a recumbent beast upon my chest.

It came time for me to go to school. It was agreed at the last minute that great-uncle Salomon would accompany me to the schoolyard, as mother claimed to be busy and papa had already left for his printing works. I was by then nearly seven. I had been to kindergarten; I had mastered the alphabet and could read simple books. I was desperate for the arrival of real school. It would – I believed – mark my freedom, my going forth among the people of the world, away from my home, away from papa reading with his pince-nez and mother silently cutting grapes with silver scissors.

Uncle Salomon dressed very carefully that morning, his neat black suit set off by a white shirt he saved for Sabbaths; a four-in-hand, correctly tied, fluttered at his neck in the early morning breeze. His homburg was set upon his head and he had combed out his beard until the white strands seemed separate and distinct in the Assyrian manner. He was ready at exactly seven o'clock and, after a hurried coffee and toast, he took my hand, receiving last instructions from my mother who kissed me on my head and pushed me off with an insistent hand, as though she were launching a toy boat. We walked along the street, my left hand held firmly by uncle Salomon, my right hand clutching a satchel in which empty pads and sharpened pencils lay ready. We passed a small park and instead of continuing a circuit about its iron fence, uncle Salomon directed me to a bench inside and seated me. He turned to me, his face drained and weary, and with an open palm quickly raised, slapped my face. It hurt and it did not hurt. It was a horror to me. That was all. It was a horror. He said sadly: "You go out among *them* for the first time. Never forget, child, what you are: *you are a Jew*. A sudden slap is not the worst that *they* can do."

I never forgave uncle Salomon for that lesson. On the other hand, I never told my parents about it either. I did not understand then what he meant. Years later (now as I write this), I understand almost everything of what he did that morning. Only the slap itself remains incomprehensible.

Uncle Salomon lived to be more than eighty. He died in a nursing home near Berlin in 1937. His veins had been injected with air.


Beloved uncle Salomon. To you who were eighty-three and murdered. How much you taught me with that slap. I have known teachers who used their leather belts. Enforcers, now reinforcers; once simply punishers, now psychologists. But you, dear old man, were neither. You didn't slap *me*; you slapped your niece and her husband. We both knew how they ridiculed your *kashrus*, making sly reference in front of guests to your vegetarian habit. They refused to wait quietly until you said your prayer at meal's end, instead bolting to the library for coffee and leaving me to watch your lips move. And on Sabbaths, how they sometimes left you in the dark when you couldn't ask for light.

Oh dearest uncle, how I delighted in being your Sabbath handmaid. I knew nothing about it, but it gave me secret pleasure to turn on your nightlight Friday evenings in the winter when darkness came early and walk with you to Synagogue where the old men gave me candy and patted my head. "This is my daughter," you announced proudly. And we all let you say this without correction. The old men knew you had no daughter and, as for me, I was delighted you loved me so well you claimed me for your own. It isn't hard to understand why I loved you. You had no duty to love and care for me and yet you did, willingly and wonderfully. And when mother and papa went for their walks on Sunday, leaving me behind, you invited me to your room and told me stories. It made their indifference less painful. We were both outsiders in their home and we came together for warmth. And then you slapped me. Isn't it true, uncle Salomon, that you were warning me not to be like them, not to forget as they had forgotten? Not only that. You had had terrible experiences in your stamp shop. Commercial travellers insulted you and once a porter heaved a rock through your window and shouted obscenities at you. What kind of obscenities? I asked. "Jewish swindler," mother answered, smiling complacently. I didn't know what that was but I remember running to you, seizing your arm, and shouting, "He isn't! He isn't! He's uncle Salomon."

The slap hurt, truly hurt, uncle Salomon, but your large, warm slapping hand was the same hand that had stroked my cheeks and pushed back my hair. The words without the slap would have meant little. And you would never have slapped me without giving a reason.

Did you imagine that you would be murdered? No. Certainly
not. You had no idea. But finally, it didn't surprise you. You
once observed to me that the most powerful and aggressive
postage stamps used black and red. And so it was. But mother
and papa? They never understood. They refused to be slapped.
If slapped, they never felt it. They temporized or became enraged. And so it was. Having understood that they would never
learn, you taught me instead – and young, impressionable, a
*tabula rasa* desperate for print, I received your hand upon my
cheek – your negative impression – and printing it black on the
white page of my books, I have devoted a lifetime to clarifying
your handprint, to making comprehensible your panic before
Gentiles and the Gentiles' fear of Jews.


My evasions, my reluctance to close the suitcase, in a word,
to flee the land of my birth, had much more to do with sentiment;
my illness was the excuse, but sentiment was its innocence.
Every time a new measure was announced or when I was informed of my dismissal from the University or papa was insulted
by one of his employees, I vowed to leave immediately. But
then, I would see some friend whom I loved or some artist whom
I admired, and I would begin to undermine my resolution. If
they stayed put, if they remained my friends, if they continued
to do their work, I found myself wavering, denying the evidence
upon which my mind had already passed judgment.


I have no clear idea what moved me towards the mind.
    One doesn't resolve upon such things, any more than one sets
one's course upon truth or virtue. It's not that they simply
happen. Obviously, there are causes and conditions. But it is
not like learning to be a craftsman or a mechanic. Not merely

a skill. The intellectual disciplines are condensations of vital curiosity. Over the years fascination, reverence, wonder, delight set forth in search of their subject-matter.

In my case, I was certain early that survival meant hiding away – under the covers with uncle Salomon or behind a book. I couldn't bear scrutinizing the proprieties that surrounded me – trying to figure out what papa thought behind his twitching moustache and mother felt behind her powdered face. In my house everything was just so; nothing was moved, nothing out of order. Mother entered a room and knew instantly if a vase had been shifted an inch; it was immediately restored to its correct diameter. She couldn't put her hand down on any surface without examining her palm for dust. And papa always hung up his coat on the second peg, always put his umbrella in the brass container in the vestibule, always changed his shoes in the foyer, always napped an hour before dinner. My childhood was spent navigating the shoals of settled fixities and arrangements.

Not unusually, my only refuge was in books. For some reason my parents encouraged this appetite. Had they known how subversive it was, they would have denied me, no differently than they punished me for breaking rules by prohibiting nougats and cakes. (I am certain that if they had restricted my reading, I would have fallen apart.) But on the contrary, I was encouraged to bring home books from my school and to borrow from the library of Herr Kastner, our bachelor neighbor who spent each summer travelling in the Mediterranean assisting archaeologists in their field work. And through Herr Kastner I met other libraries and over the years plundered them. I kept lists of what I read. Now all lost. My best year was my tenth. I read three hundred and sixty-five books. It was a year of recurrent illness.

When I realized in early April that I had passed one hundred, I determined to remain ill as long as I could. I wanted to set a record. Unfortunately, I have no recollection of what I read that year. I suspect tales and ancient myths and books of travel (and I probably cheated, counting each tale or myth as a proper book). Later, I discovered illustrated histories, fat volumes with magnificent plates. I devoured them no less voraciously, but the annual number of my conquests declined considerably.

But for influences? Persons who shaped my vision of the future? Teachers, prodigious authors, public figures, family? None besides uncle Salomon, unless of course I mention Mira Freybush, my violin teacher.

Mother found Mira when I was eight years old. Aunt Mira, as I insisted upon calling her (she had somehow to be inducted into my family), was playing violin in the show window of a music store in Charlottenburg when mother passed by. She was playing a Bach partita. Mother thought her fingering exquisite. Since mother knew nothing about violin, I suspect that it was Mira's fingers – not her fingering – that dazzled her. They were what mother called "expressive," that is to say long and tapered, their advantage to Mira being less in her playing than in her employment of them as aids to mark thought and the imminent arrival of some momentous pronouncement upon literature and life.

As my mother told it, she had stopped to listen and then, when Mira finished playing, had signalled to her. Aunt Mira agreed to teach me, although she admitted she had never before given instruction. "I am not, you see, Madame, violinist. I am revolutionary. I am anarchist." Mother was appalled by the confession, but she was obeying papa's injunction more strictly than heeding her own anxieties about hiring a self-confessed revolutionary. Papa had demanded that I learn an instrument. Since he had played violin as a youth and my brother Adam was not alive to assume the mimetic burden, it fell to me. The evening of her discovery of Mira, I heard mother explain to papa that she had found a violin teacher who, though distinctly odd and unconventional, was a splendid musician. They both agreed that since I was only eight it was hardly likely I would be influenced by more than her music. (Of course! Typical! Mother thought an eight-year-old's mind shallow. She was correct, no doubt, in that a young riverbed is shallow if left unflooded, but the steady beating of a torrential stream will mark it forever. Mira was a torrential stream in my childhood.)

I was delivered to Mira at the music shop late in the afternoon the following day. A secondhand violin was rented with the understanding that if my lessons continued beyond a year, the rental fee could be applied against purchase of my own instrument. I admit to loving my violin – its dark brown, glistening surface, its molded chin rest and deftly carved apertures. I thought of it as a creature and named it "Mouse." When I was eight I spoke with "Mouse," soothing its screeches of pain, congratulating it upon an occasional sweet note.

It was arranged that I would meet Mira twice a week at the music shop and after tea and cakes (which aunt Mira insisted upon at the conclusion of her three-hour window demonstration), she would take me to her apartment and teach. Mother had insisted that our lessons should be at Mira's rather than in my room at home. She thought my practicing racket enough without having to cope as well with Mira's execrable German and incessant cigarette smoking.

It is clear to me that no sooner had Mira become my teacher than she became as well – alongside uncle Salomon – my instructor in life. The violin was only one aspect of her necessary environment. The others were black tobacco which she deftly rolled into long cigarettes and smoked through a carved ivory holder ("it was made in faraway Peking," she confided), strong tea with currant jam, black bread and salt butter, pamphlets of Bakunin and Kropotkin, and books by Pushkin, Lermontov, Tyutychev, which she plucked from her vast leather purse and began to intone, occasionally interrupting her Russian declamation to translate into a German that beat my face like ocean spume, rarely leaving on the beach of my memory the trace of a comprehensible phrase. (Ah, aunt Mira. I called to say goodbye to you when Martens and I left Berlin. You were not at home. I have no idea if you ever came home again. Our letters to you were never answered. Of final resting places, I am unhappily more certain.)

The first afternoon, when Mira finished reciting a short love lyric of Pushkin, she burst out crying and announced to me: "No revolution without poetry."

If I understood her well, Mira Freybush had fled Kiev where her father had been a factory worker and come to Berlin two years earlier, just before the outbreak of the war. "I was an agitator," she told me. I soon realized that what she meant was that she played violin solos at illicit gatherings of young revolutionaries. She had no rhetorical gifts nor talent for organization. Her subversiveness consisted in neither of these, but only in the world of feeling which – so unlike my German countrymen – bubbled like an underground geyser ready at any moment to stream up and scald the world.

It delighted Mira that she was an alien – indeed, Mira was the first person I ever met who loved being out of place, uprooted, in exile. She loved reporting to the police (who required it not because she was a revolutionary, but rather because Germany was at war with the Tsar), thinking it somehow daring and remarkable to be a dubious, vaguely alarming person. My mother didn't like it at all that Mira went to the police regularly; she couldn't help fantasizing that Mira's crimes were more severe than being an alien. It was only when papa made formal inquiries and discovered her fears were groundless that my violin lessons won a reprieve.

I had thought foolishly – but I was only eight – that playing the violin was a technical achievement, mastered with deft fingers and sight reading. Aunt Mira quickly set me straight. What was required in aunt Mira's pedagogy became clear to me during the third lesson. I was having, I remember, considerable difficulty manipulating the bow into a position which would yield the note marked in the exercise book. I knitted my brow and frowned, bit my lip with annoyance and pinched the bow like a disobedient child. Mira, puffing, puffing, jumped up from the sofa and put a hand over my face, wiping it as if to wipe away my irritation. "*Kind,*" she shouted at me, "no music without lofty thoughts." I did not understand immediately, but over the months it became clearer. Each lesson actually began at tea with a poem and concluded with a Russian proverb. For Mira, making music was no different than conducting life. It had to be done at the highest level and with exaggerated gravity.

Unfortunately, just as I was beginning to get the hang of it during the ninth month of instruction, I began to sneeze violently whenever I entered Mira's apartment. My eyes reddened, my nose ran, and I sneezed and sneezed. The family doctor placed the blame on Mira's black tobacco. I had apparently developed an uncontrollable allergy. It became a choice: stop smoking, aunt Mira, or stop violin lessons. Aunt Mira was adamant. Black tobacco was part of her life, part of her revolutionary equipment, coupled inseparably to poetry, linked indissolubly to music.

I returned my rented violin. It was the end of my instruction.

Many years later, I was attending a political meeting in the Prenzlauer Berg, the worker's quarter in which I had taken up residence after leaving home. I had gone to hear Erich Mühsam speak. Before the meeting began, a middle-aged woman dressed in peasant skirts and wearing a high-necked Russian blouse entertained the audience, playing Russian folk songs on the violin. It was Mira Freybush. We had tea after the meeting. She no longer carried Pushkin. Her German was still hopeless, but now she quoted Herzfelde and Tucholsky along with Pasternak and Mayakovsky. I explained to her what I was doing, that I was at university reading French and German political philosophy, that I knew Greek and Latin, and for pleasure studied classical philosophy and literature.

"Oy, *Kind*, you please aunt Mira so much. *Now* you should study violin. Such lofty thoughts, such lofty thoughts!"


And so, if there was no model after whom I followed and no career of fact or fiction after which I determined to pattern myself, how does it happen that I became an intellectual historian, that is, one who examines the layering of ideas the way Herr Kastner described the archaeological strata of Carthage? I don't know, and it interests me only mildly to inquire. Curious, my indifference on this point. About everyone else's history I am immensely concerned, but about my own, not at all. My origins are uninteresting, my parents unexceptional, the artifacts of my home undistinguished. And yet, perhaps all of these are to the point. Of one thing I am certain: early, very early, even before uncle Salomon's slap, I sensed that I had to put distance between myself and my family. At first only recalcitrance and uncooperation, truculence and sour silence; later, books which I would raise higher and higher in front of my face as the calls for me from below became more insistent; and finally, stubborn words which claimed for my world and its privacy a prior right, a privilege of aloofness, an untrespassable space which, at the price of longing for intimacy and camaraderie, bought me time.

I became an intellectual less because I was certain and confident than because I was harrassed and confused. I wanted so to understand and accept what my parents deemed paramount – good reputation, honor, obligation and duty, all the virtues of public *Deutschtum* – and yet I was prevented from pursuing those virtues because of my growing conviction that all they supplied was superficial good will, self-restraint, the illusion of righteousness, and a specious sense of comfort and security. For all their decency, for all their conventional loyalty and unexceptionable good manners, my parents never enjoyed acceptance by their Gentile neighbors. When they took their walks, hats went off, ladies nodded their heads – but rarely in my parents' direction unless, obliged by the necessity of crossing the same puddle at the same instant, a polite word was exchanged, a civil courtesy extended. It wasn't, I believe, that all Gentiles disliked all Jews. That conclusion requires too much abstraction. No. It was rather that these odd creatures – these Jews – seemed to pass in and out of the Gentiles' world like shadows or clouds, indistinguishable from them, as bland and transparent as shadows and clouds; but nonetheless something about them – their odd names, their furtive look, their uncomfortable demeanor, their excessive punctiliousness – indicated that they were trying too hard, harder than their Gentile neighbors, and this innuendo of excess made the bourgeois Gentiles deeply nervous. At least this is the way it appeared to me when I was a girl in Charlottenburg, where there were many Jews but many more Gentiles.

Whatever an intellectual historian may be and whatever an intellectual historian may do, the enterprise – like all others – begins modestly in setting the way to stay alive. I can assure you, from the vantage point of this telling, two years beyond my seventieth birthday and four thousand miles from the house in Charlottenburg where I passed my youth, my discipline of history — the history of human ideas, the grandeur and misery of meager intelligence treading water in the flood of events — has proved to be less a rationalization than a kind of salvation.

I spoke earlier about my admirable brain.

But brains are such a delicacy, lightly sautéed in butter and flavored with capers. I have never been able to eat them. It took me some time to manage other vital organs such as kidneys, tripe, sweetbreads, but I succeeded. French cuisine has a way of converting the fastidious. But brains were brains. Among calves, my calf might have been a genius. It wouldn't do to eat the organ even of calf-like intelligence. And certainly not by one such as myself whose distinctive gift of analysis has been concerned with analogues and resemblances.

Scruples and self-mockery to one side, the confessional truth is that I admire my brain, although I wish sometimes my brain were as slender and sensual as my legs. I wish I could make my brain shimmer in silk stockings; I wish I could display my brain in elegant black pumps with bow tie laces. I wish my friends could say of my brain what they were only too willing to say of my legs.

Even now, in my early seventies, I apply lipstick and think of something else, the morning letters, the last visitor or the one about to arrive for whom (man or woman) I sit down to what I still prefer to call my "vanity," and put on my face. I think of other things for I don't find my face wholly admirable. It commands attention, but it is not wholly admirable.

Do men examine their faces when shaving as closely as I do when I powder mine? Martens cut himself frequently. I suspect he was not looking at his face. He was always doing something other than what he should — attending to regions beyond the altitude of face or the latitude of the bathroom mirror. He nic

himself continually, usually the lobes of his ears which had
come to offend him for their fractious refusal to hear (he per-
sonalized everything, or rather he endowed everything with soul
and hence willful contrariness). But I have looked at mine and
looked through mine to my brain and the moment I make contact
with that alive, vital organ and thought begins, impressions come
leaping; I forget I am before the mirror to put on lipstick and
begin to think of other things, sometimes putting my hands in
my lap and giving up the enterprise of face-making, surrendering
myself to an association, permitting it to lead me where its
wayward logic requires, to triumphant connection or to disorder,
and only after a time (when Martens was still alive and called
or later when I heard the phone ring or the kettle hum or a
neighbor coughing in the hallway) am I recalled to the insistent
work of making my face into something I might find wearable
and bearable, even if not admirable.

My mother never helped me with my face. I think it terribly
important for little girls to be told that they are pretty. "Pretty
Erika." Had my mother said this once or twice in the midst of
my childhood it would have carried me further than all my
teachers' praise or all my father's proud approvals of report
cards, marking each with a personal stamp of recognition,
signing it with the sententious phrase "Reviewed by Gustav
Hertz, January 11, 1917" and returning it to me to hand
back to teacher. For what reason? Praise of face, joy of
grace, that's more to the point. Instead. Quite the contrary. A
little girl was stolen from her carriage in Frankfurt and found
some days later butchered in a market garbage heap. The newspaper headlines could not be missed. I saw them and was
terrified. I couldn't sleep for days. At last I asked my mother
whether Erika could be stolen. She replied, laughing, beautiful grey eyes, soft as a doe's, suddenly sparkling, "Never,
dear child. One look at you under the lamp light and they

would beg us to take you home to bed." I was relieved, but I was horrified. It was safe to be ugly, but I found ugliness a subtle disgrace and although I knew that it was my lot to bear alone I sensed in my parents a remorse, as if to acknowledge that with all their good looks they had failed with their only Erika.

Face masks are not simply curtains of separation which, like the dressing rooms of actresses, allow them – hidden away – to change over from, say, Desdemona to Medea. The ancients put on carved or molded faces in order to take part in the sacred festival – to act in the play, or step lightly in the dance, to be gods or heroes, to mime the eternities, to exhibit and educate in civilized cultures (Athens or Rome, to the extent that they were civilized) and in brutal Mexico and brutal British Columbia to frighten and terrify, reaching down into the earth or plucking from the skies, eating grubs or tearing birds apart in order to demonstrate that the living human is no separate (much less higher) creature, but only a specialization in the humming continuum from animal to man to divinity.

But I, you see, was part of no grand ritual. So I thought then, as a child. I was indifferent to the rhythms of the universe, the importunings and imprecations adults wring from nature. So I thought then, as a child. I was mistaken. I imagined that my singleminded and devoted efforts to strip from myself the skins my parents had layered upon me had no relation to the ancient function of the mask. As usual – when it came to forming judgments of my family and its history – I was mistaken.

I arose in the morning and decided which face I would wear throughout the day. If I had slept well, undisturbed by acid dreams and stomach groanings, if I jumped from my bed and ran to the window to see my red squirrel sitting before its garden hole, if the first thing I did was smile, I would set my face to guard my contentment before the world (making myself invulnerable to disillusion and dismay) by covering myself with such a lugubrious mask of sadness one would never guess how untroubled and delicious I felt. Or if truly at ease and unconscious, I allowed myself a shy smile or set my barrette less severely in my hair to suggest a kind of innocence and careless indifference. But I was already hardened up inside, ready for the onslaught that might come – from papa saying, "What have you got to smile about so early in the day?" to my classroom teacher ordering me to fix my sloppy barrette.

Only rarely does one meet a person whose face announces precisely the truth she believes. That person may nonetheless be a fool, but there is little doubt we have no difficulty identifying who she is and what she feels. We know instantly where she fits in the universe: she is reliable, she is present, she is there as completely as her face. (It was the case with Martens. Which explains something of my love for him.)


In my blue terry cloth robe I sit before the bathroom mirror. I light a cigarette and put it in the saucer beside my steaming coffee. I am looking at my morning reflection and wondering at such a long and intimate possession as a face. A face of seventy-two years, and still unreconciled to the admirableness of its brain. I can fabulate my face as many do, but I have more projects for the imagination than that. If not fable, simple narration will do.

*Forehead*: sheer like shale, hardly enough to catch a minuscule creature should it tumble to its death from my hairline.

*Eyes*: taken by themselves, in abstraction from the face, even in abstraction from eye sockets, my eyes – like children's marbles – have a kind of majesty, although they are green or, more precisely, green hued by an underwater growth of algae and plant life and, therefore, brownish-green or brackish-green.

I refer to eyebrows and eyelids. My eyes are fairly deep-set. My plucked eyebrows curve like a beige thread. Beginning almost near my scalp, they turn upwards and then descend. They are gracious, and I can raise either of them by manipulating my facial muscles (something I learned as a little girl observing my mother watching the maid scrubbing the kitchen tiles – how I wanted to raise my eyebrows like mother and criticize; I set myself the task and learned before I was twelve, but it was years before I had anything to turn this skill upon – until then I contented myself with raising my left and then my right eyebrow, making sure I was in practice and wouldn't forget how).

*Eyelids*: like white shells, very white, very pale, very thin, like calciferous vellum, although now I have a brown spot on my right eyelid.

I sometimes close my eyes when I am forcing myself to listen.

*Cheeks and Cheekbones*: high, pronounced and somewhat disagreeable in context.

Face, after all, is all context. My face is too oval, like a freshly baked bread, too overall (and nothing merely "overall" can be authentically harmonious). My face defies harmony because it is too large and overall, which means only that the items of face are set into the dough like raisins or almonds or scooped out like a Halloween pumpkin (which I first recognized as an analogue of face, *my face*, when I came to the United States).

*Nose*: if Descartes made the mistake of thinking that the pineal gland was the operative center of the affections, the missing link between soul and intelligence, I nominate instead my nose. My nose is triumphantly and explicitly the bearer of my message. It declares me to be someone, a personage.

It is, objectively speaking, ghastly. It is an object and has

been discussed as an object, derisively described as an appen-
dage, a third hand, capable of grasping and powerful enough
to hold on. It has been referred to as a Jew-nose, but that is
familiar talk, since anything that sticks to a Jew is called Jewish
and all noses – fat, thin, cracked, humped, pendulous, sensual,
biteable – can be called "Jew-nose" if one dislikes Jews.

My nose-object is exaggerated in length but not bulk; it is
svelte like my legs when considered from the side, although
interrupted by a break which resembles more the Marquis de
Sade than the founding Rothschild.

*Mouth*: should not mouths change radically over the years,
change as they have been used, large mouths shrinking or thin-
ning, small mouths growing with their capacity to speak? But
that would be more like the medievals thinking the purpose of
the Seine was to provide fresh water to the denizens of Paris.
It is fantasy finding voice; revealing something about the fan-
tasist and little more. Think from this that I would have my
mouth turned into a tuning fork, for this is what my mind was
called on the occasion of the festivities which burgeoned and
receded when I passed my seventieth year. But that would be
to honor my mind and not my mouth. No. My fantasy of enlargement and diminishment is more by way of reproof than
celebration. I would, you see, wish that I had kept silent more
of the time. Too often I spoke up and out came folly. Martens
commented acidly several times, using his new-found capacity
for multilingual punning, "*Kwatsch* as *Kwatsch* can." He was
telling me to shut up. I usually resisted outrage until he was
out of the room and couldn't read me.

*Hair*: the last in iteration, but first, foremost in the panoply
of my equipment.

I have – all say it and I hear their celebration – marvelous
hair. Why so? It is almost coarse; it can be gathered in a fist
and held like sheavings of wheat, or braided in my youth and

wound about my head like innocent tresses, allowing me to move through the world of German schoolgirls almost hidden and unnoticed. I adored my hair although I suspected its deception. Anything my parents admired about me I came to mistrust. I understood that if they remarked about my hair or my mischievous nose (they did, in fact, chuckle nervously when they observed my cartilaginous nose bending in a wind and used to say of it, "Wipe your mischievous nose, child") or my habit of pointing my long index finger at something remarkable, they did not intend praise or delight in me, but rather a begrudging irritation that it was I, rather than my dead brother, who seemed so dubiously endowed.

I had, however, glorious hair, full, rich, an immense head of hair, a whole field of auburn hair, reddish-brown like the trees of the Hudson Valley that Martens and I visited during October, the year of our arrival in the United States. There was nothing memorable about that visit except the sight of a hundred miles of my hair hugging the hillsides around us (there was no job, it turned out, at the college that had invited us to visit).

In my childhood, mother brushed my hair in the morning while I dressed, following me about the room with a hairbrush and combing out the knots. The ritual of hair forced me from bed earlier than other children, but in those credulous years I believed that it was mother's love for me that obliged her to call, "Up, up, little one. It's hair time for the little one," and I would turn over, pressing my face into the pillow while mother began to brush me out, slowly, languorously, with an even gesture that made my whole body tremble with the pleasure of what I took to be her love.

Only later, when I came to think about those early years of hair brushing, did I understand the rumble of discord in her affection. A voice from below would call upstairs, "Leave off, *Liebchen*, leave off. It's time for morning coffee." Papa had called from the dining room; the slow hand would gather speed, knots would be wrenched free, my scalp would smart, and at the end I always began to cry.

I stopped braiding my hair and refused my mother's brush its tyranny; I combed out my hair myself, parting it so that at liberty it would fall over my left eye, to be held in place with an antique barrette or else pushed to the side behind my ear with my notorious index finger.

My hair aroused jealousy – "But Erika dear, your hair is glorious" (Martens when I spoke ill of my face); "Who has such auburn hair?" (papa trying to make up for one of his spasms of irritation); "Your father thinks your hair a festive show of lights" (my mother praising me through my father, killing two birds with one stone) – but jealousy may, as in this case, confirm assurance. I have spent my life, even to my seventy-second year, certain in the knowledge that my auburn hair was a ravishment swirling about my head like the glitter of rubies. It has been no shattering of knowledge to see my hair each morning in the mirror, almost completely grey, what remains of red glinting pallidly, grey coming like the winter of my age, covering everything that I had known in that long ago springtime when I still believed that mothers brushed and braided me in love and fathers only wanted their morning coffee.

My lips are painted and I am done another day with this agony of disagreement.

(My teeth are white and even; my chin is fleshy and without distinction.)


Despite the evidence of my father's vans, there was no *Sohn* born to Gustav Hertz and his wife Siegelinde. Or to be more accurate, that aborted foetus, inverted and blown out the trumpet horn of my mother's womb in the sixth month, was for some reason given the name Adam and buried. He was the first and last *Sohn* my father had and early on, obscurely at first, papa held that foetus against me. Not me, precisely, but my brain, as you will understand.

I came into this world on October 25th, 1907, in the midst of that era graciously designated as Wilhelmine, to signify the triumph of broad avenues, monumental architecture, public gardens, white dresses and parasols, red stripes on grey trousers, bespurred jodhpur boots, pomaded mustachios, and unspeakable emptiness. The Berlin of my childhood seemed invented to supply the imagination of the bourgeoisie with everything from immense cream puffs to endless military parades.

I deeply resented my brother his premature death. He would have borne the outrage of growing up in Wilhelmine Germany. Had he lived, all would have fallen to him, indeed upon him. My birth would have passed virtually unnoticed. Girls could be piteously ignored; for those without energy and imagination, mediocrity was destiny. But for the few with gifts the options were considerable, if one possessed stealth and cunning. The art was in concealment, and I quickly mastered the art. Unfortunately, I was the sole repository of my parents' confusion. They were never certain to which gender they wished me confined, for at the same time that they demanded I be an inconspicuous girl, they allowed my mind to press forward as though it inhabited the body of a boy for whom the real world had been created. I learned to take over for myself the advantages that were reserved for dead Adam, and to shelter myself with the blushing cheeks and coiled braids that marked out the prescribed manners of little girls.

If there is any doubt, I did not like my parents. I loved them in that extraordinary and incomprehensible manner that has only lately come to be understood. I loved them for they could not be avoided. I needed them; I required them; I lived upon them;

for those reasons love, that bubbling seepage of emotion, showed itself in unjustified enthusiasm for their approval and concession. Only later, when I had come to stand upon a social soil they had neither inhabited nor domesticated, did I begin to understand my love as something fictitious and ungenuine. I loved them as the immensities from which I had emerged, my welter, my nest of snakes, my cauldron, but not the hearth and home of my affections. I loved them. I scarcely liked them.

My parents, you see, were exemplary bourgeois.

The notion of the bourgeoisie, although it is used by Americans anxious to exhibit their international fluency, is generally misconstrued by my new compatriots. The bourgeoisie is not marked by mere habituation to *luxe* and product, inurement to ease, and mindless exuberance for fashion. These are specifically American contributions to the hard crust of bourgeois essence. No. Not at all. Smugness, self-righteousness, innate conservativeness – those normal tendrils of the bourgeois plant – are, of course, elements of the sensibility, but the bourgeoisie of which I speak (which my parents exhibited like a proud order whose sponsoring saint was no longer mentioned) derives differently from that which emerged in America after its Civil War and industrialization.

The bourgeoisie of Europe, of Germany specifically, sinks its roots into a patrician past which is pre-industrial. Its true origins are in the soil, the soil of Prussia and the Rhine, where peasants turned another's earth, held their tongues, and surrendered the privilege of feeling to the aristocracy. All German literature before Goethe is the desperate enterprise of finding (and failing to find) a voice for true feeling, albeit dissimulated in the language of nymphs and wood faeries that abound during its baroque era. And after Goethe, the effort has been to recover from Goethe.

Goethe made the bourgeoisie a holy cause, supplied it with

a ready fund of wisdom, apothecary jars labelled Art, Nature, Truth, and appropriate alembics in which they might be mixed for ready cosmology, ready naturalism, ready metaphysics, anything and everything that a young culture needed to set itself on the fast road to civilization.

My parents had everyone's complete works in standard editions; moreover, they read them like the Bible. Every evening before supper, papa would give us a sample of Goethe, Schiller, Lessing, Herder, sometimes Jean Paul, Fontane, Kotzebue and Hauptmann. The gang, in short. Heine, oddly, he discovered late in life, almost before it was too late, and Hölderlin, never. And no philosophers.

Jewish reading was on Friday night. Why? I could never fathom, although once I asked papa why he bothered to read Jewish books aloud since he had no interest in religious ceremonies or observances, hardly participated in Jewish civic events and, excepting a brief visit to the Reform temple once a year to say memorial prayers for his parents, paid as little attention as possible to the fact that he, his wife, his daughter were Jewish. His answer was that "it is fitting that we should know from where we come." As a child, I thought being Jewish was travelling equipment, like tickets and luggage, since knowing from where one comes implies that the travelling goes on and that the journey is never over.

Papa read us Heinrich Graetz's *History of the Jews*. It was many volumes and took many years to complete. He read for half an hour before Friday evening dinner. Mother lit candles which were placed in a silver candelabrum on the table; however, since she did not cover her head, or close her eyes, or say any blessing over the illumination, I understood that these candles, like papa's reading, were gestures whose meaning had been forgotten long ago − like those Spanish Catholics who observe curious rites that only now can be understood to be the remains of rituals they had conducted centuries earlier when they were practicing Jews. By the time papa had completed his reading of Graetz some ten years after he had begun, mother had stopped listening, papa himself mumbled and rushed to complete the tedious obeisance, and I had discovered that Graetz and I violently disagreed and that I was probably right. There had to be something more in the waters of Israel than Christian salt and Jewish tears. What can I think about Adam, my non-brother, my incomplete antithesis, my doppelgänger, who survives not as apparition, but as lesson and instruction? Adam, dear brother, how cruelly you were used against me, you who had no life, no distinctiveness, no personality of your own. You, like all ruined foetuses, were nothing but expectation and dream. But what a powerful weapon you became, precisely because you were nothing. Nothing, you were everything I did not become and did not choose to be. Sometimes, in a rage, papa would pounce: "Adam would behave differently." I had to stop my weeping to remember who Adam was. And mother, no less tormentingly: "Adam's hair would never knot like this. Boys' hair is so easy" and again, mystified, I would wonder about this perfect child who never existed.

Clearly, then, I was no *Sohn*. My difficulty was that I discovered no less definitively that I was no daughter. I was something that resisted parents. I had no dreams of being an orphan, no fantasy of being found by accident, a changeling, a lost child of royalty; I never speculated discovering my real parents. The inquiry, even then, was not conventional. I imagined not parents but origins, my descent (less from the womb than) through the tunnel of time.

My mother admired music. My father required that I take violin lessons. My mother called for me to leave for Mira Freybush. I didn't hear her. My father announced I would enjoy a puppet show set up in the square. I didn't hear him. Both called out to me. "Erika, daughter." Habitual speech, as though trying to assure me of an identity of which even they were in doubt. But the one contradicted the other. As daughter, I was their possession, but as Erika Margaret Hertz, I was someone else. They named me, but they settled that name upon a bundle of indeterminacy that already at birth was distinct and separate. It was for me and only for me to decide what an Erika Margaret in fact signified.

When their voices called to me or the maid came to inform me that they were calling, or my old nurse, Swabian Teresa, who spoke to me in dialect, solemnly repeating, "Erika, daughter" – imitating her employers with a sneaky smile – I put away my books and finally, at last, appeared with my violin or my patent leather going-out-among-the-people child's purse. But I did not fake. I refused a smile of gratitude. I never settled for a pout of irritation. I was blank. I was incapable of describing my sense of oppression. I was a child of the bourgeoisie and I could not name my feelings. It is now clearer why leaving Germany was easy. It was an emotional action I had concluded in my mind long before physical removal had become necessary.

Martens and I left Germany the week after the aborted subversion of Austria and the murder of her Chancellor. He came home in tears one afternoon. His eye was swollen, already purple. He had been walking by a newspaper office when the news was blazoned in its window. Berliners crowded before the *Schaufenster* waiting for news before it was published. Such people lived on news. As soon as they had a choice item, they would disappear to spread it.

Martens was crossing the street near the newspaper office. He cupped his ear in order to hear better, but he didn't understand quickly enough. Everyone burst into applause when they posted the bulletin announcing – falsely, as it turned out – that Austrian Nazis had seized the Government. Swastikas turned on their sides as arms shot up in salute. Martens didn't wear an armband; he didn't salute. Someone cursed him. A middle-aged woman punched him in the eye.

We made up our minds that afternoon. The following day, we finished packing. I put the manuscript of my essay on Henriette Herz on top, wrapped in oilcloth. Martens packed his glass slides. We took our money from the bank – a little at a time in five withdrawals over the next few days. I gave our ginger cat to a neighbor who always patted it even when it was no longer prudent to smile at its owner. It wasn't difficult for me to leave Germany.

We announced that we were going to France for a brief holiday. We took very little luggage to forestall suspicion. The money we sewed into the lining of Martens's suits. Late in the afternoon, we went by my parents' home to see them for the last time. Only mother was at home. She seemed upset by our unannounced visit. She kept apologizing for having no fresh cake. She spilled tea on the rug and rang for the maid who sullenly dabbed at the spot with a dustcloth. I had never seen the girl before. Mother explained that it was suddenly difficult finding help. Papa returned home about six and after changing into his slippers entered the sitting room where we were having tea. He shook hands with Martens and kissed me on both cheeks. Papa sensed something. He took my hand and held it for the longest time while he explained how difficult his business had become. New restrictions every day. Workers were beginning to leave. One of the presses had been sabotaged. Moreover, business was falling off. If it weren't for the big department stores, many of which were still Jewish-owned, it would be catastrophic.

"But they'll come to their senses when the French and English

realize what's happening here." I couldn't argue. I said I hoped
so. It was only when the clock struck the half-hour that I realized
I had to get to the point. Our train left at eight. We had already
been by the station and checked our luggage.

"Papa, Martens and I are going on holiday to France."

"A holiday? At a time like this, a holiday? You must be
joking."

"You're leaving Germany," mother said suddenly. Martens
kept looking from face to face, refusing to settle down and be
still. For him, it was pure pain. Perhaps he hoped they would
say something to persuade us both to stay put. I nodded. Mother
burst into tears. "You can't," she shouted. I put a finger to my
lips. I didn't want the maid to hear. Everyone spied, and reported to the police.

"Now listen. There's very little time before the train leaves.
Yes. Tonight. We're leaving tonight. I don't think it'll get better.
The contrary. I think it will get worse. I won't try to persuade
you to leave, but you should. Neither of you are young and
you're not people who fight. There's no reason to stay except
out of loyalty to something that's dead. Your Germany is dead,
even if I never believed that it was once alive." Papa began to
interrupt. "Not now, papa. We're not arguing. It's not a discussion we're having. We're here to say goodbye, to wish you
luck, to tell you we love you, but to tell you we're going. We've
had enough of this Germany. Some day if there's another one,
we'll see. But for now, enough." I stood up. Mother put her
arms about me and wept. She was almost hysterical, her chest
heaving with the deepest kind of wretched sobs. Papa's eyes
were filled with tears. He stood there biting his lips, but at the
end his anger got the better of him.

"Once I let you leave home. I was reconciled because then
I knew you were right. But this? Leaving us behind like this.
No."

"Everyone has to save their own life as best they can. I'm not allowed to teach. No one will publish me. I'm useless here. There's no point to such a country. No point at all."

"Goodbye, daughter," he said, extending his hand.

"Is that all, papa? A handshake?"

He turned away and padded out of the room.


Why Henriette Herz?

And how is it that for nearly forty years I have refused to publish this work? I have reworked and revised the manuscript (which was wrapped in oilcloth at the time of our departure) a dozen times, pruning the text, incorporating new discoveries, appending a brief anthology of the remarkable letters addressed to her. But my reluctance hardened as the years passed into an irrational refusal to publish the work in my lifetime. Why? The reasons for this refusal will become clear; they are doubtless talismanic and magical. Notwithstanding, why Henriette Herz at all?

What is it that attracted me to Henriette de Lemos, wife to Markus Herz, beloved to Schliermacher, the Humboldts, Ludwig Börne, and others besides – *admirateurs*, *Mitgliedern*, correspondents, confidants? Why her alone? I might have written of others of the same era, of eminent men, for instance, of geniuses or more commonplace outpourings of talent, who clustered about the name and court of Frederick the Great of Prussia. Might I not (like my dear friend who has left before me) have written of Rahel Varnhagen – or even of Dorothea Mendelssohn-Veit, the daughter of Moses Mendelssohn, who married first within the community of Israel and then followed Friedrich von Schlegel to marriage and another altar? Why Henriette Herz, as she is known?

The name, perhaps first the name. A search for complements and collaborations.

As I've already said, what first became clear to me about myself was that I bore (or rather wore) a name that held me apart from all others, that made me distinctive despite the artificial bonds that tied me to my patrimony. I understand well the loathing that Henry James had for being the Second or Junior to his catastrophically mercurial father. How disgraceful that a parent should name a child second to himself, pressing down upon a young head a thorny crown that promises no salvation, only repetition. And so, how cursed are we that we bear family names at all. How much better it might have been had the emancipation allowed my own people to continue its antique tradition of naming children as the Bible did, first name to first names. Mine would have been Erika bas Reb Yaakov ben Ephraim (my father's Hebrew name was Yaakov and his father's had been Ephraim), but unfortunately it has resolved itself into Hertz, all *Herz*, naked heart, dispassionate patronyms assigned to Jews along with permission to dwell in Christian cities and pay taxes.

"At least be a Hertz until your husband gives you some other name," papa once chided, annoyed with me for having written a school essay in which I dared to criticize his beloved Schiller. I protested, unclear why my transgression against his little god should bring forth the rage of patrimony. But that, of course, was it. My father and mother swore by Schiller. Schiller was the healthy spirit of Germany (they didn't know that he was quite capable of being an anti-Semite like the rest, although he concealed it well with equivocations about the vulgar rabble of the ancient Hebrews). Schiller was an artery of my father's system, a conduit of blood to his stolid heart who gave him a lift whenever he saw a production, any production, of *Die Rauber* or *Wallenstein* or *Wilhelm Tell*. It was always so. There were good names and bad ones. The Hertzes always stood with the good ones.

I never told my father about Henriette Herz. It would have hurt him; he would have insisted that his was with a "t" and hence no relation. And of course not. But sound obliterated the inserted "t" and for all the world of ears we were legatees of old Markus and Henriette. And, of course, we were all Berliners. My father's family dated themselves very far back (as far as they could fake their genealogy) until the early eighteenth century, contemporary to Markus Herz, contemporary to scenes of such heated chastity as must have set the cushions of the *Herz* home aflame.

I fell for Henriette Herz. She was no "subject" for me, no *curiosa*, no issue or complexity. She was, of course, all of these, first and foremost a problem, but earliest and most profoundly, I simply fell for her.

When I was eighteen I happened upon an etching of Henriette Herz reproduced in Landsberg's scrapbook of her life and I was startled by her incredible head of hair pulled off her forehead by a silk band. Henriette's hair was like a bower of willow leaves rising from a fountain in her brain and falling to either side in cascades of curls, thick brown hair that seemed to descend in slow motion to her shoulders, light and tight brown curls; and more than these I admired her half-moon face with eyes as big as those the moon man turns upon the earth. Only her lips seemed to me bizarrely small and well-bred, little slivers of lips set at the ridge of a full and fleshy chin not unlike my own.

In my youthful days, before I reached the plateau of patient and methodical scholarship, I made many intellectual decisions only after I had tested them by passion. I had first to fall for my subject, to make it my beloved, and then latterly, scrutinizing what my heart held, I might ask it strenuous questions. The subject, however, was no longer questioned in itself, only my own heart's renderings. Henriette Herz was one of these, one of the earliest of these, and the subject of my first book, the manuscript of which I carried in my suitcase out of all the libraries of Germany to my place of refuge.

Henriette was beautiful. Later, I found out that she knew and spoke and read in six languages, including Greek and Hebrew, that she had working familiarity with Portuguese, Danish, and Latin, that late in her life she undertook Turkish, and, with the aid of one of the earliest of Indologists, Sanskrit. But she hardly used these languages except to disport her beauty among the amazing circle of intellectuals and literati who paid her court.

Paid court to Henriette Herz? Indeed Frau Hofrat Markus dedicated a salon to the cult of Goethe. Although she had no Goethean memorabilia under glass upon her mantle, she gathered a circle of the eminent to cultivate his works. Henriette had met Goethe once in Dresden – 1810 it was – when she was nearly sixty and he not much younger. What did they say to each other? No report and no conjecture. But presumably what transpired froze her face and her enthusiasm. Henriette never let up in her admiration. And at the end of her life, she continued to adore Goethe and was still thought beautiful. Henriette gathered savants about her as a queen bee congregates drones. She was essential nutriment, although she produced none herself. She was simply edible. Her husband, a physician nearly twenty years older than herself, had been born in Berlin, but poor and uneducated, had departed to seek – unsuccessfully it appears – his livelihood in merchandise. Later he returned to Berlin, where he undertook philosophy with Kant, but impoverished, left once more and apprenticed himself as secretary to an itinerant Russian Jew with whom he accumulated wealth. He studied medicine, became a doctor, married Henriette and then – trusting – allowed her to become a queen to the educated drones of Berlin.

Henriette was their regina and those who supped her fare spoke well of her beauty, her wit, her linguistic skills, her intelligence. They wrote her letters and she kept them; few of hers survive. They admired her beauty and treasured their memory of it. Some fell for her mightily, poor Ludwig Börne writing sadly of his love, poor Schliermacher in his parson's wings fluttering before Henriette. It is hard to understand why so many loved Henriette – some even threatening suicide for her – romantic children, disciples of the young Werther, suffering to death from unrequitedness.

I found it so unbelievable that all this transpired in Berlin at the end of the eighteenth century, that a beautiful Jewess could be loved and admired by so many eminent Germans and so many aspirant Germans who were Jews, that all this glitter and style could take place in spacious drawing rooms sequestered from the public's gaze, that all these celebrities saluted a woman who wrote nothing memorable, whose letters are lost, whose sole proof of eminence is the attestation of her admirers, and that a Jew of modest means could command all this.

How so? Jews were still exotica, Asiatic flora – as common as crabgrass in ancient Palestine, but restricted in Prussian Berlin (a mere 112 families in 1700, according to Friedrich Nicolai) – a rare species with strange petals, emitting curious odors like tropical orchids. They allowed themselves, set in comfortable soil, to be bathed by waters more lambent than those of Babylon, and they determined – these transplanted flora – neither to wilt nor to weep, but to thrive.

Henriette Herz made my heart pant for the ancient desert. Her good will, which everyone acknowledged; her charity and calm, which everyone celebrated; her ease and sociability, which everyone chorussed; her beauty, which went undisputed; her intelligence and judgment, which made reasonableness a German virtue; all these consolidated her position and her power.

But in none of the testimonials that we read is it mentioned
with more than hushed embarrassment that she was a Jew of
Portuguese descent, come to Hamburg in flight from the Iberian
persecutions of the sixteenth century, a Latin Jew, a Jew of
flagrant temperament, who mastered the languages of travel in
order that her family survive.

And later, at the end, after her husband had died, Henriette
stayed behind, resisting the seductions of Schliermacher who
would have her in the church if he could not (read between the
sheets) have her in his bed, caring for her aged mother and
unmarried sister until her mother died, and then – alone, having
refused all invitations to marriage and position – then, only
then, did she accept baptism.

Was it a true change of faith? Had she been wooed by some
Christian business I am unable to understand? Had she passed
through some Pauline about-face? I do not think so. No. I think
rather that in those days – with all that whispered admiration
behind her – aging alone, facing wrinkles and a sheen of grey,
whatever was curled and cascading in her soul gave way.

The Church was easy to lonely women of the emancipation.

The story of Henriette Herz, her hair and her beauty, her
languages and her wit, honey for the intelligentsia, raised to
my mind a question that had not been asked. What role did
sexuality play in the parlous estate of such parvenu intelligence?
Wilhelm von Humboldt had said it of Rahel Levin's marriage
to Varnhagen: "Now at last," he wrote with acid, "the little
Levin woman...can become an Excellency and Ambassador's
wife. There is nothing the Jews cannot achieve."

For Henriette, Judaism was at most – in the absence of formal
rites and the abandonment of all those protective limitations
which tell us Jews that certain things of the Gentiles' world are
not for us – a defect of condition, a mere defect, a birthmark
like a disgusting mole. And when we (poor Henriette in this

case) begin to waste, when our natural gifts go and all that is wild and Asiatic in our caste gives way to shriveling, it is then that the parvenu suffers most deeply and surrenders. It is then that the roots desiccate. It was then that Henriette's *Herz* broke.

I rewrapped my manuscript and, covering it with lingerie, replaced it in our suitcase.

When the train crossed the border into France, Martens was near tears. I admit it upset me. He asked diffidently whether I thought we would one day return to Germany. I bit my lip. I had no doubt the dirty business would last. There would be no going back. At least not for me. Martens could go back if he chose. He might even survive in Germany. I doubted it, but I was willing to hear him out. I had no right to insist that he accompany me.

"Martens, does it really grieve you to leave Germany?" I asked, not unkindly.

"Of course, but not the way you think."

"Which way then?" I demanded, my voice acquiring that parched timbre it takes on when the inquiry promises rigor and consequence.

"What does it matter? It's done."

"Not so. We're married, but life is more than marriage. If you wish to reconsider, even if you wish to return, I'll understand."

"Damn you, Erika. You're always so ready to understand, to provide choices and alternatives. Don't you ever see that a person can be torn apart and still have no choice? It's not Germany I worry about. It's me. It's my fragility, my incompetence that frightens me. Going back. I wouldn't survive a minute, but don't think I'm persuaded I'll survive anywhere else."

"I'm sorry, Martens." I took his hand and held it.

It was typical of me. I knew perfectly well that he was telling more of the truth than I was prepared to consider. I was younger. For me it was horror, but it was still adventure. In those days I thought exile a dramatic necessity. It flattered my integrity to believe that I had gone from principle. I know better now. Saving one's life is a principle, but it is no less a decision of the utmost practicality. Unless one considers suicide or martyrdom intelligent choices; I do not. And then, most important of all, Martens was nearly deaf and fifty years old.

We fell silent as the train passed slowly out of Strasbourg towards Paris. Our passports had been validated at the border, but our names had been noted and we had been sternly warned that we had better report to the police the moment we found lodgings.

When the train arrived at the Gare du Nord, I saw Count Harry Kessler standing under the clock near the entrance to the railway platform. I watched him carefully. He was terribly elegant, although his face was pinched with weariness. He balanced his frailty on a cane, waiting with increasing impatience for someone who had not arrived. I had recognized him from newspaper photographs. He had been photographed constantly during the previous decade, chatting with Einstein, visiting with Maillol, attending theater with Piscator. He was everywhere, our most eminent literary magpie, but nonetheless a man of considerable fibre and imagination. I followed his career, not without envy, I confess. As an aspirant myself, I was always curious about those who had been born to clean linen, casual friendships, fine china, and the best cuisine. Not that I aspired to possess and employ them, but rather, like Count Harry, to possess them and then disdain their transparency and irrelevance. I recalled these feelings as I observed his grey suit and grey silk tie, his white handkerchief breaking the edge of his breast pocket, and the yellow tea rose in his buttonhole. Such fastidious elegance; what a ravaged face.

The porter arrived with our luggage and Martens and I pressed forward out of the station, leaving the Count behind. As we neared the foyer of the station, I looked back. The Count was just behind me. His friend had not arrived. It seemed ominous. As we passed the newspaper kiosk, Count Harry went over and asked with evident impatience if the latest German papers had come in. Not before evening, he was told. Count Harry pinched the ridge of his nose and rubbed his eyes. Later, we found out for whom he had been waiting who had not arrived.

I speculate on this entry.

Why is it that I took such careful note of Harry Graf Kessler, describing so fully his aspect and attire? The conjunction of our flight from Germany and his railway station apparition (juxtaposed and linked within the text) I suspect now is only subterfuge.

It is not true that I saw my own flight as similar to his. Or that I wished to cover my exile with the celebrity of his. The flight of Martens Berg and Erika Hertz was mentioned in no foreign office dispatch nor noted in any Berlin newspaper. We disappeared, hardly noticed, hardly missed. My friend Lotte Schiff may have been sad; Mira Freybush never found out; my parents wept and chafed at my stupidity; my university colleagues probably thought our decision prudent – moreover, it relieved them of having to witness our degradation had we stayed on and the pinches and tics of guilt it might have provoked for a week or two. But Count Harry – he was missed: missed by the Nazis who wanted the pleasure of murdering him; missed by the Left who coveted his innocent support. And condemned by the artists and intellectuals whom he patronized and was thought to have betrayed.

It was rather the case that as I stood in the vast Gare du Nord, waiting for my luggage and watching Count Harry, I felt the premonitory clarification of my life vision. As all decisive intuitions, mine began in denial. I was nothing like this splendid German aristocrat. I shared nothing of his ground. I was not raised as he. I was no international German, no creature of universal culture. I could not turn my eye with dispassion and lively curiosity upon all the works of European art and literature. I was, despite my Berlin upbringing, not yet a creature of the world's diasporas. If Count Harry was a wayfarer in luxury who took up his abode in the sticky stuff of the world as a millionaire dabbler and patron, I was at most a lodger in Being whose home had been a working-class flat in an apartment house whose hallways smelled of cabbage. For me to become a member of the exiled of my race, I had before me incredible labor and art.

The rooms we took off the rue de Vaugirard were extremely cheap, a narrow foyer, two small rooms, and a half-kitchen. I planned to stay in France for as long as possible. In fact, I had no thought of leaving France. I assumed that Germany was closed to me forever, but I could not conceive that France would soon join the register of the inhospitable. It seemed to me then that the traditional enmity between France and Germany would redound to the credit of those who had fled Germany early, who made politics rather than necessity the compass of their wanderings. I thought France more stable and stability meant then (as I suspect it still means for me) moral clarity and national integrity. How naive I was! In all events we (that is, Martens and myself) intended to conduct ourselves as though we had arrived in our second home: in Paris our second home, international despite being as well the capital of national France. I put it correctly. International Paris *made international* by the fact that so many foreigners overran its boulevards, speaking a multitude of languages the French loathed to acknowledge, much less to understand. But in those narrow days it was France's Paris that we trespassed upon and despite her culture appearing the most generous and openhanded, it was from a stingy heart that her welcome proceeded. Her sense of clarity and honor was monitored by a prideful exiguousness that required all things somehow to be purified of the imperfections of alienage by speaking to the world in French accents. France was (I know this from Heine's experience) international because it believed France to be universal, not because it was prepared to recognize that the word "humanity" could be spoken in other languages as well. This was as true of its intellectuals as it was of its concierges and shopkeepers – the three classes of French society with which Martens and I had most immediate and continuous contact.

The first week was spent settling down, acquiring the modest requirements of our lodgings, furniture and crockery from the *brocantes* and open markets. We made ready to have our first meal at home about ten days after our arrival. We had already made an acquaintance – not a friend, but an acquaintance – a bookbinder named Ewald, whom I had sometimes patronized in Berlin (it was he who had bound my St. Augustine). He had left about four months earlier and come to Paris after brief stays in Switzerland and Italy. Although he was a master craftsman, it was necessary for him to resume his *apprentissage* with one of the ateliers that filled the orders of the likes of Paul Bonet. He was a charming man, large-boned but graceful, his fingers tapered like young asparagus, his face quizzical, his eyes amused as they traced the parameters of our small quarters. He had left with his wife and infant son shortly after Hitler had been made Chancellor. He had been a Spartacist, although he loved book-binding more than politics. "I don't have to bind German books. I'll bind anything." It was his credo. He bound wounds as well as books, cheering Martens immensely. I knew because Ewald was one of the very few people in those days whose lips Martens learned to read.

We were just about to sit down to table. It was Sunday noon. Ewald's wife would come by later with the child, but had insisted her husband accept our hospitality. She knew how important it was for us to inaugurate our world, and for Ewald to enlarge his own. I had made a large fish soup and broiled some bread with garlic and paprika. We sat down and Martens opened the liter bottle of table wine. There was a knock at the door and I went to open it. Two gendarmes filled the doorway. *"Vos papiers, Madame,"* they demanded. It was then that I remembered we had not been to the police. Our names had gone in with our passports several days before and I hadn't bothered to inquire after their return. The concierge, a gruff woman who puffed cigarettes *sans cesse*, would not have replied. She never answered questions if she deemed them of no consequence to her. Ask for permission to do something in one's rooms which might interfere with her sense of order and *comme il faut* and she would invariably say no. No to pets. No to another electrical outlet. No to leaving garbage for a few hours in the hallway. But ask for passports or mail or messages and there would be no reply. Civility was wasted on Madame Beauchamps.

"Papers, Madame." A return to civility.

"But you have our passports," I answered.

"You need papers to live here, Madame, to live here and work in France."

"I have no employment," I replied calmly.

"That doesn't interest us, Madame. Whether you have work

or not doesn't interest us. We are only interested in your papers." He spoke meticulously, enunciating each word as though it were an idol. He was delivering a message from his superiors, from some authority that decreed the universal law of papers, and he delivered the message as though it were an oracular pronouncement. He was tall and young and should have preserved his innocence of the lies of power longer than he had (but perhaps, I feel now, he was preserving innocence by speaking each word to me as though it were an idol to be syllabically worshipped). I couldn't answer. It was all beyond reason.

Martens called out in German: "Who's there?" Although our lodgings were small, the doorway was invisible to the living space, where a small desk served as our dining table.

"It's the police asking for our papers. Do we have any papers other than passports?" There was no reply. I thought Martens might have said something, until I realized that he probably couldn't hear me. But then Ewald?

"You have somebody with you, Madame."

"My husband."

"May we speak with him?"

"He's deaf, you see. I'll have to bring him to you." The other officer – he was thin and ashen and I remember thinking that he would not live too much longer – pulled at the sleeve of the younger policeman, obviously his superior, and shook his head. He didn't think he had to see my deaf husband. I thanked him silently.

"Never mind. To the point. Have you no papers?"

"We have none other than our passports. I understood that when the passports were returned, then we could apply for a residence permit. Isn't that correct?"

"It is, Madame, but you can't continue living here without a residence permit."

"And I can't secure that until I appear with our passports. Isn't that so?"

"Correct. Now then, when will that happen?"

"When I receive our passports from the concierge."

"She has them."

"But, for heaven's sake, why didn't you just give them to me? Then I could have answered everything."

"That isn't the way it's done. The concierge gives them to the police and the concierge receives them from our hand."

"Ah, I see." But I saw nothing and understood less. It was a hopeless roundabout, a play of mindlessness, procedural inanity. It was everything I loathed. I must have turned red with anger.

"There's no point being angry, Madame. It upsets everything being angry. We are terribly decent for the moment to all of you," the young officer said ominously, motioning to my small lodgings and all the numberless aliens it no doubt concealed. "All you do – you foreigners – is make trouble for us, trouble and more work. We don't need more of you, but here you are imposing upon our reasonable requests for registration and permits. Now, do be at headquarters on the rue Grenelle tomorrow morning at ten o'clock with your husband and your passports." He put his hand to his blue hat, saluted perfunctorily, and then turned and went down the narrow and poorly lit staircase, followed by his aging subordinate. I stood dumb before the gloom they had vacated. After a minute of staring at a grey patch peeling from the outside wall opposite our lodgings, I slammed the door in fury and returned to the living room. I shouted at Martens: "Where were you?" He looked embarrassed. "Where's Ewald?" Martens pointed to the armoire. Suddenly I understood. "Oh God, Ewald, come out. Dear Ewald, what's the matter?" Ewald emerged. His face was white, drained of geniality.

"I have no papers, Erika. No papers at all. No passports. We're trying to buy them on the black market, but that takes much time and money. I don't even work for the binder I mentioned. He gives me the odd book to mend and pays me less than anyone. I don't know what will happen. If they catch me, they'll ship me back. Then it's the camps, and you know." He snapped his fingers, snuffing out his life.

I apologized to Martens. I apologized to Ewald. It was Ewald's disappearance that had terrified Martens into silence. He hadn't heard my explanation, but Ewald had and, frightened, had gone to hide in our armoire.

What kind of a world was upon us? People with wives and children fleeing homelands, scraping before supposedly friendly police, hiding in armoires. Suddenly I hated everyone, hated myself for being so tough-minded, hated being alive. Briefly, all briefly. The hatred gave way to confusion and vulnerability. We ate our fish soup in silence, mopping the bowls with our bread. Ewald's wife arrived. Their baby was beautiful. And then, we drank wine and laughed. We had to. There was nothing else to do but drink wine and laugh.

The window was open and a breeze blew warm and fragrant. We stalked a bee and smashed it. Again we laughed, almost too hysterically.

After Ewald and his family had left, Martens and I had an argument about language. He confessed that he had faintly heard my conversation with the gendarmes, but had decided not to intervene when Ewald turned pale and bounded to the armoire to hide. I observed acidly that his logic was dangerously askew. Had he come to the door, I suggested, to be by my side, there would have been little likelihood of the police entering the apartment to look for other occupants. And, had it not been for the sympathetic subordinate, that might well have happened. Rather than admit his notorious pusillanimity, Martens turned on me for having spoken French with the police.

"But I speak French fluently," I replied irritably.

"Not as well as the French. You have a distinct Berlin accent."

"In every language I speak," I admitted, and that included Greek and Latin alongside French and English. "But still, better to talk French than pretend."

"I don't agree," Martens persisted. "Remember how we avoided a speeding ticket four years ago when we were driving through Alsace. I pretended not to speak French and they let us go. 'Couldn't be bothered,' the policeman shrugged at us."

"Damn, Martens. Don't you see the difference between a speeding ticket and a residence permit? The one costs a little money (which, granted, we didn't have) and the other could be our life."

He ignored me and continued persistently, his characteristic stubbornness in full view. "If you hadn't shown off your perfect French, we could have bought time, until they got around to sending out another officer who perhaps knew German."

"Ha!" I roared, "a French policeman who speaks German. You're dreaming, Martens. And furthermore, to what advantage? To what advantage? As you must have gathered, he didn't like us much anyway. And anyway, it's a lie. I know French. I speak French. When I don't know, I keep my mouth shut or I ask."

Martens dropped his eyes. He was tired of my lips. He was tired of me. Actually, I didn't blame him. And perhaps, even, he was the smallest bit right. I was proud of my French. I was proud of every language I knew well (including German). I spoke languages with the same density of passion as I sometimes made love. Even trivial conversation, if undertaken in another language than my own, was charged with excitement. It was a gamble precisely because the other would know from the very beginning that I wasn't a native. Hence, compliments. Hence, praise and the deliciousness of daring rewarded. I was as delighted when a *guicheuse* at the Metro praised my French as when Bernard Groethysen admired its dexterity. All the same. The artifice of expression.

And it is true, as Martens reminded me late that night, neither of the gendarmes had praised my French. They had come about business and none was transacted.

Madame Beauchamps returned our passports the following morning. Rudely. She greeted us as "*mes métèques,*" a disgusting French expression originally intended for Italians, but long since internationalized to show French disdain for any foreigners. I told her the expression was contemptible. She laughed, showing her pink gums. The little apartment house in which we lived had no other foreigners besides ourselves. We were Madame's special property and she conserved us as property; however, by the time of our departure months later, she had begun to understand our anomalous position, worrying about our comings and goings, as though being foreigners also meant that we were children.

Martens had no work and with his degenerative hearing had no hope of finding any. It was up to me. We got our residence permit, but without permission to work we couldn't possibly support ourselves. There wasn't much money, although my father sent me a small draft several times that year. I went to a language academy that specialized in teaching French to German emigrés. I got paid by the head, which meant that I had to hang about the few cafés where the emigrés congregated to drum up business. Not very efficient. I managed a half-dozen over the first month and these, together with the academy's own registration, gave me about fourteen hours' teaching a week and a modest income.

My real reason for wishing to stay in Paris was to get on with my own research. It was in Paris that I designed the outline of a major project that even now, decades and a dozen other books later, remains unfinished. The scheme holds, some of the material has been given as lectures and published in American journals, but the grand thesis is incomplete. It is part of the roundabout of my life. I doubt it will ever be finished. Perhaps posthumously my notes and essays will be gathered by some loving friend and offered as a portion of my legacy.

*Salon, Coffee House, Café: The Society of the Intellectuals.* Self-evident and delicious, isn't it? I don't need to explain it, except in five hundred pages, closely annotated. Much of the argument is already alluded to by others. What interests me is the architectural frame — the enlargement and anonymity of space that marks progress from the salon's crammed and fetid quarters through the smoky draftiness of the coffee house to the relatively spacious disharmony of the café, where the furniture of class has given way to individuation of intelligence. For instance, the salon was rarely accounted a triumph of design during the Age of Kings — it was most often an interior space, guarded from public scrutiny, accessible only by invitation, managed principally by clever women whose gifts ran at most to versifying, letter-writing, and intrigue. The coffee house, which emerged as a sober alternative to the wine and grog shop, was at the center of English, Dutch, and German class politics. Like the salon it was not fashioned or designed as an architectural form, but grew and shrank as commerce and patronage required. The café, which flourished in France after the Revolution and reached its apogee at the end of the next century and the early decades of our own, was respondent, unlike either salon or coffee house, to the motility of the urban mass and was, therefore, conceived and elaborated as an architectural invention. Everyone of importance in the early architectural avant-garde designed a café, from the German Muthesius and the Austrian Adolf Loos to the De Stijl masters, Van Doesburg and Rietveld.

Cafés required a specific form for they reflected in miniature the swirl of the select mob, the movement of the faceless and anonymous through a semi-public space. The space – not they – conferred order and distinction and, hence, the need for architecture. The café was the promontory of the street, its escarpment, but no less was the street the outcropping of the café. The hand that extended from the uttermost table of the café (although no hedge or balustrade or elevation separated table from street) was protected by unspoken civilities from the beggar's reach; it could extend and descend, if it chose, for it was the café's arm, but the beggar could not reach in and snatch a roll from the table. There were orders of discrimination that money ruled – money, and before it profession, and before it the arts, and before them ideas and the intellectuals who espoused them.

The café was the last social institution of the intellectuals. The anarchy of their world (its dissolution of coherent values and social exuberance) spilled over from the café to the street and prominent scribblers inside became the ideologues of the mob without; and schemers of the café who never drew swords between tables were liberated to skewer each other just a few feet away.

I intended in this unfinished work to evoke the intellectuals by fixing upon their media of sociality: their furniture (literal and figurative); their preference for beverage and light cuisine; their addiction to press and periodicals; the camaraderie of persons and the publicity of personality; free language and ideological ritualization; stratifications of vulgarity and politeness; the political iconography of posters and prints; the habits of greeting and goodbye; sign languages of class (how savants, sycophants, and servants behaved); the distinction between intellectuals who plotted violence over their teacups and those who made theories of violence or wrote violent poems. All there. All in the salon, coffee house, café. However, none of it will be written down or rather all of it is written down, but only as quick notes and jottings, filling the flyleafs of primary sources.

I have not completed this book nor allowed my book on Henriette Herz to be published during my lifetime. It is, I know now, a judgment I have passed – unconsciously at first – upon the times of my life. I came early in my maturity – indeed, during the period of our brief stay in Paris before the long flight to America began – to think of both these works as my joy and delight, my personal romance and pleasure, and hence appropriate to another age than the one through which I have lived. They are projects of mind which a creative age, strained by the abrasions and angularities of disordered classes and ambitions, makes possible. But ours, this age of ours, is an age of war and murder, not of delicious friction and mental contest.

Forgive me, but I must break off this explanation.

What am I doing renewing the passions of Paris in my seventy-third year? Surely, a kind of joyous profligacy that the circumspect grey eyes of my physician, Dr. Bamberger, advise against.

I have been in bed for two weeks. A chest scan detects a small shadow on my left lung. Smaller than small, it is a fly speck upon the film. Some weeks from now when my lungs have cleared of the present bronchitis and I am flourishing again, they will do another series of tests. Dr. Bamberger tries to reassure me, but the little arabesque his pink hands trace in the air to underscore the shadow's speck-ness leaves me without conviction. If it should prove to be something else, it will not surprise me terribly. I have lived hard. I am seventy-two, after all, alive longer by a number of years than many who have been within my life and have already disappeared. People like myself spend so many years becoming familiar with death, they are hardly surprised by unpleasant medical information – after all, so much of my thinking consists in building both fortresses and flimsy gazebos against dying. We ward off and we fabulate, we magicians of the mind. But in the meantime Dr. Bamberger sits by my bedside and observes the piles of books that press against my thighs.

"You do too much, Erika. Perhaps you should lighten the burden and give some of the donkey-work to others. No?"

"I have given up so much already. I scarcely do anything these days but read and write."

"But with the usual frenzy, I suspect." He laughs.

"Of course." I join him laughing, but then I begin to rasp a hollow, dry cough that leaves me gasping with pain.

"No more smoking, you know."

"I assumed that prohibition. I've stopped. At least for now."

"Please, my dear. We need you for a bit longer. It would please us – me and your other admirers – if you took better care of yourself."

"I can promise no more than a try. And with the usual frenzy of trying."

Dr. Bamberger leaves. It is a late winter sun that streams, cold and ungenerous, over my bed. And soon, it is night.

No more then of my unfinished works. Condense those passages. My Paris project. I think of it like Beethoven's Sixth Symphony, complete, splendid, but a light thing, nature's own, my pastoral of the mind. Nothing heroic or victorious about it, nothing sounding too large; simply my work of catching breath, of flushing the system with air and red blood, acquiring health for the hard days that would soon come upon me.

We hadn't yet made the mistake of settling down in Paris and fabricating a Parisian life. It was possible, you know. I cannot bear to think of all the remarkable Germans (and later Austrians and later Czechs and Poles) who arrived in Paris like Moses before the Promised Land, mistaking the Eiffel Tower for the cloud of fire that showed by day and night.

Astonishing as it may sound, Europeans didn't travel between the wars. I, for instance, knew Germany: I had walked through most of it as a young woman. I had visited Danzig, I had been to Vienna, I had delivered a paper at an international congress of Renaissance scholars in Copenhagen, I had spent three weeks in Paris, virtually locked in the Bibliothèque Nationale, re-searching Heine's miserable Paris years, and Martens and I had toured Alsatian France, but I had never been to Italy or Greece, the Low Lands or Eastern Europe. During the 1920s, the in-flation had made movement either impossible or frivolous (either we had nothing or a friend might call and take us for a car ride, using up expensive petrol to reach some country restaurant 100 kilometers away). But travel? Meditated travel, moving slowly down from the Alps through Milan and fanning out to Umbria – those leisured trips which every Northern intellectual required for education had virtually ceased by the end of the First World War. I do not believe *Death in Venice* could have been conceived and executed much after 1911 – that languor, that atmosphere of idleness and narcissism, that vision of art had all but gone up in smoke by the time the World War ended. We couldn't do it anymore.

So what did Paris mean to me? It was not a place I knew. It

was only a dream country, familiar from the reports of exotic travellers. Many of my old friends and some of the most eminent of the exiles mistakenly thought otherwise. They knew everyone – *tout le monde* – and they imagined that *in extremis* everyone would help. They couldn't have known that the intellectuals and artists, augmented by the occasional professional and government figure with a double life (*vide* Paul Claudel or Alexis Leger), had no real power. When it came down to it, slowpokes like Rudolf Hilferding were plucked off departing ships by the SS and sent to their deaths. And that bizarre foursome – Heinrich Mann, the Werfels, and young Golo crossing the Pyrenees on foot – very nearly didn't make it.

It was Martens who said one morning, "Just in case, don't you think we should find out how to leave?" It was the way Martens usually put things to me. A collective, shared question to which I alone was expected to provide the answer. Martens hadn't always been helpless – certainly not when he was inventing ways to persuade me to marry him – but he had become helpless. The deafness had arrived later, as if to seal what character had already outlined. And so he would lay out a speculating conundrum for our croissant and café au lait, and by evening he expected I would have the solution.

"Why?" I asked, unpersuaded. My work had begun to go well. I had had a series of remarkable conversations with Bernard Groethysen; I had met old Leon Brunschwieg and Henri Bergson and been invited by both to return; but I had not been reading the newspapers, certainly not *Le Journal des débats* which recorded the deliberations of the Chamber of Deputies. Martens read newspapers. His café life continued. He either retired early to the Dôme when I went off to teach or walked down to boulevard St. Germain and settled himself, unfolding his newspaper, wherever the sun was strongest.

Our breakfast discussion of our fate was already echoed in
the national press. The trickle of political exiles which antedated
the fall of Weimar had become a steady stream, and too many
of us were – unlike the eminent Kessler and the Manns – either
Jews, or academic intellectuals with radical politics, or out-
and-out anarchists and Communists. The French didn't oppose
Germany's reoccupation of the Rhine, and Hitler's support among
the French Royalists and the Action Française had already
produced a number of violent street confrontations.

Naturally, anti-Semitism was on the rise. Several days before
Martens asked his question, we returned to our apartment after
an evening stroll to find the foyer of the building daubed with
a charcoal graffito of unmistakable clarity: *Mort aux Juifs*. No
Jews in particular. All of us. I took it personally and Madame
Beauchamps frowned at me the following day when she passed
me in the hall. The graffito was still there. I didn't ask her to
remove it. Several days passed. It remained. It was as though
Madame Beauchamps was informing everyone in her apartment
house who was Jewish that we could go to hell, even if it mucked
her premises to announce the sentiment. I had briefly thought
she (or her drunken husband) might have been responsible, but
that was hardly possible. Madame Beauchamps was above all
a *bourgeoise*: she would never soil her own nest. But once done,
let it stay awhile, like hanged bodies at medieval city walls
reminding the inhabitants of their own proximity to crime and
warning them of the consequence.

Martens's question several mornings later seemed to me wholly
unwarranted. It's only that I – realist that I am – would not
have posed it as a matter for deliberation. When the right moment came (my selfish moment, I confess), I would have been
already packed, and would have simply taken Martens along –
exactly as it had happened when we left Germany.

The truth is that I wasn't ready to pull up and move on. My eyes hadn't seen the evidence. Anti-Semitic graffiti? Nothing unusual for a German Jew.

I was treasuring my Paris days; I didn't imagine that they would end. It wasn't that I didn't feel the tension mount around me, that I couldn't hear the noise of war, that I was blind in Paris as I had been prescient in Berlin. It was rather that I was happy – foolishly, irresponsibly, briefly happy. We were ridiculously poor and I didn't mind at all. Food had never interested us; coffee, bread, cheese, and a few red, red tomatoes, luscious as passion fruit, were quite enough, once a day, sometimes twice. We lost weight, but we walked everywhere and were fit. I treasured every moment because (I now see) it was all invented, made up like a child's tale, to divert and disarm me. Those early months, I lied to myself every day. I had decided that Baron Hausmann had elaborated his astonishing city principally to receive young Erika Hertz and her loyal husband, who had fled their birthplace and rushed headlong into the arms of his Paris. And why not a good lie now and then? It harmed no one. Quite the contrary, although the awakening was harsh, the time of my deception was rich and long enough to supply me with unfinished notions and devisings that even now push me to the window of amazement where I look out and see, not clarity nor comprehension, but the lineaments of that dazzling city.

It was, however, during one of those exquisite days of Paris springtime, the 5th of May, 1935, that we came upon our own intimation of doom. We had taken an afternoon walk, Martens and I. As we crossed to the island around which the traffic of Raspail, the rue du Bac, and the boulevard St. Germain usually swirled, we were immediately struck by its emptiness. Bright buildings were shuttered and café chairs were piled behind box hedges shielding the plate glass. Posted before each building were helmeted soldiers, bayonets fixed, smoking cigarettes, hardly speaking. No pedestrians. Only soldiers and a few scavenging dogs. Smoke curled from three overturned automobiles down the boulevard. Rocks, torn from the pavement, covered the street. Ripped banners billowed in the breeze. I saw the leg of a chair with a steel spike attached to its tip. Links of chain. Someone's hairpiece and odd shoes. Even a child's glove beside a lead truncheon. And thousands upon thousands of leaflets, soiled and soaked. Martens's hand was on his open mouth, amazed, frightened. I looked down, disgusted by the battlefield, and saw at my feet a pool of blood already mottled with horseflies.

In the distance, far down, almost as silent as we, thousands of demonstrators continued to battle with each other and the police who tried to contain them. All we could know of it was the heave of a distant mass blocking our view and all we could hear of it was a low thunder of voices compressing a louder silence than our own.

The Communists had been battling the Action Française, and the police, trying somehow to restore order, had cracked heads indiscriminately. There were several trampled dead and numerous wounded. We read of it in the morning press. The riots that had just begun near the Sorbonne, at the Arc de Triomphe, around our corner on Montparnasse, along the length of St. Germain, from the Chamber of Deputies to the Eglise, would become much worse in the months ahead. But Martens could not hear and I, I was at the Bibliothèque; or visiting with philosopher friends, or teaching languages to foreigners. We didn't know, although we knew. Surely we knew, but we determined like children stamping their feet before the inexorable to refuse to know and not yet to understand.

The pool of blood diluted by sewage water began to stream along the gutter towards a drain. A mile behind the riot, two sanitation trucks were routinely sluicing the street, cleaning up.

Paris would be calm again by nightfall, but clearly it was time for us to go.

I determined to get Martens the answer he required and bring it home.


If we have an invitation to teach or perform or conduct or lecture or discover the secrets of the universe," I announced.

I had gone to the local headquarters of the American Friends Service Committee, which the American Embassy had suggested could be helpful. Actually, not the Embassy, but a young woman with a dazzlingly reassuring smile who, after she had given me the bad news – quotas filled, months to wait, months, perhaps years – had added in a whisper, "unless, of course, you're immensely talented and someone wants you." I was about to snap something guttural and peevish, but thought better of it. She smiled so beautifully. "But why not try the American Friends on Raspail. They have a list of desirable Europeans being sought in the States. You *could* be on it! Or if not on it now, you could perhaps maneuver to install yourself."


*The Emergency Committee in Aid of German Displaced Scholars.*

The lean and bony secretary of the American Friends Service Committee had handed me the memorandum bearing this endless name. He waited patiently while I struggled through its text. It was only two pages, but it took me so much time to understand. He probably thought I couldn't read English. I could. Excellently, in fact, although I rarely spoke the language in those days. No. It wasn't the language that impeded me. It was its meaning.

I had no difficulty assimilating the notion of "Emergency." I took it to be *my* "Emergency" rather than theirs. In this, I was mistaken. I came to understand later, after I had arrived in the States, that "emergency" described haste of formation, rather than any objective crisis: it was *their* emergency responding to our own that defined the attitude of speed. Emergency, indeed! Committee? A few names, a list of names ("*in the process of formation*"), some known to me, others wholly unknown, scrambled the left-hand margin of the memorandum. By the end of the '30s, names would fill both margins – it had become a mark of fashion and chic to be included on such lists, in protest advertisements, as signatories to this or that hue and cry. No notable wanted to be omitted. How many times during the years that followed did I have to explain to some irritated genius of the culture that his/her name had been omitted from something or other by sheer accident! By then, my name had joined the left-hand margin.

The Emergency Committee surely wanted to give aid – material aid, support, affection, hands-across-the-sea solidarity *with us*. And who were we? German? To be sure, German. Indeed! At least, we thought we were German. The ambiguity began in earnest at that point.

I retreated from the official desk and sat down to consider and reflect. Was I German? I spoke that language. Assuredly. The proof was that when I opened my mouth certain words came out which principally Germans understood – although occasionally I found Czechs and Polish Jews and anti-Communist Russians who spoke German. And I still used a German passport emblazoned with the swastika, although I frequently forgot to carry it in my purse. I had left freely, after all. I had travelled across the border and out of Germany. I was in that sense still a German with passport. I *could* return, although I hardly thought it likely I would return to Germany under Hitler.

Freely? That's the critical notion omitted from the name of the hastily convoked Committee. Wouldn't it have made greater sense to have called the group *The Emergency Committee in Aid of Freely Displaced German Scholars*? We uprooted ourselves, after all. We left of our own free will. I lit a cigarette. I was becoming upset.

I had left Germany because Germany no longer wanted me or anything like me. More than that, it was clear to me (even then) that once a nation sets its foot on the path of extremity, it will not turn away until it vomits its demons. There was no way for the Germans to be rid of me and mine until it had destroyed us. My freedom was merely my dim, clouded reading of events before they actually unfolded. I was a prophet upon whom no God had laid a hand. We had looked at fate and been aware that it looked back, straight into our eyes.

The Immigration Act. The Johnson-Reed Act. The National Origin Act. Three titles. Same law. All passed by the United States Congress in 1924, in response to the rising anxiety that America, more than flooded by the immigration of the poor and ill-equipped that had subsided in 1910, would – in the aftermath of Europe's post-war upheavals – be positively inundated. The authentic, pure, native stock, like Noah's congregation of the chosen remnant, would be all that would remain after the land was covered with the flood tide of poor Europe. Agitation and racist polemics. The new immigration law reduced to two percent the number of immigrants from each national origin as calculated during the first small year of the immigration (1890) rather than as of the census taken at its end (1910) when immigration had reached record numbers. The fiercely contested but finally legalized "national origin" provision of the law reduced to a trickle the tide of immigration from precisely those lands from which the new flight would come.

The law contained one loophole. Perhaps the only time that intellectuals were permitted to displace the rich getting through the eye of a needle. Clause 4d of Section 4 of the Act suspended quota considerations for religious leaders and certified teachers at institutions of higher education (and their families). At the same time, the provision was somewhat compromised by the fear that such exemptions, unless confirmed by an offer of a teaching post, would attract intellectual freeloaders. It became necessary to prove not only that you were an intellectual (or artist, composer, writer, musician), but that somebody wanted your services and had a position awaiting your arrival.

At last, then, I understood the *Emergency Committee in Aid of German Displaced Scholars.*

I was one and Martens was another. At least we qualified for attention. Aid was another matter.

"Let me see if you're on our Want List," the young secretary said with that careless insensitivity to language I have come to think so typically American. He put on his eyeglasses and slowly examined the stapled registry of names. "I'm afraid you're not here, Madame Hertz. But let me see about your husband. Also Hertz, yes, but what's his Christian name?"

"Not Hertz, sir. Berg. Martens Berg."

"Berg?" He paused, lines of confusion suddenly straining his otherwise unemphatic face. "But since you're both Jewish, Madame, why you don't use your husband's name?"

"First, young man, I don't think it's any of your business. Second, I use my name and my husband uses his. Third, my husband isn't Jewish. He's quite Aryan. He's leaving his homeland because he loves *me* more than Germany.

But why do I have to explain this to you? Why don't you just look to see whether you have a Professor Martens Berg on your list? He's a distinguished art historian. He's published three works of scholarship, six monographs, and forty-three essays in German and French periodicals. I'm becoming very upset. I'll come back. Please, sir, when I return, if you are here, do try to understand that behind every name – whether on your list or not – there's someone in trouble."

I had replied to his English with a torrential French already glistening with impending tears. His mouth fell open, as if to reply. Perhaps it was a shock. I left quickly without waiting for his reply.

I can recall vividly, even now, returning to the Vaugirard after my conversation with that indescribably callow young man. It was a fifteen-minute walk, obliging me to turn from Raspail beyond the Hotel Lutetia into the Vaugirard and then, at a certain point which interests no one but myself, angling to the right down a narrow one-way street to our lodgings.

For many years, I had been approaching the notion that all our lives were merely transitory way-stations of Being itself, that we – personae, personalities, personifications – had simply taken up lodgings in Being, fitting out the immensity of Being with the specifications and requirements of our light passage through its corridors. Nothing could have struck me more forcefully in the aftermath of that excessively emotional conversation with the young secretary (who, after all, in his own obtuse way, was only trying to be helpful) than confirmation of my ultimate view of things. I was definitively a transient in Being. This was no espousal of the Oceanic view of reality which Freud debunked so resoundingly in his reply to Romain Rolland's letter.

Mine was something quite different. It was not that I was part
of the swim, the galaxy of Being. I was not merged; neither was
I an emanation nor a unit of Being. I was – I have said it – a
lodger-in-Being or, as Hermann Broch was to instruct his Virgil
to assert, I was a lodger in my life. And *that* young man (who
would undoubtedly have offered me a tissue and a glass of water
had I begun to cry) had unwittingly confirmed for me this metaphysical self-judgment. I became certain at that instant (utterly
certain and persuaded and prepared as never before or since to
stake all my intelligence upon its veracity) that my life inhabited
a domain within Being that was imperishable. My specifics and
details – the temporality of Erika – would pass, my habitation
would change, the drapes and comforters and cushions of my
occupancy would pass away, but the permanence of Being had
conferred upon the room in which I lodged and, hence, in some
measure, upon me, an order of indestructibility which obliged
me to hold fast. You see, when I answered that young man as
I did, I was not defending Martens Berg from being thought a
Jew or protecting myself from some aspersion of concubinage,
or making claim to the durability and fame of Martens's works.
I was only making the claim of Being. I was behaving as any
truth-telling metaphysician must behave: I was offering my life
for the truth.

No small thing, and with what joy I walked home to Martens.
And, I should add, with what joy Martens received my telling.
At that instant, although I had brought home the news for which
he had asked, he was unmoved by its detail. He had noticed
the flush of my cheeks and the glitter of my eyes – sure signs,
he observed, that I had made a discovery I wanted to report.
And so I told him everything, recording carefully the epiphany
of my homecoming. Martens understood all these things. It was
he, more than you know, who had strengthened in me the metaphysical turn that marks my works. His was a similar gift, the

ability to read a painting as a speculative text, as a document that revealed not merely a social view, a cultural attitude, an aesthetic doctrine, but a vision of the whole. Martens greeted my report with a shout of pleasure and he produced a bottle of sherry to celebrate Being itself, our way-station and abode, and to toast our pledge to triumph over mendacity and misrepresentation of its charge. Martens, more than anything else, adored thinking about the highest questions along with me.

Many years after all this, Jean-Paul Sartre repeated to me the story, already legend, of his loss of faith. He was then a young boy standing at a bus stop in La Rochelle, waiting for two girls with whom he had an engagement. It happened there: Sartre lost his faith. He no longer believed in God or even the possibility of God. Unlike Descartes, who had passed a cheerless night during November, 1619, at a German inn, weary of the winter war, seeking with increasing desperation an indubitable piece of knowledge and coming, at last, upon one – the famous *cogito* – Sartre did not publish the argument of his twelve-year-old atheist intuition. Presumably, when the girls showed up, Sartre boarded the bus and that was the end of it, until he recorded the episode in *Les Mots* as a biographical addendum. When he repeated it to me in Paris during my visit with him in 1969, it was mentioned without a twinkle. He didn't smile as he slipped the autobiographic matter of fact into our conversation. I think he was rather pleased with the ordinariness of its circumstance. It seemed so right to him that his atheism should take shape at a bus stop.

Sartre thought all the time. It was this more than anything else, Simone de Beauvoir told me, that had attracted her to him. She admitted that she had been told before they met by a mutual good friend that there was this young fellow, Sartre, who began thinking when he got up in the morning and didn't stop until he fell asleep at night. He thought and he smoked cigarettes and he was indifferent to material things.

No wonder he called his autobiography *Les Mots*. (Are there not then only three types of people, those who would call their autobiographies *Les Mots* and those – a vast body – who would proudly call them *Les Choses*, and a considerable group of others – large, small, I do not know – who cannot make up their mind, desperate for *Les Mots*, but terrified of losing the guarantees promised by *Les Choses*?)

I, on the other hand (not having been raised a Catholic but knowing myself to be a Jew in whom the commandments lodged like the rotting apple in Gregor Samsa's carapace), did not cease to believe in God at a bus stop. I had never raised the question of God as such. *La question de Dieu* is preeminently a Catholic question and even more a French Catholic question: one can understand Sartre coming to his decision no differently than Mauriac or Claudel coming to theirs. It's the kind of thing French Catholics are expected to settle early. As for myself, and for Jews like myself – loathing the bourgeoisie, betrothed to thought, annoyed at the necessity but finally accepting the ineluctability of Jewish flesh – the issue was not God, but Being, the *ontos on*. And my revelation occurred in Paris, not far from the café where Sartre told me about his atheism. He was in retreat from the omnivorous luminosity of Being, and I – a Jewish Platonist, I suppose I would be called – was drawn to it as a tiny star searching for her galaxy.

I didn't bother telling Martens the details of the procedure necessary to secure an American visa. I saved all that for the next day.

It was enough merely to announce that all would be well with us "if we had an invitation to teach or perform or conduct or lecture or discover the secrets of the universe." It was such a long sentence, Martens chose not to hear it out. He looked at me and smiled and his smile – travelling to his eyes – dizzied me with its incomprehension. Martens could do that. His eyes transmitted his intelligence, but no less unequivocally they bleated his confusion. I explained patiently and he understood. It seemed to please him that I was not on the list. That sounds cruel, but it wasn't. Martens and I had some problems on that score. He, at least, was not definitely excluded; I had left before the young man hunted his list in search of an Aryan Professor Berg.

Martens rarely acted decisively. When he did, however, he was a monument to speed. Some might attribute his general lassitude to weakness. Not in Martens's case. Martens was weak in other departments. His body was weak, his sex was weak, his hearing was weak and all these aspects of a weak body and a weak *élan* may well have contributed to a febrility of spirit. I don't know and I don't speculate on such matters. My husband is dead now and I cannot show him these papers for his comment and correction (as I would – even nasty and contumacious passages). I am, after all, a scholar and I have the obligation of preserving accuracy, without conjecture, even when it comes to the evocation of my husband. Martens was rarely decisive; however, when he made up his mind, he was firm and final and he acted, it could even be said, with immoderate alacrity. I think this as well may be ascribed to his debile hearing. He heard so little that when a complicated notion, vested with urgency, accompanied by vigorous signs and lip-read repetitions, at last penetrated, Martens acted. He didn't fold up – folding up he used only for beginnings, to avoid if the matter wasn't really important or to put me off the scent if it was.

However, if the issue deserved it and got through, he was as instantaneous as a breath.

Several years before, someone by the name of Cook had come through Berlin and looked Martens up. It turned out that he ran the Institute of Fine Arts in New York and had admired a monograph Martens had written on mythological iconography in rococo painting. They had lunched together at the Café des Westens where Martens showed off, introducing this Cook to the whole crowd – Däubler, Mehring, Herzfelde, Grosz – all of whom shook Cook's hand, clapped his back and got a brandy and coffee in return for their collegiality. Cook had spoken kindly to Martens, kindly and softly, and Martens had preserved his neatly printed *carte de visite* for future reference (usually Martens threw them away with a line like "Who needs to remember *him*?").

Martens sat down that evening in May and wrote this Cook a letter announcing that he and his wife were out of Germany (permanently, he feared) and currently stranded in Paris without regular work. He put it neatly, without the finished indirection I would have used for such propositions. His exceptionally brief, almost peremptory, note read: "Our funds are running very low. Is there the possibility, I ask you, for work in your Institution of Fine Arts? I write English intelligently. I speak English not badly. I have many books to write still in my life. I look forward gratefully to the courtesy of a prompt reply."

Only now am I certain that his letter of some sixty words contained not less than seven errors of vocabulary, syntax, and usage, not to mention mistakes of spelling and punctuation. It did, however, do tricks. Six weeks later we had a reply, inviting us to come to New York, stating unequivocally that we were welcome at the Institute, Martens as a teaching associate at $4,800 per annum and myself as a research assistant at $2,600 until I could find permanent employment in my own discipline.

Cook described the procedures to be undertaken to secure a visa and commended us to the care of the American Ambassador, who he mentioned was an old college classmate. He concluded his letter with the assertion of a conviction he obviously felt so deeply that he repeated it to others (I have the testimony of Erwin Panofsky to this effect): "My dear Professor Berg," this Cook concluded his invitational response, "I can only consider Hitler to be my best friend. He shakes the trees and I gather the apples." I presume he regarded Martens as an apple, although his reputation was well-enough matured to be a plum. In those days my reputation was still small. A crab apple perhaps, but not more or larger. We were being saved, then, it appears, by someone who thought Hitler was a fortuitous asset of American civilization.

But we did get out.

We got our visas and we left by freighter on December 30 from Marseilles. We arrived in New York five weeks later. On February 6, 1936.

I add *in memoriam*: our friend Ewald tried to reenter Germany, where a friend had left money for him at a *poste restante* in Stuttgart. He was caught and sent to Dachau. Of him nothing more. Alas, Ewald was no tempting fruit of culture.

When I reviewed these pages, I felt compelled to make several insertions before I could continue:

> A week before I left Paris for Marseilles, I saw the elder of the two *gendarmes* who had come to the apartment to inspect our documents. He recognized me, smiled, and stopped to talk. I told him that my husband and I were leaving for the United States. He said he thought that was a good idea and he wished us *bon voyage*. He touched two fingers to his kepi,

bowed slightly and moved away into the sunlight. I was struck by the burnished shine of his old and threadbare uniform.

Martens and I had our last meal in the Luxembourg gardens. We brought a bread, some fresh goat's cheese, a brown paper cone stuffed with black olives, and a bottle of red wine. We sat under a chilly December sun; we hardly spoke and we ate little, but it seemed very important to us both to have our last Parisian meal in the open, in the Luxembourg gardens, where history was brownish-green, orderly, and remote.

At the train station, for the last time, I saw Count Harry again. I had seen him at a distance several times during the year we had spent in Paris, but only twice had I seen him close-up. Now, it was at the Gare de Lyons. He was waiting for a train to take him south to the vicinity of Nice, where many of the better class of German intellectuals had set up their refuge and their reprieve. He seemed ailing, immensely tired and drawn. (I neglected to mention earlier that I found out what had troubled him the day of our arrival. One of his closest friends, a writer who was supposed to have come on the same train as ourselves, had been found beaten senseless in his apartment in Munich. Naturally, the perpetrators were never found. It happened to many of Count Harry's friends.) What was left to him at his age hardly mattered. He died little more than a year later.

Lastly, to our surprise, Madame Beauchamps wept when we left for the station. It made no sense to me. I thought she despised us. She thanked us for the perishables we had left in the icebox. She had obviously rushed into the apartment the moment we started down the stairs. She had been lying in wait. I had anticipated Madame Beauchamps and had put a note in the icebox, telling her that the milk and cheese were for her. And, also, the fruit juice. Why was I generous to her? I don't know, but it seemed fitting. The only eyes from which I want an eye are those that fancy them to be without mote. Madame Beauchamps's did not qualify. In everything she was open and undeceiving: she hated us and we knew it.

Uncle Salomon's slap had deprived me of sentiment. I left Paris without a whimper, without a look-back, without so much as a catch in my throat. It was another city of our age whose people had forgotten at what price its stones had been bought.

# PART TWO

# AMERICA

▼

New York was under snow.

In fact, as our freighter entered New York harbor, it was still snowing. Large snowflakes continued to fall and melted as they touched the deck. Everything seemed to melt, or disappear, or turn into something else when it entered New York harbor. Melting snow became a metaphor for Martens and myself. We had stood on deck for more than an hour, freezing in our insubstantial topcoats as the ship passed the lighthouse, turned up the river, and met the tug which guided it to its berth on the West Side.

We were pleased to enter the city from the West Side. For many years, we hardly left the West Side. It became our side of the city.


After we had cleared customs, we realized that we had no American money. Martens had nothing to give the young Irish luggage handler. He was good-natured and accepted our situation. He even carried our suitcases to a taxi. We had the name of a cheap hotel on West 72nd Street and we went there immediately. The hotel – to which we had written giving our Mr. Cook of the Institute as a reference – paid for the taxi and loaned us ten dollars. While Martens unpacked, I went to a bank downtown to change our little money into dollars and open an account.

The red-haired bank clerk asked me for my German passport. I explained that I was not a German visitor but an emigré. I had been issued travel documents in Paris by the American Embassy. I was a person *in medias res.* (I sometimes imagined myself standing on a block of moving ice between two shores, desperate to arrive somewhere solid before the ice beneath me broke up.) The bank clerk looked carefully at my face when I handed him my travel documents. I don't know what he expected to see. My face read care and complexity. It appeared to satisfy him and he took my French bank notes and calculated their value. About $300, perhaps a bit more. Not terribly much, but in those days probably enough for a few months of strained existence. At that moment, however, I felt confident we were employed.

We had arrived and no one was waiting for us.

We had arrived to nothing except an invitation from the director of an Institute, with whom my husband had once had lunch. It seemed utterly improbable. Years later my friends would inquire whether our ship had been met, whether the nation had been alerted to the arrival of the glorious Erika. The "glorious Erika" was then a young woman of twenty-nine, with a half-dozen essays under her belt, a nearly finished manuscript in her luggage, and a satchel full of unsorted notes. She was accompanied by a vastly more eminent but depleted husband whose reputation had earned them entry visas. That was that. The foghorn sounded in the snow; it was the only noise that attended our arrival in America. We couldn't even see the Statue of Liberty; she was invisible through the snow and nobody pointed her out to us. I don't think I've ever seen the Statue of Liberty except in photographs and movies and although I owe something of my freedom to her emblematic presence in this nation, she remains a ghastly piece of sculpture.


We settled in.

By the time I returned to the hotel, Martens had unpacked our belongings. He had even removed his collection of glass slides from the bottom of his "unacademic suitcase" (as he called it). That was something he had not done in Paris. He was holding up a cartoon of the David fresco at Versailles and studying it in the dying light when I returned. He had put our clothes away and stored our empty luggage in the closet; he had secured additional hangers from the maid and retrieved a wilted rose from the trash can in the hallway and placed it in a drinking glass. Most significantly, he had removed two chromolithographs of execrable quality that had hung above the bed and hidden them behind the cheap chifforobe. In their place he tacked a reproduction of an exquisite Chardin which he had bought at the Louvre during our last days in Paris.


Martens didn't call the Institute. I had suggested that he call and make an appointment to meet Mr. Cook. He insisted he couldn't call, that his accent was unintelligible, that he couldn't be sure he would hear, that he needed to buy a hearing device but had no money, that telephones had frightened him even when his hearing was excellent. It was an endless no, no, no. He had been preparing for it. I knew my Martens. He knew I would tell him to call and he knew he wouldn't. He was ready for me when I returned to the hotel. The new Chardin, the glass slides, the small mound of his papers, the modest stack of academic offprints, and one copy each of his several books were neatly arranged on the desk. He was telling me that he was ready to go to work immediately.

"Why don't you call and make an appointment?"

He began to say no, however instead of "no" there followed the reasons for saying no. I called instead. That's what he wanted. I spoke to Mr. Cook's secretary.

"Who did you say you are? Is Mr. Cook expecting your arrival? Please wait one minute while I speak with Mr. Cook. He's on his way out of the office. One minute." Before I could reply, a hand cupped the phone, and mumbled sound, incoherent, edged through the openings between her fingers. She returned. "Oh yes, Mr. Cook remembers. Can Professor Berg come in tomorrow at eleven?" Before I could consult with Martens, she said, "Fine then for eleven," and rang off. I repeated the conversation to Martens several times, accenting the secretary's words as favorably as I could, moderating her interrogations from sheer ignorance to stupidity, finding it more optimistic to consider her slightly subnormal than merely uninformed. Surely she anticipated our arrival. Surely she had typed Mr. Cook's letter. Surely she expected Professor Berg. But then, I knew better. Something about her vagueness warned me.

It was no surprise, surely, that nothing promised was delivered.

When Martens entered the café the next day he was trembling, his face drained and exhausted. Herr Loewe, the proprietor, brought him a cognac and waved aside Martens's embarrassment at his generosity.

"Nothing. There's nothing," Martens moaned.

"Did he remember you?"

"Yes. Yes. But remembering me? What's remembering me? A hunchback. A dwarf. An amputee. He remembered the impression of me. He recalled Berlin. He vaguely recollected drinks at the Café des Westens, but me, who I am, the man to whom he wrote — vague, very vague."

It seemed impossible. Martens had received a letter, an enthusiastic letter, promising him a position.

"He said he sent dozens of them. Some people answered right away and others, like myself, never thought to answer."

I was thunderstruck. It was the first time he'd mentioned it. "You never answered?"

"Does a cripple ask for a crutch?" he replied.

"It's not a metaphoric matter, Martens. You never answered?"

"No. I didn't think it necessary."

He gulped his cognac and slammed the glass down on the table with such force it almost shattered. He was filled with rage and bravado. They always came together. Discovered in some momentous carelessness, Martens would tremble first and then become enraged.

The position promised to Martens had been filled weeks before. Martens had never replied to Cook's letter for reasons that neither he nor I could explain. He had simply assumed it was understood that he would come as soon as possible, that the offer was a standing invitation, that stranded Europeans ("displaced German scholars") didn't need to waste time on the formalities of gratitude, but should simply pack up and make haste. Our little money was enough to keep us for a few months, modestly, very modestly, but certainly no longer. Martens suspected the Institute of bad faith. He believed Cook reneged when he discovered that his hearing was impaired. I didn't think so, although it's possible. As for me, the $2,600 per annum was only for the Immigration and Naturalization Service, a ruse to persuade them that we would not be a drain on anyone, that we were gifted, wanted, employed. Fortunately, a week later the library director at the Institute called and offered Martens donkey-work sorting out an archive of slides and photographs just bequeathed to its facility. They paid him $1.60 an hour and indicated that they thought the work was good for about six months. We were off the hook of penury. It bought us time. Or rather, it bought me time.

It was up to me again. Herr Loewe at least had told me where to start.

"Go by the *Aufbau* during the next day or two and see their want ads. The newspaper comes out regularly. The next issue is a few days off. Mention my name. They know me. We always advertise the Café Danube."

Herr Loewe was pure accident. In fact, it was the unrelieved café-lust of Martens that had brought us together. The second evening in New York, before returning to our hotel after supper, Martens was overcome with longing for a café. He had arranged the names of all the Berlin cafés he knew in rhythmic order and to a jolly tune began to sing them. It was an invocation. As we turned the corner towards our hotel, there it was: the Café Danube, windows steaming, snow melting at its lead seams. Inside, we saw our people, our whole people with enormous hats and homburgs, canes beneath chairs, three-piece suits, drinking tea from glasses held in little metal receptacles, eating Linzer torte and Black Forest cake, spooning jams onto toast, stirring thick cream into black coffee, playing chess, arranging dominoes, reading a variety of newspapers and magazines held by mahogany binders. Usually, I avoided such cafés. The menopause of the bourgeoisie, I thought them – not at all the aggressive, pulsing cafés of great cities, but local oases where third- and fourth-rate social pretensions replaced the howling-yowling of the real thing.

"They heard you, Martens," I said, nudging him. Martens

turned and saw the café. His face brightened. "There's hope for this country after all," he added, rushing towards the door.

The café's owner, Herr Loewe, a bulky man with a gold watch chain cascading over his ample stomach, came to greet us, seizing my hand for the ritual kiss, shaking Martens's and with the other propelling us towards a window table.

"I can tell you're new. Just arrived. Off the boat yesterday."

"The day before," I said, not displeased by his friendliness.

"It has to be. Anyone here longer than a few days knows my Café. It's not Budapest or Berlin, but New York will have to do." He spoke to us in German, but confessed quickly that he had owned a clothing store in Budapest. "I arrived three years ago and went looking for a café. Nothing. Americans think a café is a coffee-shop with counters and rotating chairs where you get a cup of see-through coffee. I had to do something or I'd perish. And such necessities give birth to inventions, as the American expression goes. So. So. Welcome to the Danube. Tea or coffee? On the house tonight. Tomorrow is time enough to pay." Herr Loewe went on to lay down the ground rules. One coffee and you could stay all day reading papers and magazines. The food was good – more Hungarian than German, but the distinction was often lost. Brandies and liqueurs of all kinds. Tables were shared if there was room for others. He ticked off the customs of the house and then handed us a little printed brochure where they were set down in order, from general welcome to the denial of credit.

Martens and I went through the Berlin newspapers for the first time in months. They were unbearable. Later, Herr Loewe returned. He placed a hand on Martens's shoulder, a hand of *gemütlichkeit* that Martens found uncomfortable. He smiled at us and wished us well. Martens told him that the next day he was to see about a job. Herr Loewe congratulated him, but added that if things went wrong, there was always the *Aufbau*.

He pointed out various people in the café who had found their jobs through the *Aufbau*. "Terrible jobs, but still jobs. We have professors running elevators and selling furniture and being night watchmen. But in this country you have to start some-where, *nicht wahr?*"

I shuddered.


I didn't get to the *Aufbau* until the following week.

Martens fell ill. Not seriously, but enough. A terrible cold, complete with cough and intermittent fever. He made it worse than it was, sneezing with dramatic gestures, following each eruption with an exaggerated cough made louder and louder, more and more miserable, soliciting comfort and commiseration. The truth was – he admitted it later – he couldn't bear his stupidity with Cook. A plausible reversal – despising himself, he demanded sympathy. It was all right. I gave him sympathy. After all, I loved him. Moreover, I was content to stay inside. The snow had begun again. The streets were covered with slush and ice. I went out in the morning for provisions, borrowed a hot plate from the desk clerk, and fixed our simple meals in the room. By afternoon, Martens had quieted down, drowsy from aspirin and cough medicine.

While he slept, I studied English, holding conversations with waitresses, professors, bus drivers, subway clerks, elevator op-erators, every sort of city functionary and potentate with whom I would be likely to come into contact. I began my conversations with expressive formality, thinking my habituated "*bitte*" needed to precede every request. Only later did I realize that "thank you" was far more critical than "please." And even "thank you" could be, and frequently was, omitted. After a time, I wearied of reviewing English, and unpacked my books and papers, my few books, my several folders of papers, and arranged them on the windowsill. My library of flight contained my St. Augustine, a first edition of Kant's *Kritik der Reinen Vernunft* that Martens had given me on our first anniversary, the three-volume Medicus edition of Schelling, Ludwig Börne's letters to Henriette Herz, a Greek Plato I had bought in Freiburg when I attended Heidegger's seminar, and assorted volumes of Heine, Hölderlin, Novalis, and a Bible in German and Hebrew. I had arrived in America with fewer than a score of books from my own library. The selection, however, was not quite random. They were the books that had nourished me into maturity.

Now, nearing the end of my life, I have started to dispose of books again. In my early fifties I began with Martens the process of winnowing our library, but in those days it was still a decision of sovereignty, determining that certain books had exhausted their usefulness, that certain ideas no longer needed review. We dispatched the lesser and diminished gods to Fourth Avenue. The weeding was renewed several years later with considerably greater aggression. By then, there were piles of books beneath my desk, cartons of books in the closet, double rows of books on our bookshelves. We had begun to forget what we owned. The day I came home with a second copy of Jacob Burckhardt's *The Age of Constantine*, we made up our minds that the books were beginning to take over the apartment and would – unless we fought a disciplined battle – overwhelm us.

In those early days, I never expected to see any portion of my Berlin library again. Almost true. Many years later, when my reputation had begun to return to Germany, I received in the post a small package from Köln with an unsigned note: "I found this in a local bookstore and seeing your name on the flyleaf thought you might be moved to have it again." It was an edition of Henrich von Kleist's essays and stories that contained his meditation on marionettes which was to influence the whole of my later work. I was overjoyed to have this volume although

I would not have known what to say to my benefactor. The truth is I would have said nothing, not even thank you.

Already at this juncture one critical difference between Martens and myself was clear. I was an itinerant. Not a vagabond, but an itinerant.

It didn't matter to me where I set up shop and taught or put myself down and thought. While I was at university, I was always taking excursions out of the city to meet other scholars, to hear their lectures, compulsively visiting libraries and archives, tracking the echo of great movements and the impulsion of great ideas.

Martens, for some reason obscure to me, feared chance and accident; he found meeting strangers unbearable unless I accompanied him; he thought his little office at the Institute, his table at the Danube, his sofa in the apartment permanently reserved. Makeshift or happenstance confused him, refusing to prediction the inevitability which he required of events. It wasn't that he evaded freedom or denied passion, merely that he guarded them for internal play and reflection. He never understood that public freedom belonged as well to others and for that reason was never absolute except as dream. As for myself, set times, fixed places, stated duty, ordinance and regulation were intrinsically loathsome, an illegitimate imposition upon my freedom that was not part of the original social contract. All of the requirements of civility I took to be prescriptions for the convenience of masters. I had no jealousy of such masters – the ordainers, the employers, the caste- and class-bound – it was only that I had no wish to join them. What I wanted to accomplish most during my early years was to strip from myself the plaster such masters had trowelled upon my freedom, to be rid of their sense of priority and importance, to make something new of

myself which discerned the reasons and listened to them, which
made up the ground of myself without heeding their notion of
its limits and parameters. How can human beings be expected
to think hard, to take account of the world, to understand events
and to adventure, if long ago, without choice, they have been
subverted by hours of rising and bedtime, requirements of dress,
clean fingernails and brushed hair, recreation and sport, re-
warding marzipans and punitive denials? And yet, that is the
enemy against which every one of us who wishes to think free
must fight. We have first to destroy origins in order to come to
true beginnings. I have always been about that work.

I was not at all frightened when the office secretary of the *Aufbau*
suggested I apply to a fortnightly that was looking for a German-
educated intellectual to report on the culture, politics, and
society of that doomed nation.

"But you will have to popularize," Martens objected.

"I will, then, but I will say things important to be said nonetheless."

"You don't know English well enough," he continued.

"Then I will master what I need."

"But you will never have a style," he insisted.

"Perhaps not theirs, but certainly, finally, in the end, one of
my own. I'm an itinerant, Martens. I go where I have to go. I
master what I need."

As an itinerant, I began with piecework.

I came into the office twice a week: Monday mornings when
they had their editorial meetings and Thursdays when I was
expected to come by with my copy, pick up books for review
and discuss ideas with the editor-in-chief, a large man, always

covered with cigar ash, whose glaucous eyes seemed hooded with weariness even in the morning. He was well-known in the New York of that day, although by the end of the '40s, when his particular brand of smarmy Stalinism had finally begun its overdue descent into public ignominy (he was already held in contempt by the knowledgeable furies of the day), he was good for little more than drunken assaults on the cabals of Trotskyites who he imagined had successfully broken him and destroyed his magazine.

I met him many years later in a dairy restaurant having a glass of tea into which he was (not so surreptitiously) pouring brandy from a flat perfume bottle he carried in the inside pocket of his jacket. He called out to me as I came in: "If it isn't our Broadway Plato." But that was the end of his rudeness. For the rest he was sad; he eked out a living running books he scrounged on Fourth Avenue to the better antiquarians uptown, still wrote what he thought prose for the few Communist publications left in the country, and complained bitterly that the younger radicals, whose groups he occasionally got twenty-five dollars for addressing, read Marx in English. I was amused by this complaint, since he read Marx in Russian.

He was well-known when I came to our magazine. I won't mention his name. By now he must be dead, but why mention his name? Those who know the magazine for which I worked will know of whom I speak, and for the rest, they don't need to know.

When I entered the office the first morning, the editor-in-chief was alone. He was the first to arrive and the last to leave. He was sitting in the center of the office, where there was a table and chairs at which our conferences were held. Around him was a series of cramped quasi-private cubbyholes, each with room enough for desk and chair, and a small overhead bookcase. But that first morning, Max (I'll call him) was settled into the lone chair of majesty in the center of the empty office, his large hands spanning the desk, a cheap cigar jammed between his teeth, staring glumly at a WPA calendar that hung on the wall.

"Young woman," he said growling as the door opened. "What can I do for *you?*" The emphasis sounded instantly suspicious, but I realized later that Max accented English incorrectly, forcing simple sentiments and normal courtesies to perform the work of ingratiation and often seduction.

"The *Aufbau* suggested that I apply for a job you offer. I have just arrived from Europe. My name is Erika Hertz. I am a German intellectual. I understand that you need a German intellectual."

"Good God, I said I needed someone who knows the German scene. I didn't ask for an import." Max began to laugh furiously, wagging his large head from side to side. I had no choice but to raise my right eyebrow, strike a pose of irritation, and wait until he got through with his antics. "So what do you do?"

"I'm an intellectual historian by training and passion."

"And what the hell is that?"

"If you don't know, why did you ask for one?"

"Okay, okay," he subsided. "It's too early for an argument. Do you write English well?"

"Probably not, but in six months I'll be brilliant."

"Not bad. Not bad at all." He liked my answers and I determined to keep it up, but Max became canny. No one had arrived yet, although it was nearly ten in the morning. He took his chance. Later, I discovered that he had taken advantage of me by offering less than the standard rate, but it didn't matter as I had already moved on elsewhere. "We pay by the page. $8.50 a manuscript page before cuts. You do an assignment, that's what you get. Do an original piece and you get $10.00 a page. Book reviews are $15.00 apiece – and you can keep the book or sell it as you please. But if you can't write English, three strikes and you're out."

Actually, my English was much better than I feared. I had learned English early. My father had insisted on it. He had the fantasy that one day he would have a printing works in London as well as Berlin. Naturally, I was expected to take charge of the London branch. It was for that reason I spent two summers during my adolescence in Sussex at a work camp, learning English, hoeing cabbages and hosing Herefords in the early morning. It was dreadful work, but I enjoyed the countryside and admired what the English called "bearing up." Naturally, I already had English essentials, although writing for a fortnightly required a different order of expression than an adolescent's needs. Since I had to produce at least one essay and one book review each issue in order to provide an elementary income, it meant not less than four thousand words of publishable prose every fourteen days.

The first month I produced nothing, but I went to Monday conferences regularly and came by the office every Thursday for a chat with Max. The magazine was foundering; its circulation was fairly steady – somewhere between thirty-eight and forty thousand – but its influence was already waning. The Moscow Trials were about to begin, but so was Max's drinking as he tried to take account of them. I suspected there was a connection between that ghastly spectacle and his emerging alcoholism, and I proposed it to him one day, but he became irritable and defensive. He knew I wasn't of his persuasion. Quite the opposite. I had no use for his politics and he knew it.

I understood only later that I was expected to have a politics; however, during those early days, my political sense was dormant.

A word of explanation, nonetheless, about my political innocence (not naiveté, but innocence, for I was never naive):

Germany never had a French Revolution. One of the charac-
teristics of the German debate during the century after the
Revolution of 1789 centered upon the ferocious envy German
intellectuals felt for the experience of France. France had made
it clear that no point of view was non-political: everything was
subject to the pressure and pain of power. This wasn't the case
in Germany. There was no medium for the political reality, and
whereas politics – like a porous bread plunged into thick sauce
– absorbed everything in France, politics was restricted in Germany to the rich, the landed, and the hereditarily empowered.
Literati, artists, scholars were the performers of the culture,
amusing to the powerful, recipients of their bursaries and ap-
pointments, but expected to be well-behaved. When they got
out of hand, they went to prison or into exile. There was never,
however, a concerted effort to define the libertarian style, and
where the liberal spirit found voice it did so on its own, without
popular backing, without the threat of sharpened staves and
cudgels. I can recall my gymnasium teacher of French extolling
the achievement of Diderot's *Encyclopédie*. After describing the
difficulties which surrounded its publication, its suspension, its
censorship, its bowdlerization and later its pirated publication
in Lyons, he paused for a moment, and looking at us with a
preoccupied amazement: *"Ah, mes enfants, les Français (pas
comme nous) aiment bavarder des idées."* Not like the Germans,
he meant. For us, there was no "gossip with ideas" since ideas
were not our currency. Currency was currency, hard gold tha-
lers.

All this is perhaps one reason why in my day, political ideas
were principally slogans of the street, dragging after them the
mob. I, who had all my life resisted mobs and with them parties,
movements, ideologies, had to learn what politics meant from
scratch. I had no cause but my sentiment for human beings and
my conviction that I would have lived well and usefully if I

succeeded in persuading one or two of them to step back from the mob (into which all of us sometime or other would love to plunge and be lost or borne aloft) and reflect.

In many respects I was out of touch with what was required by Max and his Stalinist cohorts. Since I have always believed that ideas were among the most endangered, fragile, and therefore human creations, I took special care to make certain my ideas at least were well-sheathed by historical evidence and documentation. My journalism tended to be didactic even though it was immensely rich. I always began a piece – whether on Bertolt Brecht or John Heartfield or the murder of Erich Mühsam or the suicidal intransigence of the Spartacists or the absolute idealism of Rosa Luxemburg or the machinations of Dimitrov and the Comintern – with a setting of ideas: where they had come from, and by what route. I traced the ideas of my *dramatis personae*, their sources, their conspicuous blind spots, their misconstruction of the times. I was not going to fall victim to the charge of Burckhardt that contemporaries refuse to be historical about their own history because they falsely imagine that their age is the summation and triumph of historical processes that have been bubbling through time's caverns for centuries. I knew the opposite. *My age – yours and mine – is no summation, much less a triumph.* Quite the contrary. Ours, if anything, is the nadir, and not even that. It is an age that has demonstrated more wildly than any other what happens when the state consorts with its industry and military to secure power and together delude themselves into believing they can hold it forever.

Max could barely tolerate me by the end. Every time I turned in a piece he read it aloud at conference, flourishing his red pencil like a conductor's baton, until his eye settled on some undoubted grammatical error. By wizardry, the baton became a weapon of annihilation and he drove it into the manuscript and carved up my prose. He couldn't argue ideas with me because he had none. He had polemic, he had doctrine, he had faith, but he had no ideas. He had no notion from where he'd come and by what route; he couldn't trace the source of his own blind faith. Before me he was helpless. When he shouted and denounced, his staff chorussing behind him, I waited until he subsided. I would then ask, in a deliberately calm and measured voice, whether he knew Aristotle's *Politics* and quoting some passage or other, first in Greek and then in translation, I would suggest that he was mixing categories of justice or confusing right and truth, or forgetting the categorical imperative. I was as foolish as he, of course. With such people, finally, one cannot discuss. There is only screaming argument and depression in the aftermath.

Notwithstanding, it was during the late spring of 1936 that I came on the American scene. I was employed. I wrote more than forty essays during the two years I was at the magazine and I signed most of them. The few that I found indifferently constructed and trivial I gave to a variety of pseudonymous inventions, all of them signifying folly. But, for the rest, I succeeded in forming a sense of my capacity to articulate, to see all the artifacts of culture prismatically channeling and riveting light. It liberated me – those years of journalism – to read and be paid for reading, to release half-thoughts into print while retaining the other half for more intensive scrutiny.

I served my time on the fortnightly. It was like being trapped in a rat's maze, figuring out where the electric charge was hidden and devising a circuitous route to evade the tyranny of shock and preserve myself. It wasn't easy. Many times I failed. Sometimes Max suppressed me and I threatened to quit, but he took me to lunch and begged. He apologized that his Stalinism (he still dignified it as Marxism) had got the better of him. He admitted once — it was a terrible admission — that sometimes he wanted to chuck it all, that he wearied trying to anticipate the party line, that frequently there was no line at all, merely the invention of a line in anticipation of the line that never came, that his life was a tyranny of ritual as unreal as his poor childhood in Vitebsk. He concluded his apologia saying: "It's all habit, habit I can't break. I would fall apart if I broke the habit. If I didn't have the party line to track — like many of Pavlov's dogs — I'd go insane."

Those years before the war, Martens and I were in training. Alongside the others (most of whom we met at the Café Danube), the few years that remained before the war — although drained of optimism — permitted us at least to fill time worrying about ourselves. There were others (many others) who simply could not forget Europe, who pulled at Europe's heartstrings and ended by ripping out their own. They couldn't learn English, didn't want to learn English, grew to hate it, rebelling against its exquisite irregularity and what one aged scholar called its "whorish vocabulary — borrowing from every language their best words and making them sound dull and tedious." The fact that whorish English had the largest vocabulary of any Western language proved no temptation. The French refugees stuck together writing Alexandrines and the Germans listening to Mahler and reading Wilhelm Dilthey and Max Weber for the salvation of souls.

How laughable we must have been to our American colleagues. Or rather, how laughable we should have been to our American colleagues and weren't. Now that's a point. We weren't ridiculous for a number of important reasons, not the least being that America hadn't had an immigration like ours since Colonial times. We were so ponderously well-educated, we were so gifted, so talented, so creative, that we couldn't help but be awesome even when we thought ourselves turgid and unintelligible. People like Albert Salamon quoting Condorcet and St. Simon instead of Walter Lippmann or Dorothy Parker, people like Pan tracking pictures as though the trail led straight to the Holy Sepulchre, and Alfred Döblin, Thomas Mann, Hermann Broch, Kurt Wolff and all the lesser constellations, the minor poets, the best-selling novelists, the musicians, composers, social scientists and physicists. And all reading books and making music. It was the most sustained cultural assault of these shores since the arrival of the Puritans and the English dissidents and, by and large, completely different than theirs. It was not that our folk were seeking a liberty we had never enjoyed. We had known an order of freedom. It was rather that we were escaping certain death. The Puritan dissenters were coping with a scrupulous conscience; we were responding to the knout and the jackboot. And so, on the whole, the early immigration of the thirties arrived with books and no bank account, manuscripts and no employment. Had it not been for the activities of Alvin Johnson and the New School for Social Research that he founded, and the occasional university that took a chance on foreigners, we might all have found ourselves running elevators at Macy's or washing dishes at Nedick's. And many of us did precisely that.

Whatever aspect of adventure my immigration to America had enjoyed, whatever delight I had taken in my adaptability and readiness to learn, vanished however one morning in January, 1939, when I received my mother's last letter.

It began, *"Geliebte Tochter."* I had not heard those words, that precise resonance of words, for more than four years. I had spoken to my parents several times when we were in Paris and they had spent those expensive calls warning me about drafts in our apartment, about keeping warm, eating properly. They had not yet taken as finality the fact that I had left Germany and was not returning. I couldn't ask for money and although at the beginning, before papa was forced out of business, he sent us some, his generosity stopped abruptly. I wrote them infrequently. Sometimes for their birthdays I sent a note. Sometimes they wrote back. They told me little. They had little to say. Their silence and mine reflected the depression out of which we addressed each other. To speak about the situation would oblige me to be harsh and them to lie. And so our correspondence was vacuous and trivial. They rarely mentioned politics. Once, my father remarked in closing that "things were going to get bad," but it seemed to me that they were already terrible and could hardly get worse. (Obviously I was wrong about this.) I blamed him in my heart for the same kind of shortsightedness for which I had always berated my parents. But the letter that arrived on January 11, 1939, will send shivers through me the rest of my life.

My mother's letter read:

Berlin, November 9, 1938

*Geliebte Tochter*
I will try to write you again, but I do not think it will be possible. We are being forced to leave Berlin. Papa and I are each allowed one suitcase. We are supposed to be at the Brandenburgertor tomorrow morning at 7 a.m. Where they are taking us I do not know. Our only happiness now is that you are not here. It is so cruel. We have not known you as well as we should. Even though you and uncle Salomon (he is already dead, you know) were so different, he understood you better. I think we were too convinced about Germany. It is hard to admit that we were wrong. It is so cruel. I wish I understood what was happening to us. Papa sends his love, but he is so tired. I do not want him to know that I am writing.

It would pain him to have to admit that he was wrong, too.
God bless you, Tochter.

The letter was signed: "Your mother who loves her daughter."

Only after the war I learned that on November 10, 1938, many of the Jews of Berlin were deported to Sachsenhausen Concentration Camp where most of them died. My father had a heart attack at the end of August, 1939; he died before the war broke out. My mother lived for several months longer but I was told by a survivor (who had seen her several times) that after his death she gave away her food to the children in her block. She died of starvation.

I cannot bear to write about all this.

It is not that I have a reputation for stoicism to protect, but I have a mistrust of pathos. I am clear, all too clear, about my parents. And *my* parents I shared with most of those – living and dead – who were born into the German bourgeoisie. They were not exemplary, neither did they set out to harm me. But I am unable to deny that the way they lived and the thoughtless trust that they bestowed upon their world undid them. They believed they were home. Since I did not believe – ever – in the home they made for me nor in the world they trusted to support their home, I am cut free of sentiment.

I mourn their death. I mourn deeply the passing of any person who dies out of this world without having advanced their knowledge of its possibility and limits. The fact that my poor mother, nearing her end, had to admit that she was wrong the whole of her life dissolves my criticism of her. The fact that my father, nearing his own end, could still not admit that he was wrong persuades me, despite all my irrational passion for him, that he had never gotten himself a heart of wisdom. I take no pride in my hard way of judging. It gives me no pleasure nor peace. On the other hand, I don't know how I can say other than I say. I am also a prisoner, but to other things and other allegiances.

There are children, you see, who close the door on their parents' home and never return. They close the door decisively. They do not shut it violently, but they make certain nonetheless that it is firmly closed, soundlessly closed. They have no wish to make a noisy departure. They want no scenes, no clarifications, no explanations, neither loud voices nor tears when they close the door. And it seems that in closing the door they succeed (as I cannot) in sealing off chambers within themselves they no longer care to enter. Perhaps in time they even lose the key, and if by some chance they return to that house and look for that room, they no longer recognize it; perhaps by that time, the room is concealed behind plaster, and where once there was a room with mauve wallpaper in which they passed their childhood, there is now only a blank wall.

I have known such people. They have claimed to me that they hardly remember their parents. They have no pictures of them and they cannot be certain whether they are still alive. They forget the address of their parents' house. Even the city in which their parents live is obscure to them. Martens was like that. Once, after we had married, I travelled with him when he gave a lecture in Saarbrücken. It was late in the afternoon and our train left to return to Berlin at ten o'clock in the evening. We had been in Saarbrücken two days. A filthy city, perpetually silted with coal dust. Martens said as he closed his suitcase, "You know, I think my mother lives in a suburb near here."

"How is she?" I asked, assuming that he had called her.

"I don't know," he answered softly, "I haven't spoken to her since I left home." There was nothing I could say. If he had spoken to her a year before, I might have suggested we call and drive out to the suburb and visit with her for a half-hour. But

twenty-four years was a long time, too long for me to say anything. Martens didn't even sense my unease. It didn't cross his
mind. There were many closed chambers in Martens's life for
which he had thrown away the key.

I, too, had left my home and closed the door. I took a room
in the Prenzlauer Berg, a working-class quarter of Berlin where
many of the Spartacist beer halls were to be found. I watched
the trucks fitted with armor plate cruising the streets in 1927
looking for their enemy. That was my neighborhood when I left
home at the age of twenty. I had had enough. I had had enough
smiling, enough brushing my hair, enough dressing neatly, enough
talking in whispers at meals, enough, enough, enough. Papa
hadn't changed, nor had mother. They were both entwined like
predatory vines that bloom and flower, that attract hummingbirds
and praise, but nonetheless have the strength to pull down
unsupported walls. I was an unsupported wall, I believe. And
there came a moment, of no particular importance, when I
thought it crucial to make my exit or topple over.

We were having afternoon tea. Mother was serving an elderly
woman whose grey hair was piled elegantly like a tray of cakes.
Mother's visitor wore violet gloves and a white silk dress with
a broad black collar of *crêpe de chine*. She was very beautiful,
but she spoke out of the side of her thickly painted lips, as
though disdaining in my parents' home to speak openly and
forthrightly. And my mother was unnerved by her being in our
house, to tea in our house. The woman, it appears, represented
some charity on which my mother served. She was obviously
a Gentile. Otherwise, my mother would have been more
peremptory, even if she had remained as formal. At a certain
moment, my mother turned to me and said: "Daughter, would
you bring me my engagement calendar?" I had no idea what
she meant. I didn't even know my mother had an engagement calendar, and I couldn't for the life of me imagine where

she kept it. I looked at her, amazed, but she hardly noticed my confusion. The other woman smiled at me a crooked
smile, for she smiled as well out of the corner of her mouth.
My mother began to tap a finger, waiting for me to obey.
But I, I stood up, nodded graciously to my mother's guest,
went to my mother and bent down to kiss her forehead,
and left the room, left the house, closing the door quietly
behind me.

I stayed with Lotte Schiff that night. The following day, I
found a room in the east end distant from Charlottenburg, across
the city of Berlin, where neither of my parents would ever come
to visit me. I had some money put away, not much, but enough
to make the decision without first begging my father's permission
(which most certainly would have been denied).

Several days later, I returned at suppertime. There was silence at the table, although curiously my place had been laid
(it might have been for uncle Salomon although that day he was
on business in another city). Before papa could inquire, I spoke.
Usually, papa didn't speak at dinner until he had finished his
soup and begun (oddly for a bourgeois who prided himself on
his correct manners) to rub bread about in his soup plate. Then
he would begin his daily round of inquiry: "What did mother
do today?" And mother would tick off her boring routine. And
uncle Salomon would grunt his "nothing unusual." "And what
did Erika do today?" He still addressed me in the third person.
Before he could turn to me, for he always began with mother,
I interrupted.

"As you know, papa, I've left home. There's nothing to explain. I'm not angry or unhappy with my home. It's only that
from now on I need to be on my own."

He replied solemnly: "It's not done. Daughters do not leave
home until they leave with their husbands."

"But now, papa, it's done because I've done it. I've broken

with tradition. Presumably, I must take the consequences. What are they?"

Papa wasn't prepared for this. When I begged for punishment during my childhood, to avoid the long wait until he decided to set my fate, nothing I could say would hasten him. He waited until I had almost forgotten that I stood under the sign of judgment. And then the sword would descend. I was confined to my room or obliged to eat supper alone or some such torment. On this occasion I calmly asked for the punishment straight away. He realized for the first time that I was no longer afraid of him, that I was twenty, that I could – if he pressed me – close the door tightly, silently, and forever.

"Well, I don't know."

"I can't wait until you make up your mind, papa," I said in a low voice, but with audible determination. "If you no longer wish to pay for my incidental expenses at the university, that's quite all right. I'm able to work. I don't need much. It would be different if this were England or America where you have to pay tuition. The point is, papa, do you feel you have to punish me or, for once, do you wish to accept that I'm grown up, that I can leave my home without having to break with my parents to do so?" My voice was very calm, although I felt a tightness in my throat. He listened without looking at me, his ear cocked to attention while his eyes scanned the white tablecloth and he drew patterns with his fork across its surface.

"Yes, all right. I don't like it. I don't approve of it. But perhaps it will be better for us all if you leave home. No blessings, no curses. Now, may we continue with the roast."

That was the end of the discussion. After dinner I packed my things and several hours later, as I had arranged, Lotte Schiff came by in a taxi to collect me. Papa was at the door to shake my hand and kiss my cheek. I could hear my mother sobbing in the library.

In other words when I closed doors, they were still left ajar. I rarely came home after that, but when I did, it was always a surprise and papa told mother to bring out the remains of some special cake or open a crock of glazed fruit or preserved walnuts.

I have a photograph of my father taken when he was home on leave from the divisional headquarters where he served in the quartermaster corps during the first war. I am looking at that photograph now. It is the only one I took with me when I left home. It is the photograph I kept under the blotter on my desk in Berlin. Sometimes I stole a look at it when I was writing. Papa is posed beside a marble stand on which a bowl of flowers seems to float. He is leaning on its edge, his right arm gently supporting his handsome head. Papa had black hair which he wore parted low on the left side, brushing the great mass of it straight back until it nearly touched the stiff raised collar of his uniform. In the photograph his jacket is buttoned. All you can see are gold buttons from his braided neck to beneath his waist. He was slender and he remained slender. His eyes were blue, his cheeks were high and sometimes became flushed when he was excited. And, *à la mode*, he sported a moustache which, although cut sharply, tended to droop at its extremities, an infallible sign that it needed trimming. The face and body of my father were very handsome. Everything else about my father I am afraid was less pleasing, but the first impression of my childhood, being held in his arms and tickled by his moustache, was one of ineffaceable pleasure. Although I grew to dislike his world, even now in my own late years I remove the photograph from beneath the blotter of my writing desk and admire my father.

My mother, on the other hand, I never admired. I have no photograph of my mother. I realized that I had no photograph of her when her last letter arrived. I looked for one. I wanted to see for the last time what my mother resembled, and there was nothing. I suspect it was this that produced the nightmares that followed. Not the certainty that my parents were going to their death, but the absence of *memento mori*. I had nothing but my own recollections to evoke my mother. Those recollections did nothing to enhance her. Every time I conjured mother, I kept returning to her Sunday walks with papa when they would leave me alone after luncheon and their nap and walk through the streets of Charlottenburg without me. (Mother would be dressed with meticulous care, all light and air, all grace and pleasure, resting her gloved hand on papa's arm. They were tall and they were in love, but I do not recall with certainty the color of my mother's eyes.)

And without me! I did not understand then what it all meant. Even now, now that I understand, it does not ease the pain of that abandonment, worse, that betrayal. Mother was to blame. The rage begins against poor mother. And now, I cry for her. The guilt begins. And so it is. We hardly remember those earliest of years, their images like growing shadows mark out only large undifferentiated patches of gloom in our past and yet, indistinct as they are, those impressions are imbedded in us like geological fossils.

They were not easy days, those student days in the workers' quarter of Berlin. Forget the discomfort of scarce food and cold flats. Those were not real discomforts; I shared them with everyone. No one – or nearly no one – was exempt from the distress of post-war Germany. Regardless of whom we blamed in our hearts – whether as some the French or others the Communists and the Jews or still others the army and the industrial Right – the fact remained that all of us were hungry amid our sticks of furniture or our elegant Biedermeier.

What struck me then and even now arouses me to fury is the outrageous suffering of the young.

When I moved into my flat, I overlooked a small garden – it measured not more than a thousand square feet – which abutted a workers' school. It was what we call now a day-care center. But there, unlike the genteel arrangements of our day where children are dropped off and collected, fed and fêted with play and games, my little *Arbeiterschule* was as much an orphan asylum as a care center, as much for abandoning children as for guarding them while their parents worked.

I was expected at university lectures only two days a week. For the rest I studied in the library, gathering materials for my dissertation, or wrote in the back room of the flat, on the second floor above the small interior playground. The walls of the grimy plastered apartment houses sloped into the playground like a dizzying Feininger, cutting off sun from the muddy earth. Between two large boulders on which, in the afternoon, the children would scramble and sit somnolent, unsmiling, drinking their milk from metal cups, rose a stunted plane tree.

Isolated from the pack of children I noticed a young boy (at most eight or nine years old), hair straggling to his shoulders, upon his head a black peaked cap, wearing a coat that reached just below his pants, his legs sheathed in grey wool stockings – no doubt a Polish Jewish boy, left out of things by his unfamiliar strictness of dress and the unintelligibility of his dialect.

One day (spring had come slowly), the children shed their winter coats, but the little Jewish boy remained dressed as for a winter that would never end. He had noticed me several times standing before my window or sitting on the ledge reading, one foot braced inside my room, the other straddling the windowsill. I smiled at him and tentative, so very tentative, he returned my smile. I motioned to him to wait for me as I had shortly to leave my apartment for the university. When I reached the playground, entered through a narrow courtyard from the street, I smiled again and handed him an apple. He put out his hand, rubbed the apple in my palm, and took it at last, thanking me silently. From then began our friendship. Every day or so, I would bring Yankel Moishe – that was his name – something during play period. A piece of chocolate, a boiled egg, an apple, a crust of bread with cheese. For Chanukah, which I knew began in early December that year (I had attended the gala thrown by the Berlin Zionists), I brought him a hand puppet of Charlot.

I knew that Yankel Moishe was one of the abandoned, that soon the *Arbeiterschule* would transfer him to a Jewish refugee center and he would move on to yet another way-station of his strangled childhood. I do not use such language as unfairness or injustice. Since I do not believe in God as such, I neither blame God's exalted distance nor chastise the cruelty of our everyday life. All I say is this: the forlornness of that child confirmed for me the hopelessness, more, the irresponsibility even, of imagining that life is meant for happiness. When I spoke to that little boy (and we learned to speak, his Yiddish becoming clear and lyrical to my ears, my German, slow and without condescension, spoken perfectly), I tried to show him something of tenderness. I made up for him a story in which he was no longer a child but a man with children of his own whom he would one day love and care for. I named his children for him, giving them each one of his names. One became Yankel the Very Little and the other Moishe the Very Little. I presented him not with a vision of happiness but with a conviction that one day he would have the task of loving even smaller pieces of himself. He delighted in that invention and each day, after my gift of food, he would plead with me to tell him something more about the life of Yankel and Moishe – where they lived, what they ate for dinner, what games they played, what dreams they had, and whether they, too, one day would have little Yankels and little Moishes of their own.

We met, as I said, once or twice a week, each time for not more than half an hour. As much as he waited for me, standing off in the corner of the play yard, I looked forward to him. Our meetings lasted more than a year. It was in March of 1928 that I came to see him with a dish of kashe and milk that I had made for him. He was gone. I found out from the director of the school that he had been transferred to a camp outside Berlin, where she surmised he was being trained to go to Palestine.


I left my parents' home without any project of liberation. I was not out to prove a point to them. All points provable to parents tend to be points already missed or of an order of insignificance as to be unworthy of proof in the first place. Leaving home is quite simply taking one's unique singleness in hand and removing it from a mangled grasp. Only the liturgically bourgeois are endlessly ringing up to make certain their parents are in their rocking chairs or at their card games. And everyone else is dimly aware that it hardly matters. My parents, no less than myself, were completely alone. Leaving home was simply a physical confirmation of this commonplace realism.

And in his own way Yankel Moishe was a witness to this information. I could get that child to smile; I could coax him to guarded affection; I could reach under his skin to where his heart beat, but there was nothing I could ever do to demonstrate that it was a safe world in which he lived.

And so my mother and father perished in concentration camps built in the very heart of the nation to which they had given their life-long trust and confidence. Better a little neurosis and disbelief.

Shortly after I received my mother's final letter, I was asked

by a publisher to submit the manuscript of my book on Henriette
Herz. It was then I decided I did not wish to publish that book
in my lifetime, although it would have been undeniably useful
to my emerging career to have published it at that time. Although
I was already teaching at the New School for Social Research
and had begun to lecture here and there on the East Coast, I
was still an intellectual without portfolio. A book whose subject
was as obscure as mine would have been well-regarded. But
with the news of my parents' deportation, my mind was made
up that I could not donate any portion of my sane intelligence
to an interpretation of the cultural insanity that had produced
Hitler's Germany.

Until then, I had never dedicated anything to my parents –
not a scrap of my published prose. But I determined to dedicate
this non-publication on Henriette Herz to their memory. My
problem was that I could no longer press German questions as
*my* questions. I was no longer interested in tracing my flesh to
the German nation; it was no longer important. If Germany
survives, there will be Germans enough left to make sense of
it all. They can then explain to me the history of the salon and
the fate of its Jewish celebrants. It is a project of exegesis that
will take Germany a thousand years to complete. After my death,
however, when it is clear that I have left Henriette Herz as a
portion of my *opus posthumum*, it can be published. Its dedi-
cation will read:

> *Long after their death and my own*
> *let Henriette Herz explain*
> *why Germany was home*

By the war years, I had become part of the American world.
My essays and book reviews appeared frequently. I published

a small monograph on Heine and edited and introduced a selection of documents and writings by the members of the German-Jewish literary community who abounded at the end of the
eighteenth century. I was invited to give lectures. I attended
symposia. I met many of the most distinguished of the colony
of the fled. I became a tenured professor at the New School for
Social Research. I was competently on the scene. But I had yet
to meet many Americans. I lived beside them, but was not yet
among them.

I felt increasingly isolated and alone. It became more and
more necessary to join up with someone, with others who could
relieve my pain before Martens's disconsolation and unrest. My
life with Martens, you see, had become difficult again.


It was a beautiful day in the spring of 1929 that I met Martens
Berg.

I had taken a bus with a girlfriend (the same Lotte Schiff who
had helped my departure from home) to buy tickets for a concert
that Otto Klemperer was to conduct. I was feeling very lovely
that morning. I wore a string of amber beads a friend had brought
me from Italy. My hair was still long and wound about my head.
I felt my eyes shine; I held my head high, bearing my proud
nose like a trophy. I was fairly tall for a woman in those days
and I carried myself slender and erect, my waist cinched almost
unnaturally by a broad belt studded with cut steel ornaments.
As the bus came to our stop, I noticed a good-looking man,
much older than myself, walking across the broad avenue. He
was dressed in black gabardine and he wore a hat of white
Venetian straw with a black silk band. His shirt, however, was
not conventionally white. It was mauve. Mauve, indeed! And
his black silk tie, figured with a subdued underweaving of grey
stripes, completed his array of elegance. His face was grave,

but he wore a fair moustache which set off his auburn sideburns. He was grave, I've said, and he was older than myself by many years, but he exuded a kind of bonhommie that I thought both youthful and exotic.

He passed alongside the bus. Our eyes met and dropped away, embarrassed being caught admiring each other. He admitted later that he had seen me first as the bus slowed and that he had crossed the street to see me better. But he did not stop, and had vanished by the time we had exited behind a disabled war veteran. I sighed that that was that and went on with my friend to the concert hall. As we approached the inevitable line which formed for anything of value in Berlin, he reemerged as though an apparition. He had not been there and now he was suddenly before us. He removed his hat gallantly and bowed slightly.

"Forgive me if I intrude. My name is Martens Berg. I'm an artist – I hope you believe that! – and I should be pleased, very pleased, if you would allow me to make a drawing of you."

Lotte burst out laughing. She had never seen an approach like that. Nor had I.

"Please don't laugh. I really *am* an artist. And, whatever my talents, I have good manners."

(Ah, dear Martens, whom I married out of love.)

The sittings were real, the easel a fact, and Martens did draw quite well. It was part of his education to draw. He confessed, however, that his real talent was in his selection of subject. He knew what was right and authentic to sketch. Unfortunately, Martens lacked inspiration. His was a wholly learned skill. There was the dextrous hand, but that was all. It would be like a poet knowing how to match the words, to cull the images, to join the lines, but having no critical center that held. Martens, alas, had no vision of the form. And so I emerged after seven lengthy sittings well fantasied but unreal. I was beautiful, more beautiful than nature had allowed, but I had no subtlety. I was frontal; I was outlined in black, I had colored passages, but that was all. I was a German-Jewish *fauve*. I had been grasped, but I had not been reconceived. It had served well, however, for despite the failure of my portrait I had fallen in love with the painter.

After a month of playing at the artist, Martens admitted that he was a scholar, an art historian, not a painter at all. His ability to draw had come early. His father had been a railway conductor based in Düsseldorf. They had lived near the central station in a cheap apartment whose bedroom looked out over the railway coal yards. Martens called his childhood that of a "van Gogh of coal." Not potato pickers but coal handlers; the dust of the coal had been everywhere in his childhood – in his bed, in the tap water, in the soup. His early drawings were dark, black and brown like van Gogh's. He knew, however, by the time he was an adolescent that his gifts were meager.

But Martens, as I have said, did not tell me all this until much later, after my portrait was finished. He was afraid I would break off the sittings.

When I arrived the first time, I suspected the truth. A small two-room apartment behind the Akademie der Künste, filled with books, was hardly the atelier of a painter. The one large room facing a broad tree-lined avenue was filled with light. There Martens asked that I seat myself while he took up his position at an easel he acknowledged afterwards he really used to keep open a bulky folio of Piranesi's Roman vistas. He hadn't drawn in years and only after several visits to Der Sturm Galerie had he decided Jawlensky's bright portraits supplied the most easily adapted style for a rendition of my "unfailingly interesting face."

And so he worked. That first sitting, interrupted by breaks for coffee and frequent cigarettes, he sketched in charcoal. He showed me nothing. I didn't ask. His conversation was oblique and unfailingly polite. He never referred again to his artistic vocation. I asked no questions about his incredibly rich library.

At the end of our second sitting the following week:

"You're a difficult subject."

"How so?"

"Poets (who can't paint) speak about portraiture as though it were a process of excavation − carving from the inside out, making the heart of the subject beat at the surface of the canvas."

"Is it nonsense? I remember Baudelaire saying such things."

"Baudelaire, exactly. Poets' talk."

"And the real truth?"

"Portraiture is seizing one moment, one perfect moment, and pretending that it speaks the whole. No less nonsense. The Italians Balla and Boccioni at least have the imagination to make painting photograph motion. They create the illusion of a sequence of moments in simultaneity, but even then they don't make any romantic demands upon their invention. A sequence of moments, that's all, and no more profound for being more than one. Portraiture − even when it's ugly − flatters."

"You'll make me better than I am."

"I don't mean that."

"What then?"

"The portrait argues for pretense − that the painter's single moment is the true one. It's all a pretense of eternalization."

"And which image of me will you make eternal, Herr Berg?"

"I'm not certain yet. I haven't really begun."

"What in heaven's name have you been doing the past six hours?"

"Taking notes. Taking notes. That's all. Figuring out your ears; forming an opinion of your nose, your chin, your hair. The first part of portraiture is the vague outline − the scale of the face. The rest is taking notes."

"And the grand intuition? When does that come? The intuition of Erika?"

"That's first-rate. When I get it, I'll call it that. *Intuition of Erika*. When it's finished, of course."

"And when will that be?"

"Weeks from now. Perhaps after we've had dinner together and gone to hear Klemperer."

"You're teasing! There were no tickets."

"Ah! But there were. I bought us two. You don't mind, I hope."

I protested. I knew that scalpers' prices for Klemperer concerts were exorbitant; but Martens insisted he hadn't paid for them too dearly. A friend of his was first cellist of the orchestra; he had gotten the tickets from him. Martens had even sent one with his compliments to Lotte Schiff, who had begged off chaperoning me to Martens's although he had suggested she was welcome to do so. Lotte had a ticket in the mezzanine, which was inaccessible to the orchestra – she was allowed to hear the concert but not share our first date. I thought it marvelous. I thought Martens marvelous, but I still believed he was a painter. During those early days, I preferred to think myself the subject of a portrait rather than the object of a life. I pretended indifference to men in those young days. The truth was that they frightened me.

No, the real truth, I suppose, is that all along my loathing of romanticism was the other side of my unspeakably romantic view of persons. I recognized in myself the willingness to shave the hard truths of human action, their naked revelation of motives and sentiments that thought successfully conceals. True thought takes time but never as much time as a feeling wastes in self-concealing. Thought invents and obliterates, but feeling and sentiment stretch the sweet events of life like sheets of apricots beaten flat and sold for pennies. By the time I met

Martens I had had only one affair, of no consequence or duration
– with a fellow student as weary of solitude as myself. The
niggardliness of that episode deprived me of nothing but my
virginity, an estate already compromised by my inevitable fantasy. My body told me that sex was delicious; my imagination
of life with uncle Salomon or my father persuaded me that sex
was somehow illicit; and my happenstance collapse into the
arms of my lonely student persuaded me that it was still unreal.
But sex, like everything else, cannot be left to the imagination
too long.

And so now, years beyond his death as I frame this reminiscence of his courtship, I ask myself why it was that I fell in
love with Martens Berg and married him a year later. So much
about him seemed improbable and unsuitable – his age for one
thing, his character another still. But what do these amount to,
really? Age – irrelevant: for some he was impossibly ancient,
for others (who can only love heroes) too young even, while for
me his age was a matter of indifference. I never thought about
his age or, when I thought about it much later, I took it as a
fact, no different than any other determination. And character
– his evasiveness, his refusal to gather and sort out the information necessary to any considered adjustment to the real, his
mechanisms of denial and avoidance, his childishness, and so
forth. Matters of seriousness. Yes. But even on issues of character I temporize. I always felt it necessary to maintain reasonable doubt about persons and their behavior. It was enough to
be tyrannical about ideas.

The question remains unanswered.

Why did I marry my Martens who has from time to time
irritated me so mightily? It falls to me to explain because this
is *my* memoir, the memoir of admirable Erika whom everyone
knows and for whom, presumably (since I am eminent, famous,
a serious woman, a genius mind), everything must be perfect.

That's part of the stupidity. I have gathered sympathy, while
for Martens – immensely private, even secretive – there is little
gathered affection. Hence, the burden of justification falls on
me: I must explain why I suffered Martens, why I sustained
him, why I bore our marriage when I could have had – as Cynthia
Arnold remarked later, puffing on a cigarette, a red index finger
emphatically rapping the luncheon table – "anyone, anyone at
all." But as I said then, the truth beginning to dawn upon me,
"How stupid you Americans can be. Who wants anyone? And
who would anyone be?" I wanted Martens and Martens loved
me and that seemed sufficient. Although surely no explanation.
Martens came to the young woman of twenty-three and doffed
his hat, bowed, honored, instructed, illuminated my life when
it was just beginning to unfold into freedom. He grasped my
arm firmly and led me through galleries; he whispered slowly
into my ear the secrets of nature and imagination; he brought
all the ideas that I had closeted in my head to play in the open;
he introduced me to a world of studied cultivation, where artists,
actresses, and musicians worked terribly hard to be unpredict-
ably daring and original, while all the time scrounging for food
and heat and making themselves up to be gay and gallant at
dinner parties and entertainments.

Berlin in the late 1920s was already gone mad. What was I
doing living by myself in the Prenzlauer Berg? I was unpolitical
and yet there I was, throwing in my lot with the proletariat
because I couldn't stand any longer being a spoiled bourgeoise.
And so? What was Martens – my cicerone? my duenna? my
concierge? And all the time that he was exposing me, he was
also training me to protect him, to make him speak up, to show
him off, to tell others how charming and wise and elegant he
was and made me feel because of him.

None of us remembers the detail of infatuation and romance.
Only much later (if it thrives and flourishes) are we able to string

a necklace of perfections that explains our long-lasting warmth and compatibility. Or, if it fails, the grim recital of defects and inadequacies that we claim to have intuited from the start. We're all liars about feeling. We do the best we can, shimmering and gliding towards each other. Only if we knock up against something insupportable, something that threatens what we take ourselves to be, do we recoil and sometimes break it off. For the most part, decisive moves – moves of career, marriage, friendship – are made with less attention than opening the morning mail. At least, with the mail, we know to throw out the junk immediately, to hold on to a tantalizing solicitation, to read the hand-written note with the morning coffee. Our sense of priority is much more strenuous with the trivial than the immense. But this is too hard on our condition! The truth is probably more sinuous. Let the analogy alone. Persons rarely declare themselves with the clarity and force of the morning mail. They reveal themselves slowly, not because they're devious, but simply because they're as unknowing, ignorant, and terrified as the other. Loving is a matter of summation "on balance," a conclusion drawn from many years of coping with another person and concluding that "on the whole" "on balance" this other creature is the best – best in mind, best in spirit and feeling, best in bed – that we can hope for without turning life into a single-minded pursuit of a mate. The only people who have time to work up career enthusiasm for hunting the ideal lover are people, I suspect, who have so little talent, so little imagination, so little energy, that they couldn't manage any other comparably dedicated enterprise. But I figured early – somewhat shy before men and frightened of their sexuality as I confessed – that the most I needed from Martens was hugging and a bit of loving, good talk, walking arm-in-arm, coffee in the sun, the intimacy of an interpenetrated psyche, the mystery of anticipation, the gift of protection, all the similar and dissimilar undertakings of caring and human worry. All these – consuming not more than four or five hours in a normal day – were more than amply fulfilled, no, richly fulfilled, by Martens Berg.

All this, of course, during our courtship and before the botched mastoid operation. The medical explanation delivered by Professor Dr. Langsam in a vague, slightly bored voice recited the immense difficulties of a mastoid operation. Suddenly the surgical process that he had tossed off as routine a month before had become precarious and difficult. He expressed guarded optimism that Martens would recover his hearing, but he could make no promises. I protested that he had misrepresented the surgery and his own competence to perform it. He became angry and shouted "If you want miracles, Frau Professor, go see one of your Polish rabbis!" and called his nurse to escort me from the office. That was that. Over the following months, Martens recovered about thirty percent of his normal hearing, but even that was uncertain, declining precipitously when he was tired or under stress. At a certain moment, more than a year later, Martens surrendered to the infirmity, gave up his classes at the Akademie, and resigned himself to solitary work and afternoons in his café.

It was in the aftermath of the operation that Martens began to change, to alter in the direction of that fragility and unsureness that I have mentioned, often with churlish irritation. Until that time he had been very different. He was always terribly proud of his appearance, never leaving his apartment without cutting a flower for his buttonhole or making certain his clothing was pressed and neat. He was fastidious to the point of being dandified, but I have never known anyone as meticulous in appearance who was at the same time so totally without bourgeois affectation. He embraced each day – sunny or sour – with the same sense of anticipation, springing from our prenuptial bed and making coffee, putting a record on the phonograph (none of the classics, for Martens it was all Louis Armstrong or Josephine Baker), and then bringing the steaming pot to the bedroom and holding the cup under my nose. Fresh coffee compelled me to capitulate to the day and with a flourish he smeared bitter marmalade on my toast and we sat together in bed – he dressed and ready to leave for the Akademie and me, drowsy and petulant, needing his affectionate presence to coax me to get up. Sometimes when class had been cancelled he surprised me by returning to bed and making love.

And Martens had many artist friends who admired him. His eye was reputed to be the best and every week we went by an artist's studio to look at work, to see what Otto Dix was doing, or George Grosz (and many others you wouldn't know), whose work would be propped against the wall awaiting Martens's comments. Martens was even then the gentlest of men. He never destroyed a work, but when it died before his eyes, losing its energy and reason, he devised astonishing feints to transmit the judgment without paining the artist. He would praise something – the color, a shape, the technique – but the evident narrowness of his praise meant to the artist that the whole had failed. Some recognized this device of kindness and, courageous, could take it straight, demanding that Martens make clear why only a piece or an element satisfied him, but the whole had failed. Only then, seating himself on the high stool most artists kept in their ateliers, Martens would begin to talk about the artist's power and gift and where the work in question had diverged, failing in nerve, succumbing to pastiche, falling into banality or cliché. Martens always told the truth, the strenuous truth, but his passion was to enlarge and extend the artist's vision with the clarity of his own, not to mutilate or cripple. Martens had the gift of charity, immensely rare when coupled with truth, and he was admired for it, admired deeply.

But when he returned from the hospital, having learned fully the extent of the damage to his hearing, he became tremendously depressed. For days he could hardly bring himself to dress. Once he turned on the phonograph and played a favorite tune, but midway in the music he slammed his fist upon the record and shattered it. "I can't hear it," he moaned. He never liked birds, but suddenly he missed their chatter. He was almost hit by an automobile that turned the corner, sounding a little horn that Martens never heard. These episodes of mishap and loss turned Martens away from the world outside and pressed him even deeper into the part of himself where old memories were stored, locked memories that were better kept sealed away, but which, now in the aftermath of a destroyed public existence, became the only treasures he knew to guard. What had once been repressed was released to introspective view and Martens dallied with himself as previously he had luxuriated in the world. It was not good.

Long ago, even before our marriage, Martens had begun the work of annotating his love for me, placing a rose upon the chair on which I had posed the morning after the concert. After our marriage, he contrived artifices and mementoes of demonstration, sketches and drawings, bags of chocolate truffles, bits of eighteenth-century brocade ferreted in antique shops and placed beneath my morning coffee, a new perfume when the old one ran out, and the scores of letters written at night and mailed to our apartment so that I would receive his sentiment in the morning mail, and notes hidden among my lingerie, hidden in my change purse, discovered when I dug for a coin, concealed in odd pockets where, in several cases, I didn't find them for years, for years. (One I found only last month, more than a decade after his death, folded neatly into the minuscule pocket of the russet wool suit I had worn when we arrived in New York.

The breast pocket, contrived merely for effect, was covered by a large shell button. However, if one struggled, it could be opened, and when I decided recently to remove the button and use it on something else, I found minutely folded a little message: "Beloved. You will never find this. But if, miraculously, you do, it will be a miracle like my love." It was signed "M" and dated *"Fruhlingstag*, 1932.")

All these maneuvers of loving me, Martens, were so many ways of persuading yourself that you could love. It had been harder for you than I ever imagined. I knew nothing of this until the morning, several months after the mastoid operation, when I came upon you by accident sitting with someone else, holding hands beneath a folded newspaper at an outdoor café. I remember walking by, nodding to you (a terror-stricken smile I must have smiled), but when I turned the corner, out of sight, I became ill and almost vomited. Only later in the day when you returned as if nothing had happened, proffering a single flower, I cried, but said nothing. You sat down before me, took my hands and held them. It was then you spoke sadly of your deficiency. You admitted to me that loving was hard work, a discipline that did not come easy, and for that reason an enterprise that demanded so much invention, so much contrivance, and hence so much false energy. No. This isn't all you said, Martens. The rest that follows I added to the original manuscript when the first version came back from the typist. You described to me something about your childhood that, in my wish to justify my hurt at the expense of acknowledging your own, I had omitted. It comes back now as clear as then, you seated before me, holding my hand, the flower lying in my lap where you had placed it. "I am deeply sorry you saw me with that person. Erika dearest, it was of no consequence. I have no name, no address. We met in the café an hour before you passed by. I've spent the day walking the city. I had three brandies and thought to get drunk, but I had no wish to slobber for pity and be put to bed. I hurt you and you deserve a reply. I don't know whether this will be enough, but it is my reply. When I was nine years old my father returned from a train journey to Hamburg. As he passed through the Bahnhof on the way to our lodgings he saw my mother, dressed in a leather skirt he didn't know she owned, standing at a coffee bar talking with a sailor. Mother disappeared with that sailor and returned to the apartment three hours later. She didn't know father had returned. She took off the leather skirt and put it away in the pantry in a secret drawer she kept for such accoutrements and reappeared in her housecoat. My father confronted her with his discovery. He wanted to hit her. I saw him through a crack in the door raise his hand a dozen times and each time lower it, unable to strike her. At last he began to cry. She watched him with indifference. Later, I gather, he packed his belongings and left. He didn't say goodbye to me. I never saw him again. Mother went to work in the canteen as usual about eight o'clock in the evening. She continued to be a whore whenever things got tight. I guess she felt an obligation to care for me, although she made it clear that I was expected to get out and be off on my own as soon as I was old enough. Seventeen was the age. I left and never re- turned. I went by the flat several times during the first year, but then I moved to Berlin and when I wrote her the letter was returned. She had moved; no one knew where she had gone. Ten years later my picture was in the newspaper. I had discovered a valuable painting in an antique shop, overpainted and outrageously varnished. It turned out to be a portrait of the Elector of Saxony by Cranach the Younger. It went to the Akademie that had just appointed me. A flurry of fame that yielded a postcard from a city in the south. I wrote my mother and thereafter we exchanged Christmas greetings.

"Not a pleasant childhood. It left its mark, I think. I have been happier with you, Erika, than I ever imagined possible, but each time the happiness wells in me like water about to break the dam, I become terrified. I'm tempted to destroy everything. Catastrophe seems so inevitable."

And so we recomposed ourselves, granting each other spheres of silence, where unknowing was not merely ignorance but irrelevance. We repledged then and we repledged several times since, each time repledging to be certain that we observed the bounds of unknowing. We cared to protect each other from knowledge that hurt. We made up our minds not to hurt and to that end we guarded each other with plausible explanations, with sound excuses, and with clouds of indefinition. I do think, Martens, we did well all those years.

How could you have dared blame America for your becoming careless again? You called it backsliding. I do not. I have no patience with such notions as backsliding. The only backsliders into sin (or truth?) whom I acknowledge are religious recusants — for them the issue is serious. But for you, what was backsliding? Since I'm ignorant of any time except the first, the second, and the third, and each time they became less serious (and even *they* were long ago, during the first two years of our marriage), why did I need such self-excusing rationalizations? Backsliding? Really now! That only means you lost control and I found out. You lost the ability to protect me, the will to protect me, and so you failed to protect me. When you were careful, I always knew I was the center of your life. Whoever else occupied your time was at best a satellite, a minor planet dragging about the periphery of our galaxy, drawn along by the gravitational pull of Eros. Of no interest to me! But to learn of it, to have it thrust before my eyes and to have you blame America for it, that disgusts me. If nothing else, this country has been our refuge and our salvation. We don't know it well enough to blame it for anything. When we're ready to train our intellectual guns on America, we'd better be on target. We can't afford such laughable stupidities as accusing her of wrecking our erotic controls. Don't you think so, Martens? Really, now, don't you think so?

I put all this in a letter to Martens. I let him stew and moved out. I went back to the cheap hotel on West 72nd Street for a few months to clear my head and left Martens in our apartment on West End Avenue and 100th Street. I hated every minute of the whole drama.

Europe was at war, Poland had fallen, and Martens and I were snarled in a domestic stupidity. (Thinking about it all now, years later, I am not persuaded that the habit of mind which enlarges everything that overwhelms nations and peoples to the exalted plane of world history and consigns all personal rages and frustrations to the incidental triviality of the ordinary is valid. Quite the opposite! I come more and more to believe that the real fiction, the real charade, is world history, and that the desperately real, the absolutely decisive, the true center of our experience, is the conduct of the private. As much as we are conditioned to exalt the achievements of our public heroes, I would rather have it that human beings struggled for unexceptional kindness, helpfulness, and truth in feeling which, after all, is the art of language. For the rest, if we were so in private, world history might take care of itself so much better. Since it is not so, my memoirs are left in my desk and my solid books are about world history.)

Martens wrote me every day when we lived apart. Again there were notes with my breakfast coffee – to encourage me in my work and to reassure me that we would find a way out of the labyrinth. After four months, I agreed to return home, to try once again. Martens wanted to repledge himself. I wouldn't hear of it. When he tried, I put my hands over my ears. I shouted:

"Martens. I'm deaf. Now *I'm* deaf. Don't! No promises, dear Martens."

He stopped and never tried again.

I can't understand, of course, why people as grown as Martens delight in making resolutions, why they feel better if they hear themselves promise, announce moral decisions, give assurances that they're improved and rededicated. There's no intention in God and no divine will. God is pure freedom and pure act. Poor creatures we are. We're always promising, always intending. And our acts are infected with the plague.

I know now I should have understood that Martens would suffer. I should have heard the rustle in the bush and suspected the quiescent beast.

It should have been clear to me that evening at Albrecht Warum's in late 1939. He was a composer who taught at the Curtis Institute in Philadelphia. He had arrived in the States about a year before Martens and myself, after passing a desperate time in Cuba. There were several others, like ourselves escapees: a middle-aged psychiatrist and his wife who had come via Turkey after teaching in Istanbul for several years; a *regisseur* who had worked briefly with Piscator in Berlin and was now handing out programs at Carnegie Hall and trying to make "connections"; a very attractive Viennese woman who was well-dressed, even chic, whom I learned later was the mistress of some corporate vice-president or other (her details – even her name – didn't interest me particularly); Albrecht and his remarkably conventional wife, Anya, and ourselves. Their apartment – like all those for which we lusted – was *echt Berlinisch*, that is to say, rooms opening into rooms, a continuous circuit of rooms linked by a common passageway. Alas, all heated. Into this West End Avenue apartment Albrecht had stuffed the ingredients of his past, a superb piano, German provincial furniture in dark woods, etchings of the Rhenish school. And the dinner was roast goose with red cabbage, a heaping bowl of new potatoes with dill and sour cream, a fine green salad, and, thank God, French wine.

The conversation, however, was marked by a sequence which I came to recognize was almost choreographed by our common situation. Drinks before dinner were a dirge of misery and gloom before the tidings of war. The announcement of dinner was a relief. Dinner itself commenced with pleasure and anticipation and descended rapidly into anxiety, comment passing from the luxury of the cuisine to the plight and predicament of the diners, each acknowledging an immodest envy of the Warums and their good fortune in having relatives in Chicago who regularly remitted supplements to their income, reaching bottom as the third bottle of wine was opened, with chitchat about jobs, apartments, cleaning women, inexpensive restaurants.

The turn of novelty came with coffee. Someone (I do not remember who), responding to a despairing description of the suicide of Ernst Toller, the German communist writer who had hanged himself by his bathrobe cord in his New York hotel room that year, remarked, "What can you expect? Poor man. He was alone and in exile." There was silence, as though everyone were expected to murmur a *Kaddish* and go on.

ALBRECHT: "But he was a dreadful writer."

ANYA: "The man killed himself, Albrecht. What does his writing have to do with it?"

ALBRECHT: "Everything! If he'd been any good, he'd have found a way."

MARTENS: "That's not true. He couldn't learn English. I met him several times. He couldn't speak at all. He opened his mouth to speak and out came Berlin."

PSYCHIATRIST: "Let Toller be, but who said we're in exile? Exile, indeed! I left of my own accord. I packed up everything and cleared out."

ALBRECHT: "Would you be there now if they hadn't bothered with the Jews?"

PSYCHIATRIST: "Probably not."

I ASKED: "Probably? Only probably?"

PSYCHIATRIST: "They hate Freud. I couldn't make a living."

I COMMENTED: "Does that mean you left because you couldn't make a living?"

PSYCHIATRIST: "Yes. And Gropius left because they were destroying the Bauhaus. And Mies left because he couldn't build. And Bruno Walter because he lost his orchestra. It's a reason. A good reason."

ALBRECHT: "I'm a refugee. Pure and simple. I had no place. I became a man without a place."

MARTENS: "And now? Now, what are you? You have a place here, but what are you and what is the place? Temporary or permanent? Do you struggle to speak English or does an evening like this one – a pure German evening – convince you that German is your true language and English a concession to the streets? What are we really? Immigrants – like poor Italians or starving Cubans – who can't wait to get to the land of plenty to eat a full plate? Or displaced – temporarily relocated while awaiting what? To go back? On our hands and knees? Or brought back in glory? Or exiles, who have been permanently excised? Or now, some of us – like Erika and myself – here more than two years, waiting to become citizens? I don't really know."

The mild debate, pursued casually, cigarettes lit and tamped as interest rose or flagged, proved quite common. How many times during the coming years I heard the same! The misery of human beings without their categories, askew without proper definitions and placements. It didn't affect me because I didn't look back. What I mean is that I was grateful I was alive, that I survived, and I didn't look back. My curse upon Germany has nothing to do with what was done to me. Nothing had been done to me! The air had gotten too close; I could smell the rottenness and I left. But Martens, my poor Martens Berg, he was a victim along the way. He had chosen to be beside me and had become a victim instead, a victim of my refusal to look back, a victim of my insistence that English had to be mastered, that he had to wear a hearing aid quite simply as a courtesy to others, a victim of my ambition for the large trajectory.

I suspect, of course, that had there been no German madness, had we remained in Berlin and had our life taken the course already fixed by our inner orderings and passions, he would have still been a victim, he would still have ended suffering.


The evening at Albrecht's was so subtle a sign of Martens's discontent that I hardly noticed. Quite the contrary. I found Martens's intense, almost violent, assertion of our uprootedness strangely moving. It reminded me of the old and vanquished Martens who could, threatened, rise to a kind of eloquence, defending not our misery but our grandeur. I didn't understand that his was a cry of the heart, a heart already broken by the loss of Germany. He was confessing not to them, but to me, his own forlornness. I learned only later that the "accident" – as Martens came to describe his fall from grace – had occurred two weeks earlier with a student at the Institute whom he was tutoring in the documents of German art history. He earned so pathetically little from all this. Sorting photographs, working in archives, writing art reviews for a monthly magazine, tutoring graduate students, vetting dissertations, being of help, being useful, all this amounted to about $480 a month. He would bring home his checks, sometimes four or five of them from different sources of income, picking them up at the office or collecting them from his students, and withdraw them, crumpled, from his pocket. He handed them to me and told me to deposit them. He hated them; he hated me for having to take them and put them alongside my considerably larger salary from the publishing house for which I sometimes read manuscripts and did editorial work, alongside my fees for writing or lecturing, alongside my monthly check from the New School. Each of us worked ridiculously hard to scratch out a living in those days. I tried to explain to Martens that it wasn't his fault, that he should try to work on a large project that would establish his connoisseurship in America, but my advice was washed out to sea by his self-pity and his self-contempt. He would make a show of turning down the volume on his hearing aid whenever I began to advise him. It didn't surprise me finally when I returned home from the library where I had been working and found him in the arms of his student. This student, I can no longer remember the details, slapped Martens in rage at being compromised and I, infuriated by the slap and outraged with Martens, spat out curses I had forgotten I knew. Martens began to weep and then began to shout at me and break his glass slides one by one, pulling them from the box he had been using for research on a monograph he had secretly begun on Poussin (he said he was hoping to finish it and surprise me when it appeared in the *Art Bulletin*).

I cannot go on with this. It was ridiculous; it was also sordid. I couldn't speak with Martens then. I simply packed a suitcase and left.


I had prospered. Martens had not.

How wicked and how unjust, I thought at the beginning. But did I mean it? Did I really think it would have been good and just if Martens had prospered and I had proved unnecessary? In the old culture out of which I came such predicaments were avoided by keeping women at home. Women had their kingdom which fatuous men presumed to envy, fabricating sighs of longing to be with the children, to do the shopping and clean the living room for evening guests.

"How I envy your serene life," I have heard such fatuous men extol their smiling women. How contemptible! Not a word of truth! There's nothing to be admired. But, let me make clear, it isn't enviable either that men go to their offices, go to their boys' clubs for billiards and camaraderie, fight wars, play rough games and posture their masculinity as though it were a personal attainment rather than a fatal endowment about which they had as little choice as we. Roles are historical and change. The assumption of role to replace living authenticity is one of the endemic mischiefs of thoughtless people. Martens and I had inherited notions about role which embarrassed me before him and made him guilty before me. Each of us apologized at the beginning. I realized one day how silly it was. We had no house to clean – one large room on 100th Street with a small kitchen at the back, a large bed and a small alcove where each of us had his desk and papers. Was I to stay home and polish floors or dust tabletops? And where were the babies? We had none and it was unlikely we would. Was I expected to knit ideas out of my one-room apartment while Martens went forth like a cavalier each day to sort photos or deliver copy to a magazine?

The truth is that for both of us such sexual roles had become meaningless. We were both workers of the mind and the mind has no sex of which I am aware. In fact, it is precisely because the mind has no sex that it is neutrally disciplined, requiring the same critical exposure to sources and assumptions, the same inurement to the shoddy and meretricious, the same morality of purpose and goal; it cannot be argued that the mind of woman differs in the slightest from the mind of man. It is the case that the transmission of historical roles deprived women of the education which would have enabled them in earlier centuries to progress comparably, but this is injustice and shortsightedness and in no way obedience to some anatomical limitation. I thought this through and my guilt vanished. If Martens wanted to babble, as he sometimes did, about his bad luck, I let him, but when he occasionally let slip something about his "intellectual wife," I demolished him.

It was during the war years that I realized how ambitious I was. Even now, many years beyond the banking of those fires, I find myself thinking about ambition. I receive astonishing letters from lazy readers asking me to summarize the work of a lifetime in a few paragraphs. I have old students that come by unannounced or phone the apartment and laboriously reintroduce themselves and petition me for referrals and recommendations. In the old days Berliners — having mastered their environment — called this *chutzpah*, but in America it is called ambition. Or more blatant still are those who send me books for my endorsement, books that bear no connection to the center of my enterprise, books of poems or stories or critiques of domestic institutions and the loss of faith. This, too, is called the fair play of ambition. Such maneuvers are not at all what ambition means to me. I will always assist the needy and quietly I will help to advance someone from undeserved obscurity to deserved rewards, but that does not mean for me to "aid ambition." I will buy the books of unknowns that I admire and pass them around. I will mention the names of scholars who should be honored because they *should be* honored, not merely because they are old enough to be unthreatening. What I do is done because the work commands it. But in doing this I respond to no pressure of persons for the sake of persons, and I exert none for myself.

My ambition has been no pursuit of the honors that constitute the rewards of this immensely rich and often negligent nation, which distributes its emoluments and prosperities with a fiercely egalitarian indifference to quality. It has so much in its pocket that it seems not to mind that the odd coin is frequently disbursed with jejune thoughtlessness. There are always those, however, who dance about bestowing power and mistakenly conclude as they collect such random bestowals that these are truly intended for them. I make no such mistake. I take no grants or subventions except for retyping my very long and complicated manuscripts. I accept no honors unless it is clear to me that my benefactors understand what is being honored.

Ambition, you see, has its center in the mind.

I had suspected for many years (but I did not become certain of it until *The Travail of Freedom* was finished) that my mind was itself ambitious, that it possessed its own energy and authority, its own sensorium and moral intensity somehow distinct from the mundanity in which most of my hours were passed. I came to think of my mind as though it charged an independent motor that resisted reasonable demands of time, assiduity, clarity. On so many occasions when I was writing I would find my weary consciousness willing to make do with a passage less perfect than it might be, a footnote less thorough, anxious to finish the day's work, to close my books, to leave the library, take the bus home, have a warm bath – and I could not. I was stiff, my eyes tired, bone-weary from hours of sitting. Yet my mind wouldn't let me off. It formulated its insistence, articulating censure and reproof, compelling me to return to the text and begin again. Hours later, it would be correctly done.

Such *ambitio*, such requirement for tracing the whole, for going further than had been gone, such an exigent wish to exceed what had already been said in the hopes of finding a new and original pattern of understanding, drove me relentlessly. My ambition was all a contest within myself, a demand that I made to renew the lease upon a certain seriousness which my American colleagues too often construed as an attempt to undermine their credibility, to humiliate their ignorance of languages and their frequent reluctance or inability to use primary sources. It wasn't so. I never undertook to embarrass or humble anyone. The mind has its work and its materials; it has no choice in this respect. It can do nothing else but work properly – balancing thrust with caution, intuition with verification, argument with detail, interpretation with groundwork, grand truth with the webbing of subtle argument. The working of mind is a slow and patient procedure. It cannot be rushed, but then neither can it be faulted for its ambition. Ambition is not an overreaching, nor a bravura display of fireworks illuminating a cardboard city; it is a true reaching, a true pursuit of the goal. Its task is clarification, and clarity is the moral luster of the mind. So much for my ambition.

*The Travail of Freedom* was begun just before the war. It was completed after the war's end. It was published in the last year of the dreadful decade. I cannot imagine how it was accomplished.

Each morning, Martens and I read the newspaper together. Our coffee cups shook. We could hardly eat. We searched each page, hunting for a scrap of hope. Some days we found nothing. The news was bleak. It was not until Stalingrad, the Battle of Midway, the landing in North Africa that we limned triumph. But alongside this, we knew from occasional and generally unbelieved reports that deep inside Europe millions of Jews were being murdered, millions of Jews, gypsies, Slavs, mental defectives, all the kinds and varieties of human victim. On such mornings I wonder now how I was able to work on *The Travail of Freedom*. What was it that impelled me to take out St. Augustine's *De Libero Arbitrio* and interpret its vision, to argue the importance of the Latin Church's combat with the aristocratic cloture of Christianity in Justinian's Byzantium? I cannot believe that I tracked the tracings of freedom through two millenia of European civilization at the same moment that its gut was being torn out. I attribute this, as well, to the tenacity of my mind, a feat of endurance and sheer will.

It was said, and repeated as a slogan, in the months that followed the publication of *The Travail of Freedom* that its author was a genius. The book was hailed and celebrated, borne aloft as an emblem of culture, worn – if books can be worn – as an armor of civility. I did not mind.

Or rather, what I minded could not have been avoided. In those early years beyond the war, an atmosphere was beginning to gather which in the decades that followed has become pervasive. The achievements of mind, works of imagination, grand schemes of intuition, are increasingly submerged and lost in the chorussing of biography. I was interviewed; I was quoted; I made appearances at parties whose hosts I did not know, to be greeted and introduced about gleefully as though my presence, along with others, conferred some kind of special significance to an otherwise lusterless social congregation.

"And you know Erika Hertz. She has just written that book on freedom."

At the beginning, I was flattered. My publisher urged me to attend, "to go public," my editor suggested, regarding me no doubt as some kind of closely guarded secret that required visibility for the sake of dissemination. Rarely was the title of my book known or, when known, properly pronounced – either "travail" emerged as a French word, in which case my book's title would be sometimes rendered as "The Work of Freedom" (which assuredly it was, the irony preventing me from offering correction), or where "travail" was rightly understood as agony, younger people commented that they found no difficulty in being free. In short, I had become what I learned was called "a celebrity," and briefly I was considered an immensity of mind no different than any other star of popular culture whose specialty lay closer to the surface.

It cannot be denied that my book was read – however, by vastly fewer than bought it. For too many I became something of a romantic figure, a woman who had fled her homeland, braving this or that fabricated torment to come to freedom, caring all the while for her afflicted husband (this was repeated privately, since I allowed no discussion of Martens and Martens refused to be interviewed about "how it feels to be married to such a celebrated woman"), working long hours in libraries (where else do impecunious scholars work?), typing and retyping her eleven-hundred-page manuscript (not quite!) and, at last, surviving the anguish of the war, the loss of her beloved parents in the concentration camps, she has given us this masterpiece honoring the democratic institutions of her adopted country. And so forth, on and on.

As you know, it is all a lie and it is all true. The abundance of mis-emphasis, of journalistic exaggeration and sentimentality, had seized the rudimentary details of an unexceptional passion to survive and transformed them and their subject matter into a mysterious and looming mountain of mind, unapproachable except on one's intellectual knees, unintelligible unless one has read "everything," unimpeachably moral and grave and pure. If I had believed all this nonsense, I would have begun to wear white in winter. As it is, I began to wear dark glasses some years later, but only because my eyes had become acutely sensitive to sunlight.

*The Travail of Freedom* was a good book, carefully argued

and in its own way important, but it did not justify the high shelf on which it was placed. It bore no relation to Spengler's *Decline of the West*, with which it was foolishly compared. My synthesis compassed the whole of the European tradition, but its thesis was absolutely the opposite of Spengler's. Nor was it a "Summa" of freedom, to be set alongside Thomas Aquinas. Its roots were in Plato, its imaginative scenum in the Prophets, Saints Jerome and Augustine, its political matrix in Hobbes, Locke, Spinoza, its contemporary argument not much later than Hegel and Marx. It was a difficult and, I suspect, a tedious book, but it did transmit an absolutely unqualified conviction that proved in those days to be of critical importance. Freedom, it insisted, is not given. It is educated and requires education. It can never be assumed except by the nobility who after the age of monastic education mistakenly believed it given with their birth, or by the mob who mistakenly believe freedom the motor of popular will. Although my views were and remain deeply democratic, I believed and still believe that freedom is the reward that patience, reflection, and worry confer upon those who struggle to achieve it. Freedom is then a light that suddenly goes on – miraculously, it would seem – in the midst of our efforts to understand the oppression against which all of us struggle: against powerful and pretentious historical institutions, against political subjugation, and against stupidity, despair, and boredom. Freedom comes after prolonged travail. It is earned, but one never knows the day on which the degree is conferred. It follows from study and attention, but its pursuit does not necessarily entail books and classes, nor does the study have a length of term, rewarded by diplomas.

It amazed me then and it still does that my book became famous, but I suspect its celebrity asserts something about the need for an aristocracy of achievement which this society, whatever its egalitarian persuasion, craves. We all need leaders and models. I proposed not a person, but a state of clarity. The free man, I argued, has the obligation to be clear.

Martens and I became citizens of the United States during the fall of 1949. There had been a technical delay, despite both of us – the first month of our arrival – renouncing our German citizenship and making application for naturalization. Neither of us could bear having to use our Nazi passport for identification. The first day of our arrival, when I went to change currency at the bank and was obliged to produce my passport to substantiate my travel documents, I felt ill. I couldn't stand carrying my passport after that and was constantly terrified during those early days that I would be stopped by the police and asked for my papers. I couldn't believe that Americans were not required to carry identity documents. It was one of the first discoveries about this country that overwhelmed me. The citizenry knew they were citizens. They did not stand (as we did in Europe) in an essentially adversary and subordinate relation to the state, which somehow owned its population and demanded duty more than it protected rights.

Martens and I were free without ever having had to fight for it. Perhaps this bothered me – this ease of freedom. Perhaps that very ease is the source of America's conventional indifference to its pearl of freedom. Its fight, it popularly believes, was won long ago. Once and for all. And now, with Constitution and Bill of Rights, it imagines itself protected. Possibly. Or rather, I hope so. But it was nonetheless transparently clear to both Martens and myself that even if the Nazis, by some miracle, blew away, even if the war ended on the day it began with unprecedented victory for the democracies, we would not return to Germany. And the conviction grew over the years. We were quite aware that our new country had profound problems – its

treatment of minority races and uncongenial ethnic communities, its regional antagonisms, its uncritical admiration of power
and wealth and its commercialization of culture, art, and in-
tellect. These were surely real and noisome, but not decisive.
Overriding all such reservations was the openness of spirit, the
fundamental good will (naive, innocent, uninstructed, no matter)
of its citizenry, the splendor of its judiciary and the moral
independence of its higher courts, the vulgar directness and
passion of its politics and the almost contagious enthusiasm of
its elections, the absence, then, of subversion, assassination,
violence as instruments of achieving power. Ah, we were en-
tranced by America – in love with it and having loved it, later
on, becoming partisans for its protection and enhancement, we
became once again European in our sophistication and cool in
our evaluations. But, above all, at the conclusion of our first
decade in this country, we were deeply moved, deeply moved
beyond understanding, to become citizens. We recited our vows
of allegiance, we studied for our examinations and passed them
without mistake, and we took it as a grace that we were now
Americans.

The emigrés had settled in by the end of the decade. We were
still impossibly burdened with our foreign accents, which some
of us – fearing to assimilate – exaggerated while speaking nonetheless a compulsively colloquial English. It was wonderful to
hear university lectures in which the street language of "gangs,"
"bums," "hoboes," achieved such elevated employment as "that
intellectual bum De Maistre" or "the Saint-Simonian gang" or
even, as one visionary sociologist had put it, "William Blake
and Walt Whitman, those Anglo-Saxon hoboes" – he was a
Russian, via Berlin, and hobo was pronounced "*chobo*." We all
burst out laughing. But we loved him and he always reserved

the front row at his lectures for "the visiting intelligentsia" as he called the half-dozen of us who regularly attended them. By and large, we stuck together, checking up on our progress at the same parties, the same concerts, the same benefits; we knew who was working on what and how much everyone earned. Curiously, we were all pretty much the same, although some of us were undeniably more gifted and capable of coping than others.

And we gossiped and gossiped, hating each other lovingly, full of jealousy and insinuation, naively persuaded that pre-war conditions still prevailed – that only the smallest slice of American success had been slotted for the intellectual migrants and anyone who seemed to be getting an inordinate bit of the minuscule was endangering the subsistence of all. Needless to say, I suffered from all this. My special gang took particular pleasure in demolishing *The Travail of Freedom.* I realized that the little support group on which I had relied for more than a decade was withdrawing its pooled resources from my account. I was on my own. I had broken ranks with pure spirit and beleaguered genius by having won an American audience. Even though my book had more than sixty pages of meticulous footnotes in several languages, ancient as well as modern, all scarcely readable in eight-point type, I was still thought a betrayer. When I arrived with Martens at a gathering given one evening by Manfred Riessner, a comparative linguist who taught at Columbia, I heard an explosion of excited argument as we came off the elevator towards the Riessner flat. Gisela Riessner opened the door; we entered; and suddenly, people fell silent, conversations dropped away, and small talk began to lap the fringes of what had been a conflagration.

I knew it was all about me. Manfred told me later after most of the guests had left.

"They can't stand you, Erika. All that press. All that attention. Interviews and radio talks. Who does she think she is?" Manfred laughed.

I didn't know Manfred very well and suspected from the fluency with which he reported the slanders of others that he probably shared them and had contributed several of his own. I knew it for a fact when we left. Stony-faced, Gisela had disappeared into the kitchen and never came out to say goodbye.

I confess to having found all this depressing. It wasn't only a nasty experience at the Riessners'. I knew it had gotten out of hand when someone at school the following week asked me whether it was true that *The Travail* had sold fifty thousand copies.

"Who told you that?"

"I don't remember. Someone in the faculty lounge."

"One of my colleagues, no doubt."

"I suppose."

"Well, the next time you hear such nonsense, tell them fifteen thousand is more like it."

The figure was never corrected. It continued to mount, reaching almost a hundred thousand by the following year, although the book did – it must be said – sell twenty-three thousand copies before it became a paperback. The untruth was fabricated out of envy – not of me, not even of my text, but of an abstract number of books pushed out, sold, and returned to me in the form of percentages, dollars, and celebrity.

The social consequence of such success was more devastating even than falsification and untruth. We were not invited out as often by our old friends. It was thought we had passed to another level of society, abandoning the emigrés for American stars. We had passed, it appears, from pariah to *arriviste*.

Something had to be done. If relations with my usual friends were to be strained by success, I had to look elsewhere for companionship. Martens and I were tired of spending most of our evenings at home. We looked through our appointment book for 1950 and discovered that we had been out not more than thirty times. And although we knew some Americans – the intellectuals of record – we had never invited them to our home.

We made an effort.

A large party early in December of 1950 brought to our new apartment on the Drive an almost continuous stream of what I knew were called "New York intellectuals," that is, journalists, academicians, novelists, publishers, editors, art critics, painters – the new gang as distinct from my old and familiar gang. Some of the latter I invited out of affection and they all came, anxious to see what I was up to. Martens even courageously turned on his hearing aid for the event and an energetic team of black ladies worked the kitchen, filling the trays with cakes and sandwiches I had bought from a Viennese caterer who insisted that all of her recipes were stolen before the *Anschluss* from Dehmels.

None of this transition from the old ghetto to the new would have been possible without the advice of Cynthia Arnold. Cynthia supplied me with the impetus and energy to bring it off, and she stood beside me at the door of our apartment introducing everyone who came through like a major-domo at an English country house, making presentations and supplying warranties, whispering in my ear thumbnail descriptions, mentioning their important books, their gallery, their publishing house, their newspaper, until my mind was a jumble of unconnected circuits. Most of my guests I knew by name, a great many I had already met at the parties given for me by my publisher, but I couldn't link up the title of a novel with its author's name or the author's name with an image of his face. In time I began to sort it out, but that first Sunday party was an ordeal.

When it was over, Cynthia asked for a double scotch and settled back on the living room sofa. The two black ladies were cleaning up, spilling ashtrays into a trash can, removing glasses, hunting for canapés under the couch. Martens had begged off and gone into the bedroom. I didn't blame him. I almost wished that Cynthia would go home, but that wasn't Cynthia's way. She demanded a post-mortem, as she called it. She wanted to hear gossip, but even more she wanted to transmit it.

"Did you notice how Manny Kolok went through your library with his notebook open? He must have written down fifty German titles. He's voracious. He checks people by their bibliographies. You passed. I remember him once telling me that he couldn't take any book seriously unless he found three references in the footnotes he didn't know. And Alfred found you dazzling. You are, you know. Dazzling! I've never met anybody quite like you."

I have no doubt why. Cynthia had been raised in Colorado in a family of high church Anglicans. She went to a strict boarding school and broke out at Radcliffe where she claimed to have gone to bed with every Harvard professor under forty. How she managed to study with all that activity I have no idea. And what was never clear to me was whether university professors were by species a randy lot or whether she invented that conceit with the same persuasiveness with which she wrote her brilliant stories of social deception and failing manners. The side of Cynthia that I admired – the side she treated with conventional disrespect – was her intellectual mastery. She had Greek and met with me monthly to work through Plato's *Theatetus* in the original – she was syntactically ingenious and I did the textual interpretation. Moreover, she had read philosophy and history with that remarkable energy so characteristically American, but without the slightest conviction that it really mattered. Her immense gift was for friendship. She knew that having friends required the most exacting kind of labor, that it wasn't mere accessibility, casualness, candor, as she explained to me once, which "most Americans take for friendship. They think having a friend is having someone who swallows you whole and never throws up. *Au contraire*, my dear. Having a friend is having someone who never relents in demanding of you something more, something better, but never trades on the expectation that when the extra is delivered, it becomes their possession by rights.

"A friend is so much better than a lover," she confided, which I knew in her case to be true since she had many lovers but treated me as an example of a perfect friend.

I was grateful for Cynthia's friendship. I was not quite as tough and resilient as I would have wished. Martens was growing old and although his difficult years were behind him, he had begun to plod through his days, moving about the house in bathrobe and slippers, disdaining the necessity of dressing unless he had to go off to do his teaching stint. His face had become grey and worn, his hair unkempt, and his manners more snappish and irritable than usual. He was losing interest, not simply enthusiasm or passion, for he had lost those some time earlier. Nothing seemed to matter terribly much; depression covered everything of him like a light, fine rain.


That Sunday afternoon inaugurated my brief party period.

Parties, parties, parties. They became a fatality of my everyday. The invitations would arrive, the telephone calls, even, of late, telegrams.

Parties were a curious New York phenomenon. Of course, there were parties in Berlin, but they were totally different. In those olden days, like the twenties and thirties themselves, parties were sheathed in a kind of hysteria – endless bottles of champagne, wine, and schnapps, a French brandy standing next to a peasant beer, platters of sausage without mustard or crackers, or varieties of breads with no cheese. Whatever was to hand in abundance became the excuse for sociality. If one of my friends sold an article or sang a song in public or did a play, inevitably a party would follow. Not a party in celebration or toast – for them, their momentary celebrity was the blinking of an eye – but rather the occasion, the excuse for bringing together twenty, thirty friends, glum and dispirited, to shriek and howl through the night, to dance to a tinny tango and in the early morning to finish it off walking through the streets singing sentimental songs of the *Wandervogel*.

Parties? Those parties were aggregations of misery. It didn't matter whether it was black Baker dancing nude for beautiful women in grey satin, while aristocrats drank champagne from Lalique beakers or among us – proletarian intellectuals and artists – swilling coarse Hungarian eau-de-vie, it ended the same, burnt-out, weary at dawn, heads swollen, eyes red, and our spirits – as we had begun – broken, broken and dismal, hopeless.

But in New York, beginning during the late forties, early fifties, and staggering from there, parties were so much more. It wasn't for drink or food that we came, but for talk, for news, for gossip. We crowded into Dennis Wright's apartment those years to battle over Simone Weil; he stood there, towering over all of us, the bottom of his chin beard wriggling like a lapdog, telling us the news of politics, the shifts and squirms of ideologues. Everybody read magazines, lines of magazines, stacked and serrated like the teeth of a saw, piled on tables and night stands, mounted beside toilet bowls, contending for space and attention – magazines nobody remembers anymore, but then, in those days, signifying currency, immediacy, violent opinion, the ephemeral thrusting for the eternal. Magazines were electric shock, small voltage, sizzling charge, only a skin burn. But we loved it.

I loved it. I prepared for parties like going on stage, prepared

my face, prepared my legs. The rest — the clothing in between
— offered fewer choices. I was still conventional and had never
mastered fashion. I admitted to reading *Vogue* and *Harper's
Bazaar*. My friends laughed. "Erika reads fashion magazines."
So incongruous. My name like that of a porcupine. How could
an Erika care about fashion? If I had been an Ingrid, a Grete,
a Marlene, it would have been plausible, but among names mine
was for something other than chic or beauty. But within my
budget I attended to my face and legs. I had colorings and
highlightings, gestures towards lightness or severity, and for my
legs I had grey silk, green and mauve, beige and russet. It was
the one gift friends knew would delight me. Stockings of varying
texture and subtlety of hue. And as I dressed, I thought of who
would be there. Who might come to Philip or Manny or Dwight,
who might drop in on Cynthia or Robert or Mary, who might
make their drab apartments shine with bright intelligence or
quiver with wit, who might pick up a stalk of cauliflower and,
forsaking roquefort dip, brandish the vegetable as a pointer,
strutting about the room, carrot sliver in hand, poking celery
like an English schoolmaster pokes chalk. Parties in those days
were parades, sallyings forth, receiving praise, dispensing approval.

And I was at its center. Or rather its epicenter. I was one of
several. I would come into a room, a narrow rectangle lined
with books on one side, windows overlooking the river on the
other, kitchen at one end, hallway to bedrooms at the other.
Seating arrangements took the principal space, chairs and couches
and love seats to accommodate six or fifty, camp chairs flung
oddly against breakfronts, the dining table covered with solid
food if there was a non-intellectual wife attached to the menage,
or if an artist or writer, inconsequential fare — Velveeta on
crackers, peanuts, chips, slices of salami, and too much to
drink, swilling the stomach instead of filling it. Those parties

were gaieties of conflict, fierce debate and horrid insult, Communists beaten to pulp, Trotskyites more militant than the Comintern, pretty young editors and researchers desperate to pick up an identity or a lover with an identity, Reichians trying their luck out after a month in the box, Freudians with piercing eyes spending their energy dealing out high wisdom with low language, and always someone telling Jewish jokes with raucous manipulation of Yiddish dialect.

What was it all? The cell meetings of the secular, everyone just over a life of faith – faith in blind gods, Stalin, Trotsky, Marx, Freud, the Church – and looking around to find someone who still clung to the true faith to beat up. Those parties were savage.

I bore them for a year and then one evening, as I was about to leave Martens for another party, my felt hat drawn low over my eyes, my lips red, my cheeks matted with powder, I forgot to press the button of the elevator. I stood in the hallway before the elevator door and watched an ant making its way processionally over the black and white tiles towards the immense emptiness that surrounds all ants. The ant pushed before it a crumb of bread vastly larger than its own size. I was transfixed.

It seemed so ridiculous to me to be going to a party. I let myself back into the apartment. Martens couldn't hear me return. But when I entered our bedroom with a trayful of tea and cookies, he burst into a relieved smile.


It was during early February, 1951, that I met the only man, besides my husband, whom I learned to love.

I would have omitted any reference to Simon Markus in these reminiscences if our love had assumed any of the familiar forms of entanglement popularly thought to define the repertoire of middle-aged love. Our attraction was profound, deeply felt, *passionné*, if you will, but not in any ordinary sense carnal. Or rather, as I put it once to Cynthia (and it was always to my most intimate women friends that I had to explain), attractions of persons could be carnal without perspiring adhesions of flesh. Simon and I made that definition work, or rather I formulated the definition long after I had found Simon. But having said this, I cannot leave it, for I sense a legitimate demand for more.

It is such a commonplace that love requires immediate physicality, the twining of limbs, loss of breath, droplets of perspiration upon the lip, cries of pleasure and groans of exhaustion. All these I have known and I have enjoyed – before Martens, with Martens and, indeed, after Martens's death, with Simon, but I have never thought that these copulative alliances either enhanced what was already established as love or supplied a foundation on which love would grow. It is, forgive me, precisely because fucking is so totally factual that it allows so much second-rate theory to prosper in its explanation. Or permit me the paradox on which so much of my life depends: it is precisely because I had grown to love Simon, but had remained in caring marriage to my Martens, that I determined early and Simon, more reluctantly, concurred, that we would never, as the expression goes, "make love" while Martens and I were married.

It could not have begun more undramatically. We were both reading in the park, seated in the sunshine on the same bench. I had come to the bench, as I often did, from our new apartment on 110th Street and the Drive. Martens wasn't at home. He was up the Hudson at the college where he taught three days a week, and was not due back until the next afternoon. I was never lonely when Martens was away. I would organize his desk, sharpen his pencils, establish for my consolation the imminence of his return. I missed Martens although I no longer longed for him.

Quiet years had passed. Martens, if not at peace, was finally reconciled. He had elaborated a convenient explanation for his failure and, having heard it for so long a time, I was too tired to object: it was the fault of the war; it was the fault of our displacement; it was the fault of *America deserta*, that vast wasteland where European habits of culture – slow and leisured as Martens wished to believe them – could not be assimilated. Over the years, Martens had managed to produce several important essays; he had become an expert bibliographer and his compilations of sources were often commissioned by museums and publishers; his English had become flexible and confident, although his accent remained heavy and, with his deafness, incorrigible. Fortunately, he had made some friends and one of them became the chairman of the art department of an upstate liberal arts college. It was through him that Martens was hired and over the years advanced to a tenured position.

My schedule during the early 1950s was less settled. I was teaching graduate seminars at the New School and trying to keep up with a whole series of writing and lecture commitments I had assumed in the aftermath of *The Travail of Freedom*. I found it to be the case that whenever I finished a book, I would spend the following year or two sorting through unused or undeveloped ideas it had engendered. The result would be shorter studies and essays which in the course of their turning and elaboration would provide the topsoil for yet another book. I was at that moment writing a series of small essays left behind by *The Travail of Freedom* which, several years later, would yield my even more popular and controversial essay, *On Cruelty*.

That morning, I was immediately aware that the man who had seated himself not far from me on the same bench (when all the others were empty) either knew me or, failing that explanation, wanted another's proximity in order to enjoy the better his own solitude. Whatever the explanation, we sat beside each other – two bodies' distance between us – and did not talk. I

confess my estimation of him rose considerably when I became
aware that he was not examining my face and form, as would
have been more commonplace, but was trying to see the title
of the book I was reading. It was a book in German by a
philosopher (Klages, I now remember) whose thought, it turned
out, was far more cranky than his style; however, it was an old
book printed in *Fraktur* and, hence, more difficult to decipher
from a distance of three feet. I, on the other hand, was aware
that my bench neighbor was also a reader, but it was less difficult
for me to secure an impression of his credentials, since he was
reading an English translation of Flaubert's *L'education senti-
mentale*, printed in large format with running headlines that
announced the title conspicuously on every page. I absorbed
the information, not pleased or necessarily optimistic, but at
least interested. It was only after some minutes of this mutual
scrutiny, conducted with lowered eyes and shifting body weights,
that we both returned into ourselves and left off from each other.

Why, I wondered, was I curious about this man, curious
enough to check his reading? I wanted, simple enough explanation for the moment, to talk. I had spoken to no one since I
had said goodbye to Martens the previous day. Of course, I
could have called a friend or made an appointment to visit, but
that was not the point. It was not that I needed some artificial
encounter, some specious reason for calling up one or another
colleague. For the moment I appeared to need nothing: for me
to call and have nothing to say would strike my friends as odd,
perhaps even alarming. When Erika called, it was said, there
was a point to the telephone: I called for information, to check
a fact, to have an argument, to review a text, but never as one
says "to chat." And yet there I was, somehow unnerved by the
man beside me, seeking out clues to his identity, reconciling
his reading with my recollections of the work, curious for an
instant about the point to which he'd come – was the insurrection

over? Had the *arriviste* become the lover of the *parvenu*? And what did he think? Was he delighted with Flaubert and Flaubert's unfailing sense of social detail?

I did not find out that day. We sat beside each other for more than an hour, the sun high above the Hudson, the white light of winter masking the towering constructions of the amusement park across the river, leaving them to appear in that indefinite light some species of dinosaur whose flesh had been picked clean. I saw it all through eyes that did not fully open and stare about. I had no wish finally to break the spell of the enchantment, the sense of seeing and being overseen without for an instant looking full face upon my neighbor. I was, I understand it now, preparing myself for some event, laying groundwork for a mysterious encounter and, consequently, assuring myself of that invincible treasury of the imagination where the gold is hidden and in the face of disappointment can be unlocked with the key of fantasy.

It was fantasy and it was romance. And it was all self-induced. I slumbered in myself and my reading slowed. I hardly turned a page. And it was only as he walked away, his hat replaced upon his head, that I heard the words he had spoken. "Goodbye, Professor Hertz. Perhaps we will meet again." I had not acknowledged his greeting and I could not call after his back, but I watched him move away, his body bundled in a thick warm sweater. I admired the back of this stranger.

During the days that followed, I went often to the park in the morning. Once I insisted upon my hour of reading in the open even though it was a busy day and Martens had reminded me of my seminar that afternoon. Time ran late and despite my preference for the bus, turning at 57th Street and taking me

down to 12th slowly and stertorously, I was forced after my
nervous hour in the park to take the subway.

It was not until the following week that he returned. I was
already seated, sipping coffee from a thermos I had brought
along, when I observed him walking towards me. This time, I
smiled and he asked whether he might join me on my bench.
It was as though he knew me, as though he acknowledged my
terrain and was formally applying for permission to trespass.
"Of course," I said warmly, and he approached, speaking softly,
so softly in fact that he had to repeat what he had said.

"I'm Simon Markus, and you're Professor Hertz, Erika Hertz.
Isn't that so?" His voice was diffident, but strong.

I nodded. "How is it that you know me?" I realize now that
the question was fatuous and later when I became stubborn or
relentless, Simon would often laugh and mimic the archness of
that moment. "And how is it that you know me?" he would say
and I, I would deflate into laughter. It was the first of our codes.

"I was at your lectures at the Y."

"Yes? *Those* lectures? Did they make any sense?"

"I think so. What I could follow made great sense and for
the rest I've been working through the reading list you gave us."

"Did I hand out a reading list? Oh God. How pretentious."

"You didn't, but after each lecture I came away with at least
two books I had to read. I developed the reading list out of my
own ignorance."

I began to feel immense pleasure, listening to this remarkably
guileless and open American confessing himself. It was unusual.
I didn't care if people hadn't read something as long as they
didn't pretend they had. Pretense drove me wilder than ignorance. I laughed with pleasure.

"Does it please you?"

"What? Ah. You wonder why I'm laughing? It pleases me
and it amuses me."

"Why is that?"

"A young man who takes such trouble with a lecture."

"Not so young. If you saw the grey. Not so young. Forty-one isn't young."

"In this country, perhaps. In Europe we would still think you a beginner."

"But you're not much older."

"I'm still a beginner."

"That's disingenuous, don't you think?"

"Not at all."

"For myself, *les jeux sont faits*. I've made up my mind on that one. Most definitely, most definitely. Even if it's juvenilia as the conceit prefers, I think your book will last."

"You've read it then?" I rarely dared to ask this, but it counted. I needed to hear something definite and sure.

"Yes, I have. More than once, in fact. However, I will not let you cross-examine me. Here, you have to trust me."

Later, I would hear the echo of those words, softly spoken, but with an assurance and conviction that allowed for no confusion. I became suddenly dizzy; my head was spinning with pleasure. It was true, absolutely true, that this man whom I had never met before had in some strange way bonded himself to me as my student, had learned me, mastered me, and refused to be regarded with anything less than the trust he had bestowed upon me. I was silent, but I nodded. He didn't pursue it, as he might have had he lied, forcing me to concede (as I would have readily) that I believed him, while all the time wondering why he insisted so strenuously if it were true. "That sounded badly. I apologize. But you understand why?"

"Yes and no. If I lie, after all, it's my choice, my lie, and my loss. It shouldn't really matter to you."

I thought to myself that he was right. How very much like

me he sounded, and I smiled again, my pleasure showing. "And you, Simon Markus, what is it that you do?"

"I play fiddle."

"You what?"

"I'm a musician. I play second violin in a quartet." He mentioned the name of his ensemble. It was very famous. He was the youngest member of the group, having recently joined his senior colleagues.

"*Der Tod und das Mädchen?*"

"You like Schubert."

"All Schubert — quartets, trios, piano sonatas. Everything, but so little is recorded."

It was wonderful to be with someone who knew a world into which I was hardly initiated. I loved music, but what is loving music? I was thoroughly ignorant about music; I knew compositions, I hummed tunes, I admired performers, I spoke reverentially about Bach, Mozart, Schubert, Stravinsky. Which put me among millions of others, neither better off nor worse in my unsophistication.

"We're rehearsing an all-Schubert program for Carnegie Hall. Would you come if I sent you tickets?"

"I would love that."

"How many will you need?"

"One will be enough. You can send it to my apartment or the New School."

"Better yet. What if I brought one to our bench tomorrow and we had lunch afterwards. Let us say about noon."

We continued to talk, but we had made a rendezvous. He lived not far from where we sat; his apartment overlooked Riverside Park and he often saw me on my bench, watching me while I read or scribbled furiously or looked out across the river. Many times, he had wanted to break off practice and join me, but he had resisted. He was too embarrassed. I told him I was

delighted he had overcome his shyness. He insisted shyness
was so much a part of a musician's equipment – "so much of
our life we're listening to others" – that he found it hard to
overcome.

Simon took me by the arm and we walked. We passed a knot
of people, several of whom I knew. I introduced Simon as a
musician friend of mine. It was all terribly vague. Simon hardly
spoke and we soon left them. Once again, he took my arm and
we walked. Slowly, I began to relax, to enjoy his hand upon
my arm, leading me while he talked. I don't remember very
much of what he said. Occasionally, when he laughed, I looked
up and saw him watching me. He was much taller than I and
he bent his head slightly as we walked, his sandy hair falling
to his forehead as he inclined towards me. He was telling me
about his father whom he obviously loved for he imitated his
speech with such affection. His father telling him to "play,
play," which Simon took to mean practice his instrument, while
all the time the weary tailor meant only that he should go roller-
skating or play stickball. He had grown up in Brooklyn. Va-
cations were in Rockaway Beach. I caught snatches. But I was
not really listening. I was feeling his hand upon my arm, firm
fingers holding my elbow as we crossed streets. Once his arm
even passed beneath my breasts to alert me to an automobile
turning too sharply from the avenue. If I could have hugged
myself, I might have. I felt terribly young and desirable. My
sentience was returning, coming once more to the surface, re-
acting to touch, warmth, laughter. And affection. Although we
had said nothing personal. And yet in every gesture of the man
there was an attention, an appreciation not of who I was but
that I was there. He, it seemed to me, was as delighted to be
grasping my arm and guiding me as I was to be held and led.

There would be times in years to come when it would be I, laying my hand upon his shoulder, who would transmit the warmth that he was giving me now. Such grace is reciprocal. I felt not like a woman pursued – a bit of pelf – but like a person admired, made admirable by an unguarded face, eyes suddenly open, lips speaking quiet and firm, tiny crow's feet enriching the texture of his face as it became animate and intense. And when I had passed through this (and it took more than a dozen blocks of walking towards the restaurant he had chosen), and had begun to hear him and the questions he now put to me, I realized that he asked for nothing more than meeting, demanding nothing, requiring no disclosures. I presumed he knew that I was married and I, for my part, regarded his gold band as evidence enough. We did not discuss my husband; I did not ask about his wife.

Luncheon together at the Piraeus began with all the tentativeness of a first rendezvous. It was as though walking there had accomplished one set of requirements, learning how the body moves, observing angles of cheek and neck, watching response to public events – traffic, noise, pedestrians – only to begin again as we sat facing each other at the back of the bright little taverna that smelled of oilcloth and retsina. The food was ordinary, but the place delicious, the Greek-Italian owner setting down besides the avgolemono black olives in oregano and warm bread dotted with sesame seeds. Simon had ordered before. "I didn't want us to be disturbed with food decisions and regrets. I come here every week and know the menu perfectly." The baked fish with herbs was precisely what the fall day required and although the wine was trashy, by the third glass I had grown quite used to it, my head was light and my tongue relaxed.

I was aware that I was behaving differently than I usually do with strangers. I wasn't chattering. I was waiting, deferring, watching. And I enjoyed the change. Not a drop of performance. He, after all, was the performer. But it wasn't only that. I interjected comments that meant something different than usual. At one point I observed that a shock of his hair had fallen over his eyebrow. He pushed it back and talked on. He was calling on a reserve of gossip about which I knew nothing – stories about Toscanini and the NBC Symphony, a funny story about Heifetz rehearsing the Brahms violin concerto with Koussevitsky – and identifying the names and personalities of his colleagues in the quartet. Newsy and kind. Simon wasn't inclined to be competitive. He was so tall, I surmised, he towered over enemies.

"Were you trained in England? You use your knife and fork like the English."

"Not at all, merely an affectation I picked up from my Hungarian mother. I've done it this way since I was a child. But I'm not a child now," he said pointedly, but I missed the point.

It was only later while he was fixing coffee in the studio room of his apartment that he made the connection I had been missing.

"You must have many children?"

"No. I don't. I don't have any. Why do you say that?"

"You've been making motherly comments all day."

I blushed and laughed nervously. "Have I? How embarrassing."

"To me," he replied, smiling.

"No, to me. I've never been accused of being motherly."

"But I suspect you've rarely had lunch with a stranger and gone back to his apartment."

He was quite right, of course. And then with an unaccountable girlishness, I dared ask him why he thought I was behaving this way. "You're slightly afraid, Erika," he said, bending down to refill my cup.

"Afraid?" I replied at last, staring at the word with wide eyes. "Yes, Simon. Terrified." It was then Simon took my hand, not as he had taken it to conduct me along Broadway on our walk. That was a different taking. This time, he laid his hand across mine and I felt a warmth of contact that was animal, but still the gentlest of animals.

"There's nothing to be afraid of. No. That's not quite true. There's everything to be afraid of, but not usual fear, I should think. It's not fear of me. It's not even fear of public consequence. It's usually fear of emotions we've lost track of possessing."

I wasn't afraid of this large, slightly awkward man, who spoke to me with such immense self-assurance and ease. I was afraid of my own action and its implication. And nothing had happened. I had met a man who invited me to lunch and brought me back to his apartment for the afternoon. But I remembered Martens's hand under the newspaper and I could hear Cynthia Arnold probing for information. I resolved not to tell her, and Martens would never need to know. "I should be going. It's getting late."

"Not really. It's just four o'clock. My wife won't be back for some time yet."

"And your children? Where are they?"

"You saw the photographs?" A diptych stood on the mantel of the fireplace in the studio – two black-haired boys, dressed in their football equipment, smiling happily. I nodded. "They're at boarding school in Connecticut."

"Away? Don't you miss them?"

"Constantly, but it's best for them. Betty is always off. She's head buyer for women's fashions at B. Altman. You know the store. Betty loves her work and is very successful. But it's too irregular a schedule to manage growing boys." He turned away and looked out the window towards the river. "And you? No children. But what's your husband like?"

I knew the question would follow. It would have been easier to brush it aside. Don't want to talk about Martens. Don't want to explain my Martens. But I had no choice. Simon had been clear and precise. I had his picture, the broad outline without detail. He waited attentively. "Martens, my Martens, is a wonderfully difficult man, nearly twenty years older than myself and virtually deaf from incompetent surgery. He teaches art history several days a week upstate and pads about the house in his bathrobe and slippers the rest of the time, complaining about his failed career. He's a sad man in some respects, but in many others – the ones that make a life together – he's been preeminent. He and I have always talked even when our life with each other has been very difficult. We've liked each other's minds since the beginning; we've liked each other's openness and effort to tell the truth, and willingness to persevere. Many times it would have been easier to abandon the struggle, but I think we were both quite mature when we fell in love. We were grown up. We knew who we were and who we wanted to be. It wasn't a question like it is with so many couples of marrying prematurely to flee home or because the romance seemed so splendid. No. It was none of that. Unfortunately, Martens's life didn't prosper. The injury. Leaving Germany. New country. All of that, all of that painful dislocation and readjustment. And Martens hasn't been as strong or as willful as I. But he has always been quite definitely my husband." I hadn't looked at Simon while I smoked and talked. I had looked away, talking carefully to the wall, trying without the distraction of his face to be as attentive to my language as I could. I knew that if I had watched him I would have added or moderated in response to his face and I didn't want that.

"I think I understand," he said simply. "But now it *is* late and I should practice a few hours before Betty gets home. We're eating out. We usually eat out when Betty works late. And the concert is two days off. Tomorrow we rehearse all day. My Lord, I almost forgot." He went to the desk and came back with the ticket and handed it to me.

"One is enough. You're sure."

"Quite sure. Martens finds it useless to go to concerts these days."

"Will you come to a little party friends are giving after the concert?"

"No. I don't think so. I don't want to meet everyone just yet."

"Someday?" he asked.

"Someday soon," I answered.

At the door he took my hands into his, kissing them warmly, and then he kissed my cheek. "Thank you, Erika, for a marvelous afternoon. Schubert and I both thank you." We smiled.


The ticket was for a front row seat in the center box at the rear of Carnegie Hall, directly facing, across the sea of heads, the lowered eyes of the second violinist. He knew I would be facing him, he told me later, and I watched him with a thrill of secrecy I had never known. The quartet played magnificently.

During that first concert it was difficult for me to pick out clearly the voice of his instrument. As I have said, I loved music, but hardly understood how to listen to it. I realized that listening was an art no less than playing was the great art. Over the years Simon taught me how to follow a score, showing me with great care how to track the thematic line of chamber music, to watch for transitions and shifts of emphasis which bode the intensifications or windings of the principal and minor plots of the music. But that first concert, without skills of hearing, was all watchings of Simon. I noted that he sometimes curled his feet about the legs of his chair when he was bowing ferociously, how, at climaxes and conclusions, he threw back his head triumphantly as he lifted the bow into the air, how his boiled shirt ballooned slightly at the third eyelet, his bow tie slightly askew, his shock of hair falling over his left eye. By the conclusion of the concert Simon the performer had become an utterly familiar presence. I felt a special joy to know that there was a person in my life who made music. I said this on a note that I sent backstage to him after the concert. "A thousand thanks. What a joy to know a musician. Yours, Erika." I had first written "your Erika," but in an afterthought I inserted a cramped "s" followed by a comma of separation. Was I too timid?

Simon and I didn't lie to each other. Sometimes we refused to answer, sometimes we deflected curiosity, sometimes we walked about the truth, but we tried terribly hard not to lie. I am certain, of course, why our fear of lying was so powerful. It seemed to us one of the greatest sins of civility, although I have heard others describe convincingly the intelligent procedures by which they lied through half-truth and dissimulation. They had to lie since the people they made love to were not necessarily the people they loved. For me it was very different. I understood passion and I desired it, but I had a less robustly demanding appetite for the play of sex. It was sufficient for me to have what Simon offered. I did not need all of him, all his life, all his energy, all his time. It was because I respected him finally that I could accept the limits he set as my own.

Another truth, of course, which explains much about what Cynthia called my "convent chastity," is that I was terribly busy. So was Simon. Quite simply. We enjoyed what we did and we knew quite well that reorganizing primary alliances meant far more than loss of time. It meant repositioning the gyroscope. It wasn't necessary. Time together, touching and talking and keeping still, and not even that always, was quite enough. And sometimes, of course, there were hours when I ached for Simon, but much more than changing my mind was at stake if I gave in to the passion. It was never a question of "just once" and never again. Passion doesn't work that way. Great loving is an exaltation over so quickly, embellished by recollection with such extenuating detail, it cannot help but be repeated. And, in my case, I had to stay with whom I had been for a lifetime. I could hardly kick over the traces now. And so the explanation interpreted as well. It was a busy time, as I've said. I was often away lecturing in California, doing a conference in Chicago, teaching my courses, writing my essays and my books. My life had its order and, with that order, priorities and obligations, and these were quite as reliable sources of satisfaction as any affair might be.

The essential point is that neither Simon nor myself was unhappy. If I have any advice, it is never to fall in love when you're miserable. I wasn't. I never have been. I have been beside myself with grief, with loss; I have been *distrait*, that is, at my wit's end with annoyance, or confusion, or irritation. But I knew from my past that these would come to an end, that no magic maneuver was called for, that I could handle it and come through without such dramatic gestures as breaking with the past (what a ridiculous idea) or changing my luck (a tautology) or having a turn with someone new (a penultimate stupidity).

No. Simon Markus was my beloved friend. I think that was grace enough.


I was delighted to get through the 1950s. I cannot claim that I preferred the 1960s. I didn't, but I had found the 1950s unsettling. Moreover, the founding and senior members of my generation of the displaced and fled had begun to die. Hermann Broch, Jacques Schiffrin, Alfred Kerr, Heinrich Mann, Bertolt Brecht. I began to read the obituaries before the headlines. I still do, but with less interest now. My curiosity presently is merely to ascertain whether there will be anyone I know around to attend my own funeral.

I accepted an invitation from the University of Michigan to give a series of lectures during the fall of 1962 drawn from the text of my book *On Cruelty*. The origins of the book, as I previously mentioned, lay deep in the research for *The Travail of Freedom*. Cruelty is, after all, a portion of the marginalia of freedom.

Cruelty, no less than other poorly described and emotionally charged passages of human behavior, is too often used without distinction from barbarism, and in the course of such usage loses its power to frighten (much less to persuade) us to reconsider the extremities of political passion which bring societies to its use.

*Barbaroi* (from which we derive our term, barbarian) was at most an epithet by which self-congratulating Athenians described the inhabitants of the land mass of the Near East, most particularly their Persian enemy. The barbarian was quite simply rude, vulgar, uncultivated (according to Greek lights), and hence despised.

The ancient barbarian was not particularly known for his cruelty. Indeed, war was always desperate and total: whole cities were burned, women and children destroyed along with warriors and youths who might one day grow into warriors. Total war was most certainly an aspect of the ancient world, but "total" meant city by city and state by state, wars coming to abrupt ends as leaders died out or armies melted away. Even wars of hereditary enemies enjoyed a kind of protracted casualness, a recreative function consuming lives, wealth, and much time.

But cruelty? Who was cruel in such a world and what did cruelty mean? It is a reality which hardly has its analogue in early antiquity. Doesn't Herodotus retail stories we would think cruel? In his tales of feasting upon flesh, cruelty is highly individual and imaginative brutality – incidents of calculated maiming, torture, revenge, whose key is their inventive brilliance. Whether the cruelty actually occurred or not is less critical than the tales' narrative power as instruction and allegory. They are tales of "Beware" and, as such, cautionary cruelty and an aspect of moral pedagogy.

With Rome, however, and its turning towards collapse, cruelty came into its own. For the first time cruelty reveals its source in boredom and ineffectuality. When citizens of power and position are satiated with their normal enterprise – when the conquest of the barbarian without is no longer an espoused cause and too few control too easily and too indifferently the lives of too many – there is bound to set in a weariness and ennui which no new sauce, nor delicacy (neither ice from Scandinavia nor spice from India) can any longer divert. The physical and moral palate is satiated and all things come to taste the same. Amid such ennui, sport and novelty are no longer found in benignity, for the nerves cannot be agitated nor impotence overcome nor weariness relieved by the discovery and assimilation of new *things*. The care then is to deregulate the self, to disorder, to disfigure, to deharmonize whatever constitutes settled arrangements and proprieties. Here then is the task of cruelty, for cruelty works upon others the enlivenment and agony that one imagines for oneself, tearing open, prolonging pain, slowing death that the weary torturer may see himself restored to life.

Cruelty, in my view, is the direction that civilization takes to awaken and intensify the listless sensibilities and conscience of the torturer, not to test the stamina and resilience of its victim.

The cruel man never works his discipline on those he admires or is certain are his superiors. The most ghastly cruelty is wrought always upon those who have first been stripped of their human credibility – upon slaves and frontier tribesmen, condemned criminals, Christians and Jews in ancient times and throughout the history of the West upon political recusants, heretics, witches, gypsies, Jews, creatures already cast outside civilized borders and, hence, indifferently practiced upon, as though by skewering and burning them, slowly breaking their bones, gassing them in our day, there will come upon the inflictor a renewed conviction of power vitalized by the ability to inflict and the curiosity to behold.

What begins with the obscenities of the late Emperors of Rome, reassuring themselves that they can do anything and remain gods, has become by the end of the Middle Ages and now in our century the conviction of totalitarian societies that cruelty insulates them from doubt and failure.

The phenomenology of cruelty entails an understanding of what makes human beings dead in life, what promotes satiation and boredom. Clearly, cruelty is no instance of insatiability, but rather contraction and narrowness. It is well known that the most pathetic of sadists must prepare endless hours for the orgy, and what profits that spirit but a few minutes of fantasied pleasure and the smallest increment of sexual release? The machinery groans so loudly for so little. And on the larger plane and for all of us, what is the cruelty of an age but its fright, its retreat, its constriction, its grimness and dead seriousness? There is no cruelty laughing, although the perpetrator may think laughter proof of resuscitation. Not at all! It is a laughter intended, like all the gestures of the cruel, to self-persuade, to self-perpetuate, to self-induce, to self-erect. The victim is an

epiphenomenon, a mere by-product of the despair and hopelessness of the afflictor.

These lectures I wrote out, dismayed by my analysis.

I understood then (in the very composition of the argument)
how different is cruelty from pain, for I felt pain and anguish
before my argument; I felt wounded and depleted by my logic.
It gave me no pleasure to be a genius of insight. How deeply
then was I offended when a young philosopher (I suppose him
to have been) rose to his feet during the question period assigned
to the concluding lecture and, leaning upon the large black
notebook which he consulted from time to time, quoting his
rendition of my words as though they were *really* mine and after
many disclaimers of his capacity to understand my argument,
insisting all the while that perhaps not I, but he, was at fault
in his comprehension, came at last to the one question he felt
he could ask without misconstruction. He proceeded, quoting
almost correctly the first sentence of my opening lecture four
days earlier. After shoe-shuffling modesty and stammering, he
asked at last: "What were you thinking, Professor Hertz, when
you said that?" To which I, attentive to the positivist drift of
his debunking (a debunking pursued by the legerdemain of his
disclaimers of his own understanding and intelligence, implying
thereby my stupidity and irrationality), replied simply: "I do
not *know* what I was thinking. When I wrote these lectures
months ago I was thinking, but these past few days I have not
been thinking. I have been reading."

Ah, such laughter and applause. A colleague suggested, at-
tempting irony, that I had been needlessly cruel to the young
academician. I suggested he rethink the nature of cruelty.

▼      ▼      ▼

It happened that Simon was to be in Ann Arbor several days after I finished my lectures. The quartet was giving three concerts and later he was to appear with the Chicago Symphony as soloist in the Beethoven. He asked me while we were having tea in the garden of the Museum of Modern Art if I would stay over and be with him for a week. There was nothing conspiratorial in his manner. His wife wasn't home in any event. She would be at a buyer's convention in Los Angeles. "Yes, I understand, my dear, but I have Martens."

"But he can keep for a week, can't he, Erika?"

I don't know why, but I became suddenly angry. There was something about the expression, its very language much more than its tone or intent, which alarmed me.

"Simon, dear friend, Martens is a person and no person keeps. A roast can keep. A chicken can stew in its juices over a low flame. But never people."

I had horrified Simon by my vehemence. He didn't understand. Or rather, he understood perfectly well that the answer was no, although I hadn't actually refused him. I had only repudiated his rationalization.

"But we never see each other," he protested.

"That's not true. We see each other a great deal."

"Not enough. A luncheon, a dinner, theater, a concert, an art gallery. They're all public. They're occasions in public."

"They're all human time. They're your time and my time together. You think time together in Ann Arbor is special time. I don't. I loathe motels and American breakfasts with wretched coffee."

"You're being unreasonable. I want to be with you so that I can..." It was here that Simon faltered. But I knew what it was and saved his having to say it.

"Dearest Simon. We don't have to make love to be lovers. I

have told you that I will not repay Martens in kind. It would never be understood."

"But he would never know."

"But *I* will know that *I* deceived him. Quite enough. I worry about who *I* would become if I began to deceive."

"It would never come up. He would never ask. You've told me that yourself. He doesn't ask."

"Because he's unreasonably grateful and unreasonably resentful. I've explained that to you also. He's grateful for my enduring his old age and he's resentful that I'm not old with him."

Simon acceded. He did not renew the invitation, although he called me in Ann Arbor while I was giving the lectures and we talked for such a long time. He wanted to know everything – the size of the audience, its response, the questions, the dinners, the applause, everything. I didn't speak with Martens; he never used the telephone now. Whenever it rang at home, Martens handed it to me without even saying hello. He loathed the telephone. "It hurts my ears," he complained. But more than that, the call was so rarely for him.


I was beginning my own entrance into years. *Entrar en años,* as Spanish has it. A graceful, mantilla-style expression for difficult years.

I awakened in the hotel room in Ann Arbor on the last day of my stay and realized it was my birthday. A calendar hung on the wall. A decoration, I suppose, since each month pictorially celebrated a joy of Middle America – hunting, fishing, baking pies, planting, eating turkey, ice skating, and so forth. My birthday fell on the same day as that of the first Governor of the State of Michigan. I turned fifty-five at approximately the hour of my awakening. I lay in bed. Rubbed my eyes. (I felt puffed and overheated. Menopause was joining the celebration.) Little boys were playing tag on the concrete walk outside my window. I sat up, arranged my pillows, and lit a cigarette. I never smoked in the morning, but I was surprised to realize it was my birthday. I could see myself in the mirror which hung over the ersatz chest of drawers across the room. The mirror was cracked; the crack ran across my forehead. I looked wounded without bleeding.

I had given my last lecture on the cruel. The sun was overcast, a kind of fog hanging in the air, although it was a hard bright day. An industrial sun. My face seemed unchanged. Not quite. I hadn't noticed it in some time. I tried to recall when I had last looked carefully at myself. I couldn't remember. I had put some powder on my cheeks the night before. There had been a party for me given by the President. But I hadn't looked at myself with particular attention. I treated my face in the mirror like someone else's. I had worn a black silk dress with fake pearls. And an antique gold pin Simon had given me for Christmas. But I hadn't bothered with my face. At fifty-five something ghastly should show. I knew it from my friends who were always complaining about how badly they were aging. But I swear I didn't know what to look for. A line, a wrinkle, a looseness about my neck, a grey cast to my hair. Was that age, I wondered? And did it matter? What was the point of looking closely? If I knew what to look for, it would matter to me and I would become alarmed by small and subtle details that no one else could possibly notice, a secret brown spot, a small discoloration, a loss of resilience in my skin, a touch of arthritis in a toe. So what. I was fifty-five and Martens didn't telephone anymore and Simon was on a plane to Detroit. We would have a drink at six and say goodbye.

It mattered much more, I think, that I was alone on my

birthday in a cheap motel in a university town, that I had been performing thought for over a week, that I was terribly tired of it all (interpreting and explaining), that I wanted to be home in New York, sitting in the apartment, listening to music, watching Martens looking at slides.

I made a few calls to say goodbye, left a letter for Simon at the ticket office of the Lydia Mendelson Theater, and caught a plane back to New York early in the afternoon.

Martens hadn't forgotten my birthday.

When I opened the door to the apartment, I saw almost immediately an immense bouquet of forsythia he had placed in a pewter bowl on the little table in the hall. I called out for Martens to thank him for remembering me. But, of course, he wouldn't be expecting me. He probably wasn't even home. Or he couldn't hear me. When I was away, he didn't wear his hearing aid. I shut the door, dropped my suitcase, and hung up my coat. I walked to the yellow flowers. I touched them. Their smell shook free. They were marvelous. I turned on the lights and went to the living room. The windows were closed. I opened them; a cool wind from the river blew through the apartment. I wondered where Martens could be. He had retired from teaching, although he still made occasional visits to consult with his colleagues. Perhaps he was at the Museum or working in the library. I didn't worry for the moment. I was once again surrounded by such familiar noises – creaking floorboards, door squeaks, window rattling – all so familiar I hardly heard them as noise. I settled myself and lit a cigarette and breathed deeply. It was then I heard a tiny gurgle. Water was flushing somewhere in the building. And a small, almost rhythmic thumping upon the floor. A nail was being slowly hit by a muffled hammer.

After about five minutes, I don't think it was more, I felt

terribly thirsty. I needed cold, fresh tap water. I got up from the living room sofa and walked across to the dining room and through a swinging door to the pantry hallway that led to the kitchen. I stopped briefly to look into a mirror. I wasn't looking at myself, but curiously at a drawing Martens had framed and hung in such a way that it was visible in the mirror. I heard the gurgle again. A little louder. The nail was being struck in the next apartment, I thought, but such a little nail, how could I have heard it? I wondered. I went to the sink and picked up a glass. I filled it with water and turned around to see the kitchen. I wanted to know if Martens had had lunch at home. It was then I saw him crumpled in the corner near the storage closet, cans of soup in disarray around him. He was alive; it was he who was gurgling; it was his foot with agonizing uncontrol that spasmodically rose and fell, lightly thumping the floorboard.

The ambulance arrived in a little over ten minutes. Martens had had a massive stroke. He was paralyzed on the right side. He couldn't speak.

After a month in hospital, he came home to die. They advised keeping him in hospital. I wouldn't have it. Martens deserved better than to be kept alive. Whenever he decided (if it was *his* decision) that the time had come, it was preferable that he leave me at home. He had always lived surrounded by color and form. White was absence of color; hospitals were unbearable. Once, briefly, I became curious about hospitals while I was waiting that first long afternoon and night for Martens to wake up. I thought about hospital whiteness. Martens didn't wake up that day and I went home to rest. The doctor told me it might be several weeks before he came out of the coma, if at all. I wanted him to come around so terribly. I wanted to be able to care for him. At least, his eyes would understand. The last thing of

Martens that would go would be his eyes. It was selfish. It would
have been better if Martens had died already. Less suffering,
less pain, but I needed time to catch up with the suddenness
of it. I needed him alive a little longer for myself. I was being
selfish. I knew it, but I forgave myself. He would have forgiven
me as well, although he might have teasingly wagged his finger
at me. "Selfish Erika," he might have said. But he would have
forgiven me.

I didn't call Simon. We spoke several times during the days
that followed, but I couldn't bring myself to tell him. Our conversations were short, perfunctory. I pretended to be in a hurry
or exhausted and sleepy. What would have been the point? I
never understand people reporting catastrophe to people they
love. What is it they expect? Would I have been relieved or
comforted if Simon had withdrawn from the quartet or given up
his concert in Chicago and come home? Or worse yet, if he had
temporized and continued on and played badly, guilty and unhappy. Ours wasn't that kind of unreasonable loving. We expected no theater, no special effects, no miraculous sacrifice.
What we wanted from each other, we received. Caring and
intelligence, felt intelligence, which is considerably more than
the aridities of reason. (I don't trust rational people, but I trust
intelligence.) That was precisely Simon Markus. He called me
when he got back from Chicago. I told him straight away. I
began to cry on the telephone. Martens had still not awakened.
It was ten days. I had spoken to several of my friends. Cynthia
and Alfred had come by the hospital to be with me and we joked
gravely. But I hadn't allowed myself to cry yet, even at home,
at night, when I was used to awakening at almost any hour and
finding Martens sitting at his desk reading. I hardly ever saw
Martens sleep. He did, I'm certain. He swore he slept enough,
but never more than five hours. "Past seventy, we don't need
sleep. We need awake, not sleep," he said effectively. But now

all the lights were out and I lay for hours, sleepless, thinking inevitably of how life would be without Martens. But when I spoke to Simon and told him, I began to cry. Simon told me he would come over. He knew Betty would understand. (I had met Betty several times by then.) But I wouldn't have it. He was just home; his children, home on holidays, needed him, too. And so did his wife. He was hurt, but he knew my crying was possible only before him. He called me frequently that day and the following morning, very early, he came to the apartment and we had breakfast before I went to the hospital. I hadn't expected him. He had bought fresh rolls at the corner and he carried flowers. For me? For Martens? He didn't say. He fixed the coffee and we sat in the living room and had breakfast. He put out his hand and covered mine. It upset me. I almost began to cry again. Martens had done that every morning, but how was Simon to know?

And then suddenly I said something horrible, withdrawing my hand from beneath his own and pounding on his knees. "You're anxious for Martens to die, aren't you?" I said ferociously. "Out of the way. Dead. I'd be yours completely."

Simon looked at me at first with stunned incomprehension and then, quite firmly, took me in his arms and held me. I couldn't move. I struggled at the beginning, but then I relaxed and sobbed. I knew it wasn't true although it possessed a bitter truth for which apparently I had longed for nearly eight years. I was speaking my truth, not his, and Simon knew it. My pain, my guilt, my longing. I was frightened of Martens dying, but I was ready for it. Its time had come and I was ready for it.

I knew Martens was coming home to die. I repainted our bedroom bright blue. I couldn't stand the creamy insipidity of its former face. I rearranged the furniture and made up the sofa near the window where I would sleep. I moved all his favorite objects into the bedroom and stacked his collection of drawings on a music stand Simon had lent me. I wanted to be able to show him his drawings from time to time. I arranged our bedroom as a *tableau vivant*; everything about which Martens cared was on hand, easy to touch, easy to show. He had how much time? I didn't know. The doctors thought a month or two at the most. I prepared as though there were no time at all. There wasn't, as it turned out. Martens was going to die very shortly.

It was Sunday night, eleven days after Martens came home, that I had to go to the corner to buy some cold cream to give him a light massage. The doctor advised that I try to keep Martens comfortable by giving him a rubdown and massage every night before he went to sleep. Only his legs and arms. I couldn't turn him over without help and the nurse was off on Sundays. I put on a sweater over my housedress and went to the corner. I was terrified of being out of the apartment. I was never away from Martens except when the nurse was on duty and then only if I had a class to teach. That was all I allowed myself.

I couldn't bear waiting for the elevator. It was ancient and slow. I ran down the two flights from the third floor and rushed out into the street. I saw someone out of the corner of my eye standing in a doorway a few steps away, but I didn't take notice. I had to get to Broadway before ten o'clock and then back to the apartment. I practically ran all the way. When I returned to the building, I was too tired to walk up. The elevator was there and I entered. Before I could react, I felt a hand over my mouth and a knife at my neck.

"Now, doan' you make a sound. You goin' to da third floor." I realized I had pressed the button before the elevator door had fully opened. The man was hidden in the car, in the shadows.

He had unscrewed the lightbulb. The elevator ascended. It had never been slower. At last it stopped; he pushed me out into the corridor.

"Now which is your apartment, lady?"

I didn't answer.

"Lady, I'm askin' nice. Which is it?"

"You can't come in," I said firmly, looking him in the face.

He laughed quietly. "My knife says I can, lady."

I stiffened. I almost gave in, but caught myself. "No. I'm afraid you can't."

"You *be* afraid, lady! I got da knife," he shouted hoarsely.

"I have a dying husband in there and you can't come in."

He hesitated. He wasn't sure he believed me. "You got your dyin' man in there. How do I know you not shittin' me, lady?"

I held up the drugstore bag so he could see the caduceus, but then I realized there was only a jar of cold cream in it. I held it up before his eyes to demonstrate the presence of illness.

"You can have my money. You can have my watch. If you'd like, I'll take off my clothes and give them to you, but you *cannot* come into my apartment."

"You let me fuck you, lady, to save your man?"

I didn't reply, but I looked at him with such fierceness, my face ached.

"You crazy, lady." He grabbed my purse and ran down the stairs.

I had the keys in the pocket of my dress. When I got into the apartment, I began to shake violently. I called out for Martens. "Oh Martens, Martens, Martens." I fell onto the living room sofa and wept. But I know it was the truth. I would have fought that man and probably been killed, but I wouldn't let dying Martens be disturbed.

▾        ▾        ▾

Martens died the following week.

He died softly. I was sitting beside his bed, resting my hand upon his, reading in a fading light. A monstrous pink sun was settling behind me; the page flickered dully. I was not concentrating. I was aware of my palm upon Martens's wasted hand. His fingers breathed, slight tremors of life passing through them, the shallow breathing of skin invisible to the eye. I had felt his hand for more than thirty years and knew its life. And then, it breathed no more. I do not know the moment that he died. I lifted my hand from his to turn a page and when I replaced it movement had ceased. I stared at him until night fell and I could no longer see him.

Throughout the days that followed Martens's death I found myself enraged. It was a subtle rage, submerged and buried. It came forth live and palpable, from the depths where I had encouraged it to be quiet at those moments in the drama of burial when I was obliged to be public. It would have been so much better for me, for everyone in fact, if I had been allowed to bury Martens my own way. If I had been allowed! I would have – if I had been allowed – had Martens instantly cremated. No ceremony, no visits, no poetry and music, no elocution, no visiting hours, no lying in state, none of these. If I had been allowed, I would have had a private service to which only I would come, a cremation at which only I would be present. Only I had known Martens. His life had been between him and myself. Why not his death? But I was not allowed. From the very first, from that first night when Cynthia Arnold arrived at the apartment minutes after I called to tell her that Martens had died, it was out of my hands. Cynthia had asked clear and practical questions. She assumed that Martens had wishes and I knew them. But Martens and I had not discussed his dying. Martens couldn't speak, I reminded her. "But before, didn't you ever talk about it, Erika?" I tried to remember if we had. My God, we hadn't.

"Should we have?" I asked.

"Most people do. Most people like you, Erika, talk about death. It's not so surprising."

"Most people like me think about death," I answered, "but we don't talk about it."

"Americans do," she answered. Cynthia had a way of reminding me how foreign I was and remained. "Don't Europeans?"

"I can't speak for Europe, but Martens and I did not."

The edge of my rage had begun to show. I knew I would not be allowed. By the time we had reached this point, Alfred had arrived. Cynthia had called him. She had also called Simon and Betty. Betty was nervously making coffee, constantly calling me to find perfectly obvious and visible utensils. Alfred had called a funeral home. It was out of my hands. Martens lay in the bedroom. The bedsheets were still messed and Martens's legs had not been straightened. His eyes were still open. His forehead still glistened with dried perspiration. No one had gone to look at Martens. I disappeared from the living room, from the dining room, from the kitchen for a while and went into the bedroom to see if Martens was all right, if he needed anything. I began to talk to him, little questions. Maybe he had some ideas about how he wanted to be buried. I caught myself doing this. The edge of anger showed. The edge of hysteria. Several other people had arrived. My publisher came with his wife. My editor arrived. Someone from the New School with a message from the President. The New School wanted a memorial gathering. And no one had looked at Martens. The funeral director (that's what they're called, you know) arrived with several assistants. I couldn't believe how beautifully dressed such people could be at eleven o'clock at night (do they sit around in pin-

stripes and morning coats waiting for the telephone to ring?).
Martens was lifted from the bed and placed on a stretcher. No,
no, Martens isn't sick any longer. He's dead, I wanted to say.

The director took me to one side. "Will you visit us tomorrow
to make arrangements?"

Cynthia Arnold spoke for me: "Will ten in the morning be
all right?" She looked at both of us, the business official and
the mourner. I was right. He begins as a director, then he
becomes a consultant, then a planner, and finally a bill collector.
I began to laugh. The hysteria was showing.

I turned to the people in the living room – there must have
been fifteen by then, smoking and sipping coffee. "None of you
even looked when they took my husband away."


Alfred reminded me that I was Jewish. But Martens wasn't, I
replied. The funeral director assured me he would look fine,
"just as he did when he was alive."

"He hasn't looked well in years," I answered. The funeral
director went away mumbling something. That point I won. I
demanded it. They hadn't looked at Martens when he was taken
away. But now they would have to see him.

No service. I didn't want a service. What kind of service
could it be? We weren't about to invite God's attention now.
We knew no prayers that we loved. We had different taste in
music. Or rather, Martens had no taste in music. The best we
could have done would have been to show slides of Martens's
favorite paintings and have the corps of the New York City
Ballet perform. Martens loved painting and dance. So, no service, no talks, no reminiscences.

But there *was* – as the language of obsequies required – a
viewing of the deceased from six until ten o'clock the night
before the cremation. No flowers. No request for contributions

to anything. The discreet notice in the newspaper. I won that point. An open coffin. It was unexpected. Too many people came. Simon was there throughout, standing not far away, occasionally edging nearer to touch my shoulder. There must have been three or four hundred who signed the register. I was on my feet for hours. They all had to pass through the small anteroom where I waited. They spoke, seeing the foot of the casket through the double doors that opened into the chapel. Eyes would look in and return to me. "Thank you. Yes. Thank you for coming to see Martens. Please go in and see Martens." I said this, I don't know how many times. The anger was showing. They came to be seen by me, to sign the register that I would read, to note my sad eyes and comment on my appearance. But they had not come to see Martens. I made clear that not I, but Martens, was the subject of this event. The only reason that I could accept for all this – for not simply cremating him straightaway – was that others might want to say goodbye to Martens. But most of these people had never even met Martens. They knew me, damn them! They didn't know Martens at all. They thought of the funeral as one more social event – a party in black dress, a severe occasion for saying hello to me, not goodbye to Martens. Perhaps they thought – all those famous friends of mine – that the newspaper would mention who had come. Not likely. The press covers the famous dead, not the famous living whose exhausted husband has died. I made them take a good long look at Martens. Someone said as they passed out of the chapel behind me, "He looks just fine, Professor Hertz." It was late in the evening. The young man was among the last. That was quite enough. I sat down and began to tremble.

Each one of us, I have come to believe, has a text written with oneself in mind. It can be a text familiar to everyone, but still addressed to only one or two in each generation. Most people may receive only a fragment of their text – an allusion to a principal need or an obsessive fantasy, an island idyll or an immensely handsome man; nonetheless it is still *their* text since it is the fulcrum of their dreams.

Artists, poets, philosophers are not given their text, but must go in search of it. Searching for their text, in fact, is precisely what makes them artists, poets, philosophers. Were they given their text with their youthful dreams, they would be satisfied so early that little would be left unresolved to compel them to the pursuit that agitates their inquisitive passion. No. We must search for our texts. Usually, we do not find them early. In our novice days, when we are still limbering the muscle of our talent, we attach ourselves to fragments of the text, words out of context, words not yet reshaped by the imagination. These words we may come upon by happenstance in our casual reading or hear in conversation or find by accident in dictionaries – searching for one word, our eyes fall upon another. We overhear our reality when we are young, but in middle years if we are lucky, we find our texts and then, having entered into age, we are able without fear and without confusion to pass the most pleasured time, unravelling its significance, living its consequence, and drafting interpretations as the bequest of ourselves to future times and to others whose text it will, in turn, become.

My text was embedded in another. Of course, I had read the Book of Genesis. I had read it in fact many times, but I was not aware then that my text was Genesis 3, which narrates with incomparable brevity the story of the sin of Adam and Eve and their exclusion from Paradise. I became certain this text was mine many years after I had closed my copy of the Hebrew Bible for the last time. I had come upon my text almost casually. Uncle Salomon had told me the story of the embarrassed Adam and Eve and the insinuating snake. He had made me laugh with

his telling, imitating the snake with a hiss, and solemnly miming
the Lord God as he calls out for his disobedient children. My
uncle Salomon had not really understood the gravity of the tale.
He had made it seem, like so many other Bible stories that he
told me, a dramatic invention, and a lean and bare one at that,
rather humorless considering the absurd situation of Adam and
Eve. However, had it not been for uncle Salomon's dramatic
rendition of such Bible tales, it may be doubted that I would
have carried the text around inside me for as long as I did. (It
is possible, you see, that one can mistake one's own text, and
failing to identify it, adopt another not intended. Such mistakes
can prove catastrophic. Since the way of tragedy is that of
necessity, it may be argued that choosing the wrong text is
binding oneself to the ineluctable through whose strict and unyielding fabric nothing of the light of one's proper freedom is
allowed to shine.)

I became certain that the Genesis tale was my text when the
stolen copy of my volume of Heinrich von Kleist arrived at the
apartment during the spring of 1963 after Martens's death. The
superintendent brought me the package, neatly tied, my name
written out in imposing majuscules, the stamps of the Federal
German Republic announcing its general origin, since the sender
had omitted his name and address from the outside of the package. I took it that he did not wish the book returned even if it
did not find its destination. I thought that correct. It had belonged to no one but myself, and having been stolen from my
library and having made its way (by what devious route I cannot
imagine) from Berlin, where it had occupied a position of some
honor in my small collection of literature, to a bookseller in
Köln, where it was rescued from the ignominy and misunderstanding of being shelved somewhere between Klabund and
Klopstock and was sent back to me, I instantly regarded the

book as possessing an endowment, a kind of magic (aura I should call it) which other books did not possess.

I opened the book carefully and noted, remarkably for me, that I had written my name on the flyleaf – evidently in my eighteenth year, since my handwriting had just begun to exhibit that stepping out into assertion that marked my passage from adolescent shrinking to uncertain pride. And so, I had acquired a volume of Heinrich von Kleist's collected works that contained the writings of his very last years. I began turning the pages of the volume, hunting, I suppose, for some additional message this belated homecoming might carry.

It all became clear when I arrived at the little essay *Über das Marionettentheater* which Kleist had written in 1810, about a year before his suicide. The little text occupied six and a half pages in my edition. In its margin I had written the dates on which I had read it, something extremely unusual in my habit. I had, in fact, studied the little essay four times. I read it aloud once more and noted the date, 26/4/63. It was only when I finished reading the last page that I noticed I had lightly underlined the concluding exchange between the essay's interlocutors, the question posed by the interrogator to the principal ballet dancer of the local theater whose ruminations on the mysterious grace of the marionette provided the pretext for Kleist's reflections.

Alluding once again to the dancer's earlier reference to the predicament of the fallen creatures of Paradise, the interrogator asks: "Does that mean we must eat again of the Tree of Knowledge in order to return to our state of innocence?"

The dancer replies: "Of course, but that is the last chapter in the history of the world." I had scored *this* passage years before.

What Kleist had described contained the secret ambition of

my life, yet another confirmation of the epiphany of Paris that I described earlier. My life task had been until that moment and remained confirmed thereafter to understand the unspeakable loneliness of human consciousness – the shared faculty of awareness whose every detail defies camaraderie.

The genius of Kleist's little essay lies in its spirit of resignation and hope. The curious interrogator encounters his friend, the principal dancer of the local ballet company, whom he has observed in rapt contemplation of the performance of a troupe of marionettes that has been set up in the marketplace.

How can it be, he wonders, that such a professional dancer should be enchanted by these manipulated creatures? His misunderstanding is initially challenged by the dancer's assertion that the marionettes are performers of perfect grace to whom no human dancer can compare. However manipulated, the manipulation of the master's cord is but a submission to the wooden dancer's perfect center of gravity which allows arms and legs to move in balance and harmony, needing to touch ground only to reaffirm the earth's existence, but not to provide the marionettes with any necessary firmament. The marionettes exhibit the purity of natural grace, their sense of gravity always intact; no human dancer, contrived and reflective, needing decision and reminiscence of choreography, can achieve any comparable perfection. The human dancer does well to think upon the marionette since he *can* intuit and comprehend its wooden perfection while, however desperately he desires it, he *cannot* grasp the perfection of God. The marionette is always telling the truth of its being, whereas the human dancer – always an imitation of the whole – covers his inadequacy by affectation, shifting the soul from its true gravity through an artifice of technique which serves only to confuse and obscure.

The interrogator is unpersuaded, regarding the dancer's approval, no, celebration of the marionette as a conceit, a verbal fireworks, a mere excuse for bad dancing, or worse, false humility since he is himself the finest of dancers. It is then that his dancing friend confesses the despair he guards. And what is that? It is the despair of knowing the fall of mankind. Human dancers cannot dance pure, their souls in order, their spirit correctly situated, since they are fallen into self-consciousness. The misconception of the dancer – and by extension all of us – follows from our having eaten of the Tree of Knowledge.

"But Paradise is locked and bolted, and the cherubim stand behind us. We have to go on and make the journey around the world to see if it is perhaps open somewhere at the back." The grim interrogator laughs in disbelief. (I did not laugh nor have I ever laughed at this passage. Moreover, I am convinced, the interrogator did not laugh in high spirit, but rather with grim acknowledgement of our entrapment, his thin lips nearly closed, his teeth grinding, his laugh more like a groan.)

And so, the desperate paradox of the human: we are perfect *before* self-consciousness and we are fallen thereafter. Our condition before knowledge is innocence (some might say stupidity and ignorance, but they do not understand what is meant by the Tree of Knowledge). At the same time, we are creatures who mime infinity and for us to be innocent is to be deprived of that which resembles the God in whose likeness we are made. Therefore, we pursue knowledge and lose grace, lose purity of heart, lose innocence. Whatever we do, whichever horn of the dilemma we propose to adopt, we mortally wound ourselves.

We can, however, flee the dilemma entirely by proposing to reenter Paradise by stealth, by going the long way of history and hoping to find at its back another route of entry. We are not assured that there is such an opening. Or rather, we are assured that the opening exists, but only at the end of history, at the very end.

Genesis 3 is most certainly my text. I learned from it the

deviousness of the historical way, the only weapon in fact that we retain in our struggle against being less than we are – that is, marionettes of perfect grace – and aspiring to be more than we can manage, that is, divine.


For many months after the death of Martens, I was locked in grief. I had essays to write, but I ignored their deadlines. The Collège de France invited me to deliver again the lectures on cruelty, but I explained I needed time to decide. I was unable to act; I felt drained and miserable. Some will think this odd. It is not completely believable that I should remain so immobilized by the loss of a husband with whom I had not been sublimely matched, of whom I have complained, with whose habits of cowardice and febrility I have been irritated. She is not telling us the truth, you will think, those of you who have not seen my eyes, tired and sleepless. I cannot persuade you. Nor, frankly, do I give a damn. It's not a question of wishing you the same so that you can test yourself when *your* time comes. Clearly, it comes to most of us. However, if you were blessed with a relationship – whatever its tone and texture – that was constant, that went on (enduring much and surviving) to share silence, to embrace, to miss absence, to worry, all aspects of human caring, you will grieve deeply.

And what is grief truly? Not only loss and irreplaceability, but the selfish unwillingness to change. How difficult after more than thirty years.

So precious little is original. Most of my days – despite my helplessly admirable mind – are mired in habit. The body knows from where the coffee comes, whose hand will pour the water and toast the bread; the psyche expects the door to be answered by the same hand – sometimes quivering with pleasure, news to tell; sometimes firm with irritation, interrupted in some private pleasure that required no other. My God, how I missed Martens during those first months. Once, I sat at the breakfast table half an hour, reading the morning paper, waiting to hear the perking pot and smell the brew. Then I remembered. It takes such time for death to make its way among the living, where habit and expectation plod like doomed sleepwalkers.

The unnaturalness of marriage is the learned need for another. Our domestic education is consumed with training us to solitude, compelling us to withdraw from mother and father, to straighten up to independence and then rudely, about our twenty-fifth year, expecting us to take another and to live with that person until death. It is a contradiction of all childhood that first weans us from dependence only to pressure us in adulthood to start all over.

My exuberance seemed to return. There was an event in my life. Excitedly, I rushed home. I turned the key in the lock and the door gave way before a darkened passage. I called out. "Good news! Good news, Martens!"

I had called out from some region of willed forgetfulness. I put my hand to my mouth and bit deeply. I think then I decided I had to go away.

I had just been made a University Professor. That day, in fact, the Chancellor had called me at the New School and invited me. He told me that the Board had unanimously endorsed the appointment, finding me admirable in every respect. I rushed home to tell Martens of this excellent appointment. I noticed the teeth marks in my palm several hours later.

I cabled the Collège de France to say I would come for the lectures the following month. I had to get away.

Of course, I shouldn't have gone just then. One life passes and another instantly begins even if it's hopelessly difficult to observe it gathering in the wings just beyond one's vision. Simon's marriage was coming to an end. Betty had taken a lover of sorts with whom she spent all the time she had left over from her business career. We met him once. Not a double date precisely although the oddity of the situation allowed for such a mirthful description. Simon and I had gone to a musical afternoon at the home of an art dealer who had once been a cellist of considerable note. He had given up playing professionally, but still organized marvelous Sunday afternoons for musicians to gather and play in his apartment overlooking the Park. Simon and Betty had been invited. They were still a couple, or at least Sidney Daniels was impervious to gossip and had invited them as one. Betty had begged off and so I had gone with Simon. Towards the end of the afternoon while the players were doing a Beethoven trio, Betty arrived with Sasha Borisov – not a Russian bear, but more like a marmoset, I think, with a small head, beady eyes, and sharp, pointy teeth. I couldn't stand him. Instantly, Betty moved Sasha through the gathering like a tough little icebreaker smashing up the Arctic floe. There was little conversation, the Beethoven had stopped, and Sasha made chirping chatter with everyone, saying the right thing, remembering the recording, praising the jewel, admiring the instrument of every guest. When he came to Simon, whom he had not met, he went white.

"And this is my husband, Sasha." Simon dropped his head low in an avuncular gesture of social connoisseurship he usually reserved for gushing ladies after a concert. He was magnificent.

"A pleasure," Sasha said in a low voice.

"Not at all, Sasha. You must be scared out of your wits. But don't be alarmed. Betty and I are splitting up. It's all as it should be."

Sasha threw a frantic look at Betty, whose jaw went slack with astonishment. Later, when Simon and I left, he told me over supper that it had just come upon him that instant. It seemed the right time. The boys were old enough; Betty certainly wanted done with the relatively stylized glamor of a musician's fame – not much cash and never enough action in music; and, of late, sensing as well that the time was ripe to bring it to an end, she had begun chafing at his long evenings with me, although she herself rarely managed to be home before midnight.

It wasn't sordid at all, quite neat in fact, although it raised new issues that I was unprepared to deal with.

During the flight to Paris for the lectures, I drank cognac, I smoked, and I thought about my own end of days. Long air flights alone invariably bring on thoughts of death.

Martens's death – despite his being much older than myself – marked the inauguration of my own end. It did not mean instant decay, no imminent degeneration, merely the end of all the routine of intimacy on which I had grounded the private time of my life. Trivial, irritating often, misplaced thoughtfulness so frequently, but still ongoing presence and connection. I could anticipate nothing fresh or new in that respect. At fifty-five I was alone. I did not think it outrageous or unjust. I had no longing for a replacement. And, of course, I was still depressed.

A new toothbrush. Boiling water for my tea. Fresh flowers. Rust paper napkins from Bloomingdale's. An attention to myriad details such as these marked elements of connectedness that were severed. I would use stale bristles to the end and white napkins from the supermarket. Flowers? When I thought of them or when Simon thought to bring me a bunch. Chance and accident without solicitude.

▼         ▼         ▼

(But you say instantly, how can I mean all this. I had lost
Martens. True, you concur, but then you have received a pres-
tigious university appointment, you have a faithful lover who is
now desperate to have you completely, to become something
new in your life, to make your aging years rich and full. And
instead, you bitch, grieve, and speculate on the end of your
life. How indulgent and mean-spirited. I take all this under
advisement. Everything you object may be so, but it doesn't go
to the heart of it. The heart of it is always more gnarled and
grizzled than one imagines. And what I say now, only months
beyond Martens's death, may change again further along. I write
this now in the midst of recollection and although I know what
is down the road for I have passed along its way, I cannot deny
that those early months beyond his death found me shut away
and imprisoned. Grief is as subtle as love, as torrential and as
inconstant. I needed time to click again into life.)


I arrived in Paris and returned to my own *quartier*. It was early
June. I had several weeks to myself before the lectures. The
hotel I had chosen was modest but near everything I cared to
see and the weather was clear and bright. No one knew that I
had arrived. I managed to keep my arrival a secret until late
in the afternoon the next day, but not much beyond. I met young
Denis Senancour on the quai Voltaire. He recognized me from
the publicity photographs in the office of my publisher for whom
he worked. And with that, it was done. By evening there were
messages at my hotel, a dinner invitation, and a summons to
lunch with my French publisher the following day.

It was my first time in Paris in more than twenty-five years.
We hadn't travelled – Martens and I – because we had no money
and during earlier days no one needed my services for cultural
junkets. It was very different suddenly. I could have spent

months travelling, attending conferences, giving lectures, examining European cultural institutions. We weren't – we cultural
factotums – particularly important in the order of things, but
we had our counterparts in every country. It was cheap inter-
nationalism to dispatch half a dozen intellectuals to meet the
assembled intellectuals of other nations. It kept us all identified
and on record, a way of keeping count, but it was – my friends
tell me – a pleasant enough way to break the routine.

I was in Paris for six weeks. The lectures would be done by
the middle of July and I would return to New York and go to
Martha's Vineyard for August. I had merely inserted a bright
envelope of time into the stream of numb repetition. But while
it lasted, it seemed to provide change. I met so many people.
I found myself asking Simone what it was like living with Sartre,
asking Sartre to tell me about Merleau-Ponty and Jankelevich,
and Claude-Edmonde Magny about Simone de Beauvoir. But
no less, I heard of others asking them about Erika Hertz.

I still had no clear understanding of my own fame. I thought
it ridiculous that there would be interviews with the French
press and discussions of my work on the radio. I found the large
audiences that attended the lectures, sitting on the floor before
the lectern and standing crowded at the back of the auditorium,
unnerving. There seemed to me something wrong about all this,
but I was not certain what it was.

A letter arrived from Simon. A beleaguered and self-accusing
letter. I read it quickly during breakfast in the enclosed garden
of the little hotel. I put it away. I didn't want to be returned so
abruptly to "problems." Simon called it "reality." I did too, but
I suppose definitions of reality shift as mood requires. I can

speak of the real as authentically as anyone, but I know finally that it is constructed reality, what the occasion calls for, not what it is. My deepest conviction is that reality has no opinions. It is the horizon line of consciousness, distant, undifferentiated, like the sky meeting the sea – that indeterminate cross-over from the heavens to the deeps. No opinions at all. When someone tells me that I have to attend to the real (the expression, dear me, is "reality-oriented"), I usually shudder. I shudder. Reality doesn't even blush.

I folded Simon's letter and returned it to the envelope. But why does he write me on musical notation paper? I can do without his charming conceit – noting the key in which the letter is composed and the speed at which he wants it read or played. I know he's still shy with me. (Intimidated, Cynthia avers. Of course, Cynthia prefers *her* men to be intimidated – and presumably mine as well.) But I'm beyond Simon's nervousness, even though it's all about loving me more than he thinks I love him. It will have to change.

It was time to leave Paris, but unlike my earlier departure, this was a return home. I was gathering up pieces, sorting out belongings, arranging lingerie and dirty laundry, piling copies of books (among them, *L'Agonie de la liberté* – if only the French language discriminated between liberty and freedom, my book would have been thought less Germanic), unanswered invitations and unanswered mail (among the latter Simon's letter which I had not answered, although I had written him several times), making telephone calls, saying goodbye.

I took tea with one old gentleman whom I had last seen in 1935 when he worked at the Librairie Tschann on the boulevard Montparnasse. He had always helped me in those days when I was searching for something obscure. He had retired in his

sixties; that was twenty years ago. I didn't imagine I would see
him again. We met one day on Boulevard Montparnasse and I
invited him to tea. We sat in a café around the corner from the
bookstore where he had worked most of his life and talked about
the adulteration of the book, the decline of standards, the erosion
of scholarship. Monsieur Polemarkhus – who had been born in
Salonika and had walked to Paris as a young man – was of an
astonishing literacy. It was not that he had read everything,
only that his sensibility compassed all the possibilities and
navigated among them with exquisite delicacy and precision.
He looked something like Paul Valery, the elevated manner,
the delicate bones, the ancient dress of severe woolens and
white shirts, but his mind was like running water, source water
– not effervescent or speedy, but continuous and deep. He told
me of young poets (he admired Jacques Dupin, of whom I had
not yet heard); he spoke to me of Paul Celan and the poets of
his own nation, Seferis and Cavafy, with whom few were familiar
at that time. But of what he spoke – that is, the names and
books (literary itinerary) – nothing need be noted, but how he
spoke and with what intention, that mattered immensely. He
was eighty-seven and he still read to learn, but he read fewer
and fewer books. In 1950, he informed me with an amused
smile, he had begun disposing of his library. He had decided
that it was unlikely he would have any further need for certain
philosophers, for certain mystics, for certain religions, for certain literatures, and off they went to friends or public institutions. He was left, he said, with a permanent library of about
two hundred books.

"Which would you still prune away?" he asked, handing me
a neatly written list. I thought at first glance that there were too
many French, not enough Anglo-American, and the wrong Germans, but I could say nothing. The list was magnificent. I could
see how it kept him alive, the imagination of that list, examining

his books, appraising them, changing his criteria, replacing editions, refining selections, taking himself to an excellent restaurant for a "meal of reflection," he called it, to determine whether in fact he should keep the Sermons of Meister Eckardt or replace them with the Angel of Silesia. It took a weekend in the country, he announced, to replace Hobbes's *Leviathan* with Dean Swift's *Gulliver*, but to his lights, Dean Swift seemed a more acute strategist of the state of nature than the admittedly more systematic Hobbes. I listened throughout our tea as my old bookseller (who would die before I next returned to Paris) told me of the brilliant intellectual maneuvers by which he sustained his passion for life, undiminished. And I marvelled at him. He gave me hope.

Simon's sonatina, composed in the key of E, was definitely *allegretto*, although I reread it several times, aggressively *vivace*:

> Dearest Erika:
> We must reconsider now that Martens is gone. Reality has changed. You are now alone and Betty and I are already living apart. I am not as clear-headed as you, but I feel the pain of my situation keenly. Can't we speak about this when you return?
>
> *Your Simon*

I arrived at 4:15 in the afternoon from Paris and Simon was speaking about it the moment we reached my apartment. He didn't waste a minute getting to the point. As soon as his divorce came through he wanted to marry me. I confess I acted badly. I pursed my lips with irritation. I hope he didn't notice. Simon was so tender, but he was also funny — his diffidence with me, his shyness, his abashment. It had somehow, he thought, worked

out. My old husband was dead and the new one was waiting
patiently. He had imagined all along that my refusal to sleep
with him was grounded in some kind of sentiment for Martens.
(Martens was no sentiment; he was a cause, a first cause – my
*primum mobile*, who had set me in motion and then, alas, like
the God of the *philosophes*, retired to watch me operate.) A
crucial point of my nature is that I lack sentiment. Whatever
sap of sentiment ran in my family had dried up when it came
to me. I had stared at sentiment and it had turned to salt. My
sweet Simon, it's impossible. I am alone, but for the moment I
am hardly lonely. I have to make do with empty rooms and
creaking floorboards, with unrelieved silence, hearing the click
of my own fork, my own cup rattling, but it's not unbearable.
Being alone is merely learning to fill out emptiness with
imagination, but loneliness – that's quite different. Loneliness is ghastly: the certainty of being unable to fill out the
emptiness with oneself. That isn't my condition! It isn't that I
think I'm sufficient. It's the certainty of my insufficiency that
compels me to read and write and pay attention. I'm always
learning, precisely because I'm not over and done with.
How terrible if I were. If I really accepted my fame, if I
really believed in my camp followers, I would be desperate.
The silence would rise like a tidal wave that never breaks,
suspended above me. Then, then, the nausea would be monumental. Dear Simon, I know you've loved me for many years,
but like the sense of insufficiency that guarantees life,
so patience must be your cause. Neither of us is terminal.
Neither of us will come to the end of loving. How terrible it
would be if I gave in to you now. How terrible? Do you realize how desperately lonely living with another person would
make me?

▼        ▼        ▼

No dearest, not that. I can't marry again. And why do we need to? We've been together now nearly a decade. I'm as entwined with your life as I possibly could be."

"That's not so, Erika. We live apart. We go through our petty time alone. Breakfast alone, newspapers alone, practicing alone. At least with Betty there was another voice – a pretty shrill one at times, but still a voice. I'm afraid of it."

"That's not what frightens you, Simon."

"What then?"

"You've told me the story, but you didn't listen to it. Your whole life, you've worn music as a mantle, draped about you, covering you like the warmth of a majestic and powerful sun. You grew up poor and music sheltered you. Scholarships and honors for the sake of music. And just out of the conservatory, you married Betty and carried her to Europe while you made your debut and won your fame. You've never been alone. You've never had to cope with Simon beneath the musical canopy. You misread Betty. She wanted something else. She wasn't content managing her musician and orchestrating his eminence. That was about the time we met. You were just becoming familiar with the dangerous possibility that you might really be alone, you and the music you made, you and you alone. And now, with me standing beside you, but fiercely independent (another, but different, Betty), you want me as well to give over and be there when you practice and when you want to talk and when you choose to need. It's not possible. Not just me. It's not possible for any genuinely alive woman these days."

"You've said it before, Erika. Not grown up."

"Not yet, but growing, growing all the time."

"But you love me?"

"From the first day, you gave me joy and you've never stopped."

"Tell me again. I need to hear it."

When I had finished, for it was a litany of my pleasure in

Simon, he smiled and kissed me. It was enough for both of us. He was and has remained at the center of my life. Although, to that point, we had not become lovers in the ordinary sense, I knew that would come as well and I awaited it now with confidence. It was clear finally.

I wonder if it is good for the mind to be relentless.

It would be bearable – at least arguable – if the mind were always, by its nature, relentless, if it followed its scent – like a hound – unerringly, undeflected by bones and birds to right or left. *But the mind is never this way.*

I thought about all this in a hot bath at midnight. Simon left after a few hours. I settled back to read Hannah's book (which I had decided to read only after the furore it provoked had settled) and when I finished late that night – jet lag closing in – I needed my hot bath. Midnight is always my bathing time, darkness about and warmth in the tub. I am usually so tired I rarely take up hard thoughts, but this night was different.

I am moved by my friend's testimony of her experience.

All of you know Hannah Arendt. She is as much your household name these days as mine was last year. We alternate our years in type. She covered the trial of Eichmann in Jerusalem. Her reports appeared each week in the *New Yorker*. (And why not? Our domestic *Querschnitt*. No photographs. Instead cartoons and my friends.) And now the book has been published. Until now, I have not mentioned her name. It's not that we resemble each other. No. Not that, although the similitudes are obvious and have been noted more than once. Rather than resemble, it is that we dissemble each other. My friend and I. I lie in the folds of her garments. She in mine. We hide each other and we protect. And for this reason more than any other I am so careful what I say about her. We have agreed never to mention each other in print or discuss each other on the platform. And she does not appear, except for these remarks, in the body of these memoirs. It is not that we are estranged or distant. We talk constantly and I have exchanged with her over the years since my arrival not less than a hundred letters which, like hers to me, will be sealed for a generation in the library archive that will receive our papers. Hers – she is dead at this writing – have already passed under seal. We arrived at this strategy of sequestration to humble the American passion to know everything, to have everything set down and annotated for posterity. She, like myself, was deeply private. She rumbled in public only when she was possessed of a great conception or an even greater rage. It is one of these – a great rage in search of a great conception – that obliges me to break my silence about her and speak to the heart of her enterprise. It is more in the manner of an oblique address to her – wherever she has her residence in the kingdom of eternal discourse – that I thought this out in my midnight bath.

My friend moves me to wonder if the mind dares to be so relentless when it can never be pure. Pure? That is to say, purified of subtle weights and imbalances, pure of one's history, pure of special moralities and unconscious loyalties. And what would such an antiseptic mind be worth? Precious little. A boring drudge, such a mind. If then the mind is never pure, it cannot avoid its course. It presses on, relentless, fervent, unhedged by pleadings and considerations. It has no choice but to lead the hound out into the open to catch the fox of one's own lair.

And so my friend attended the trial of Eichmann. In her book, she has assembled the evidence and she discerns. She adjudicates the decision. She remarks on the witnesses, their look and their aspect. She discusses the prosecutor and she tells us about the defendant. She inserts essential history into the holes of narrative. She makes story out of event, her language spinning into time the thunderclaps that burst upon the courtroom in a single instant. Her language is a camera, whose film began to roll long before the court convened and will roll long after, until time's end. The court has found him guilty and he will hang. His defense was his idealism. And all the while, my friend writes in her hotel room, developing interpretations to set upon the scales of justice.

I know her well, this friend of mine. I can report that there is nothing unclean about her mind. Nothing at all. Hers is a mind of unyielding severity (cauterized like a surgeon's blade) and her intelligence possesses an impudent honor.

But is that enough qualification – these attributes of probity – if one has accepted an assignment such as this? Assignment? How grotesque! Would I go to Jerusalem and write back about such a trial? I doubt it. Not that I would not be tempted. I would be tempted and I would conclude: better a gifted journalist than a relentless mind to such a task. What is wanted by the accusers is that their show trial *show*, that the exhibition be made before the nations of the world, that the reporters be horrified, that their reports set forth and numerate, count up each body and give it name. Not as my friend has done: to use the occasion to be original.

Eichmann claimed that he was an idealist. Idealism was his defense. The prosecution had no interest in countering his idealism with their own. That wasn't the issue. The matter was murder. And so they brought witnesses to testify to murder, to document the commission of murder and, incidentally, to observe that the preparation for murder was the prior degradation of the victim. They proved their case. It was never really in doubt.

But, you see, my friend had already made that point. An earlier work, another book. The mind had already discussed anti-Semitism. It had already located its role in the logic of the total state. She wouldn't repeat herself. And here is where relentlessness comes in – our mind's unease and restlessness, its insistence upon saying the remarkable word that stuns like the thud of a giant hammer on the heifer's head. Stunned? I was stunned. I had never conceived such a turn of mind.

It was then, glazed and drugged by that hour, that I took my bath and sank into reflection on the mind's way: how it drives through all conventions to the sea, how it levels travelled highways and settled communities, covetous not for itself but for the goal, caring not at all about the sacrifice it requires, caring only for new and unexpected truth.

It was Kant, I recall, who coined the phrase "moral terrorist" to describe those whose truth is so powerful that its premises are obscured from view, whose argument is so radiant that its ground in the human soul is blinded by a golden cast. My friend has dared and she brought it off. She is already bitterly attacked. I will surely come to her aid. I will try to explain – not her, but the working of the mind, since my stake in the mind is as great as her stake in its daring. But all the time I defend her I will wonder to myself, wonder constantly to myself, if this is the right way for the mind to go. Dare we be so brilliant before everyone, performing so deftly and with such grace on the high wire of culture that everyone below, holding their breath, screwing their eyes upon us, cannot help but wait either for the triple somersault of genius or sudden death? Those below pray for both. They have no idea what they want. So long as it's spectacular, either triumph or death will do. But my fright is different. It's that those below will get their somersault of genius but bear it from the scene of triumph to someone else's death.

Banality. Evil banal? If only my friend had mastered all the resonation of the language before she chose to use it. If she had felt English banality in her bones after a lifetime of stupidity, of mean-spiritedness, of insult and gossip, if she had accumulated all those sounds of meaning like so much dust flicked off a sleeve, I would have trusted her ingeniousness. For then I would have worried not about the mind's relentlessness, but about the unconscious education that is everyman's patent for using language with clever and revealing originality. But as it is, I cannot. She cheated herself by using a word identical in both her tongues. The word is the same in German and English, her original child-speech and her battle-won gift. And there's the danger. What a German thinks banal is not at all what an American thinks. The words mean the same in both tongues: commonplace, trivial, petty, ordinary. But in Germany, where I learned to say *banal* and *banalität*, we referred to military bands and pink parasols on parade, to massed cavalry on the Unter den Linden. My dead father once passed an army officer striking an insolent soldier with his crop. *"Was eine Banalität!"* my father cried out, and I never knew what he meant. The whole range of association that conjured the disasters of Weimar was commonplace and banal. German politics were banal. And so its evil and so its corruption and so its murderousness.

But now in this country. I have never heard such things as we Germans dismissed called trivial here. People chip at each other in clichés. Banalities. Trivia. Americans, however, are not inclined to think evil banal. They make other mistakes about evil, but never the mistake of diminishing it. And yet now, with the mind's insistent restlessness, with its showy commitment to the original, it tells a new and perverse truth in a foreign language. It's now permissible, it appears, to speak in English of Eichmann's evil as banal. I think this is reckless.

▼          ▼          ▼

A week later, Simon arrived in the late afternoon and presented me with a cat (a rare breed, he informed me), an Abyssinian male, ginger-colored, the prototypical Egyptian temple cat. I almost refused. Instantly I smelled the cat, I knew that it was alive. I wanted to refuse. I couldn't bear the idea that something else would be alive in my apartment. The cat was brought in a carrying case. It made little noise, but upon release instantly stalked a fly. I rather liked that. If it were a choice between a cat and a fly, I could rationalize the cat – larger, but at least a plausible creation. The cat did not catch the fly. I continued looking at the cat, the baby cat, the infant among cats, and I couldn't speak.

I didn't thank Simon. He didn't expect it. He knew quite well that I could never thank him for a gift until long after its presentation. Gifts were utterly unknown in the repertoire of my experience. My parents never gave me gifts. They gave me necessities. Even books, in their giving, were implements of use. Books and scarves and dolls. They were things young girls needed. And so often, when I needed a gift badly – when I was ill with mumps for three weeks – mother bought me a brush for my hair (admittedly, a brush with a pearl handle, but still a brush) and explained that now I had so much time in bed, I could tend to my hair myself. ("You can be grown up now and brush your own hair," she said, smiling.) And Simon's little presents – the antique pin, the Tantra painting, the Thai Buddha, the page from Robert Estienne's Hebrew Bible – would be received and only later, sometimes a month later, after I had looked and looked at it or worn it on my favorite suit or with my spring dress or on my cloth coat, could I say to him, "Oh, dear Simon, what a lovely gift. How perfectly right it is." Then I could put my hands to his cheeks and draw down his forehead for a kiss. I needed time for emotion. I could never match the feeling to the occasion straight off.

And now a cat. A generic cat. A male cat without a name. I couldn't thank Simon. I had nothing to say, watching it explore the apartment, settling itself on the armrest of Martens's chair (how did it know instantly to choose that chair?), its head between its small paws. It was a creature of exquisite grace, a miniature puma or leopard bred down to smallness while retaining all the grandeur and suppleness of large and wild cats. It followed me about; it slept at the end of my bed like a temple guardian; it stalked its dish of fish heads (which I began to buy – disgusting things to handle, but beloved by Clitus). Yes, Clitus. Hera-clitus. Not the motility and fluency of the cat, but my own. I was the river into which no one could step twice. But I was able to change. I continued to grow and alter. And the acceptance of Simon's living gift was the mark of my willingness to go on.

Thanks for living things take longer than for jewelry.

I was at last able to thank Simon in the way he had always wanted. Clitus abandoned the bed for the floor during the proceedings. He seemed bored by our enterprise. It was all anticlimax, but now it was somehow delicious and right.

One afternoon, sun streaming into the bedroom, Simon had followed me to the window where I had gone to hunt a copy of a magazine that had just published a ponderous profile of me. I found the magazine on my night table. When I turned around, there was Simon smiling a twisted, somewhat sheepish, smile. He had obviously planned to seduce me, to wheel me about, to handle me firmly, to undress me and make love to me. He would – he admitted later – have taken me firmly, refused protest, had his passion and risked the consequence. Instead, I saw his sheepish smile. He put out his hand and touched my breasts.

I sat down on the bed. He continued to stroke my breasts and to kiss me. I wanted him badly.

We loved ardently, but neither of us was particularly inventive. It didn't matter at all. Making love was no cause to be won; it was only one more clumsy expression of our need to be implicated in one another, to be part of ravelment and mystery. By the time of the event, I was so enmeshed in Simon's life, and he in mine, that making love was no longer remarkable, not a symbol, not a secret, not even noteworthy. We made love many times afterwards, not so many times that I lost count, but not so few that their occurrence was unusual. It was merely added to our language.

Simon understood, however, that making love *now* was no concession to the prospect of marriage. Quite the contrary. If I were the kind of person who required physical love as something indispensable, such a logic could be pressed. But I was not. I needed such loving the way I needed a glorious wine or a rare book or the voice of Maria Callas. I needed them as expressions of the wonderful. I could live without their presence in *my* life because I was certain that they existed, but it delighted me to know that they were in reach and available. At fifty-five, it helped to be reminded.


(I have read these pages again and again. The manuscript is now done. It lies in my desk, among my papers, gathered and tied for my executor. I am not yet dead, but I will be soon. If not tomorrow when I am scheduled for surgery, then next year or in five years: death becomes more inexorable each day. And so it is prepared for; its welcome made ready. I hope it will not surprise me as it did Martens, but however it comes, it will find me with at least a portion of my life stressed with my markings.

And for the rest, may it come when I sleep or when I have kissed Simon goodnight or have listened to the Waldstein.

I insert this here because rereading myself I see again how cold others may find me. But it is not the coldness of the shut-away, the afraid to feel, the consciously bred *froideur* one finds among some Cape Cod natives who button their lips to keep cold breath out. That's not my condition. There is heat here, but it is not central heating. I am not a creature who is all flame. I burn when I choose and then it's all hell. No. It's not my coldness you mean. It's my control, my all-control that you suspect. And you think it, mistakenly, the flip-side of coldness. Wrong. I am neither withering cold nor machine control. It is a misreading I blame on you and your world and passionately deny its relevance to me. You still mistake the boundaries of license and freedom; you still think style and expression more charming than sense; you still demand vulnerability before dis-cretion; you still admire romantic youth, rippling with anxiety; you are — in a word — still sentimental.

I am a wonderer and I am amazed. But I cannot be set upon and beaten up without a fight. I see nothing wrong with being a coward if I am warned of danger, but taken unawares I will battle like a doomed hero. Controlled? No. There has been nothing improperly or artificially controlled in my life, except the certain conviction that the next day I wanted a reasonably clear head to get on with what interested me, to get on with my work, my writing, my art, my thought. That's not control. That's purpose. And to risk purpose for some unsteady passion seems to me reckless, finally stupid.

I don't recommend my way to anyone without the steadiness to see it through, and I am well aware the very precision with which I set its course scares the hell out of most of you, but it's my truth and my life I'm reporting. I don't care if I persuade you, but I insist upon one thing, that you accept the fact that I'm trying to tell truth. That's quite enough for me.)

It was a terribly hot summer in 1963. Simon promised to join me on the Vineyard if I went up for August, but I was just back from France and disinclined to pack and travel. I had changed my mind again. Cynthia Arnold called and urged me to come up for Labor Day. She said the weather was superb and everyone was there.

"Everyone longs to see you, Erika," she added. I guess that was her mistake. The idea of being scrutinized horrified me. I was the only one of our worldly company of minds who had gone through an agonizing loss. It was commonplace to divorce, replacing husbands and wives, lovers and friends, but death was not quite as commonplace at our age. I feared little luncheons and intimate cocktails. I didn't want the attention of anxious faces worrying about Erika's well-being. Erika was just fine, just fine. I stayed at home, turned on the air conditioner in the bedroom, and began to prepare for my classes.

Fuss about my university appointment had been considerable.

Of two kinds, from two sources. Those who disliked me because I was too famous; those who disliked me because fame is considered the enemy of seriousness. In both cases I was to be sacrificed to bad faith.

One of my opponents in the University said, "Women can't think." I countered – sluicing my response through the same conduit to guarantee the sewage would return to its source – "It may be true, but better to be unable than to have forgotten how." The mean bastard had been poaching territories of younger scholars for years, raiding their dissertations and undercutting them by rushing his own abstracts of their work into print before theirs had been approved. His were the habits of the bone-dry. Others, not uncommon, simply couldn't stand the fact that I worked like a demon. Thank God for my ambition – my nose was filed on the grindstone. But Chancellor Brightman had stood his ground. He had pressed my case intelligently and he had won.

Nonetheless, I can't say that I looked forward to being a university professor. Granted, it was a well-endowed appointment and carried with it the distinction and protection of eminence. I had not simply risen through the academic ranks, but had been won like a prize and publicized as such. I was expected to be present at all important university functions; I was expected to receive and entertain visiting scholars; I was expected to close ranks with the administration on its policy decisions. Unfortunately, I was not terribly reliable in these respects. I did not believe (as ardently as did the administration) in the expansionism of the American university. I was accused of disbelieving the messianic meliorism of education. The commonplace of the decade – even more exaggerated later – was that education somehow meant moral improvement, as if the acquisition of each academic credit was like the monastic achievement of a single virtue. I argued once that St. Bernard's listing of the degrees of humility and the weighting of their disciplines of attainment bore no relation to the achievement of an academic degree. Four years of prayer and self-scrutiny might win grace, but never four years of college. It was an unpopular position. It won for me little more than the accolade of elitism which I had always thought praise until I realized it was the new curse.

It may well be true that my judgments upon philosophic questions – rendered as judgments, sure and firm – are at best skillfully wrought and deeply felt convictions of little value to others except as they reveal the convolutions and intricacies of my own mind. I am persuaded, however, that the source of this wrong-headedness arises from the fact that I no longer share a body of common learning, literacy, and lucidity with my readers.

Judgments of value in philosophy are founded upon a shared bond of education. The present-day collapse into subjectivity is an expression of weariness before the mounting dump of ignorance and disengagement with the issues and the inquiry. Students who don't care and teachers who no longer wish to struggle for elegance of intellection and clarity of language are all encouraged to retreat to the paradox, the *sic et non*, the contradiction, and to present them to the world as a golden discovery when they are in fact such poor things, such feeble and unhealthy specimens of a mind reluctant to come down hard on one side or another. The fact that judgments of value need to be argued and defended, that they require placement within the continuum of relevant information, that they depend for their clarification upon the willingness of their claimant to make explicit their ground and presupposition, does not deny them objectivity.

To be objective does not mean to be absolute. It means only to be willing to inflect reality, to code its text with stress marks, like the ancient Hebrews who took the raw text and by printing its vowels and adding cantorial markings made their God sing.

There is no longer any point in this telling of my days to mention date and year.

When Martens died, I finished marking my time. I suspect it is only for others that we note years anyway. It is to force memory that we specify dates – in order to recollect the occasion of photographs, to share the detail of travel, places visited, restaurant meals, first visits to the Louvre and walks through the Père Lachaise cemetery.

With Martens dead, I realized that I no longer remembered when the photograph of both of us laughing in a forest clearing had been taken. I could no longer set the scene. All I knew was that once, many years ago, someone (who it was no longer mattered?) had taken a picture of us holding hands before a tree. What did it mean and why? I no longer knew. It was simply that – a seized moment, without placement, a ripping out of a fragment of the perishable.

I never mounted photographs. They were kept in shoe boxes which Martens piled in his closet. He never organized them either, except to date their archaeological layers with cardboard markers, hoping perhaps for some miraculous stratification and sorting. One box was dated 1927–1930; another, remarkably full, 1936–1937 (even though I can recognize only a dozen photographs from our Paris sojourn); and beyond these, when we were already in America, two shoe boxes wholly disorganized, some with undeveloped film still in their yellow containers. It was all confused.

One day, I remember, Martens had gone looking for a single photograph of himself in the black suit and white straw hat he had worn when we met in Berlin. He never found it. His desk was covered with hundreds of photographs. He gathered them up with disgust and threw them back in the shoe box. It was hopeless. Fifty years of my life were preserved in a fistful of photographs. Of my childhood, however, the only certainty was photographs. I knew it was my father who had posed me standing upon a small rock. I remembered that rock as immense and my father asking me to balance and hold still and smile. I remember that photograph. I know I was about four. I know it was taken one spring in Bad Kissingen. But why do I remember that and not know where Martens and I were smiling, hand in hand?

Perhaps it has to do with the fact that as a child I posed for my father, my smiling face was given to him, but later on it was all for myself (or as a reluctant concession to Martens) that I posed at all. I wished either to remind myself what I looked like at that moment or else was utterly indifferent.

I could not bear any longer to look at those shoe boxes of my past. I could not bear to be reminded of what I had forgotten.

I threw the photographs into the incinerator.


Sometime, a number of years after Simon had given me Clitus, Clitus became ill and died. I don't know how old he was when he died. I had loved Clitus for many summers, taking him in his carrying case to Martha's Vineyard for our holiday, watching him at first timidly and then with increasing confidence marching across the wooden floorboards of my rented cottage, observing his judgments of my guests with astonishment – Clitus always befriended those among them who were allergic to cats. I found his instincts marvelous and his opinions generally correct. One morning, I found him dead. The veterinarian admitted that he had all along known that Clitus had an enlarged heart and would not be long-lived, but he had seen no point in burdening me with the information.

It was several days before I decided what to do with Clitus. I kept him in a shopping bag in the meantime. I couldn't dispose of him in the trash. Returning home several days after his death, I observed a concrete mixer pouring the foundations of a new building on Broadway. That night I carried Clitus in his paper shopping-bag shroud to the excavated hole in which the first levels of concrete were hardening. It wasn't a large building and the night watchman hadn't begun to make his rounds. I climbed over the chain and walked down a narrow path to the first level of the concrete fill and with a wooden spoon opened a small hole in the concrete. I pushed Clitus into the concrete and smoothed over him the grainy syrup of concrete. Clitus glistened in the moonlight. I said nothing over him. I thought about his ginger coat. I remembered his paws upon my thigh. I saw him sleeping while Simon and I made love. I smiled over Clitus. Now, he had a concrete mausoleum, not very different from the ancient pyramid in which he had once slept beside Pharaohs.

When Simon came back from tour the following week, I told him Clitus had died. Simon came over immediately. He was quite right in coming quickly. The death of Clitus was a loss. He offered me another cat. I said, "No, Simon. One husband, one cat." We both laughed, but I'm afraid mine was a wet and miserable laughter.

I don't remember the years anymore. The sixties are over and we are in the seventies. I am in my own sixties. It's enough that the time of the world and my own are correlated.

Betty and Simon are divorced nearly a decade. Simon's boys are grown. One has become a botanist, the other a sound engineer. Simon likes them, somewhat abstractly I think, but then I never had children. I had thought of wanting them – one step removed from desire – but I had never pressed my reflection into need. I never regarded the absence of children as a defect of my nature. The matriarchal principle was alive and well in me without actual maternity. It has been objected by some that I was – given the ostensible rigor of my mind – defectively feminine. But such language tries my patience. Gender was a fact having little to do with programmed desire and instinct. And, for the rest, the feminine principle, the maternal quest, the instinctual passion, the metaphysical subjectivity, the emotionalism, the *Erdmutterprinzip*, was diverting nonsense. For so much of the history of the human race men had been setting the rules of culture; it could not but be that woman was every-thing men desired or feared. Where the fear exceeded imagi-nation, woman became the enemy; where imagination subdued the fear, woman became mysterious, and where woman was left unconstrued – so rarely – she was allowed to invent herself with consequences yet to be specified.

Unfortunately, I was among the construed: my mother feared my father and punished me; my father fabulated me and loved me, untruthfully. I took my leave from them; I did it early and survived the separation. Unlike weaker spirits, I profited from having disliked them. I found myself so early burrowing into other skins and taking up long-term residence. My parents hardly knew where to find me.

I have never thought of Plato as a man. Hence, I never feared him, never feared his mind, never considered myself unequally equipped to cope with his philosophy. Nor did I fear Origen for his castration or St. Francis for his stigmata. All those oddities of the masculine I found *curiosa*, like the masculinity of cats. Did I care that Clitus was a male cat, or should I wonder about the gender of the lion beneath St. Jerome's desk?


I think often (it is always late, when only a few lights still patrol the night in the inner courtyard of this building) of the wrenched partings that have made up my life. In one sense I am blessed for having endured. Such a blessing! Too much cynicism to have believed the lies and, what is more, an almost preternatural sense, bred in me like an unintended growth, to disbelieve first, to deny trust until it had passed its trial, to hold back and resist all covenants of heart and mind. Here, among the American people whose handshakes make bonds, where drinks are deliv-ered around the table as if to plight troths, my point of view is thought merely perverse, often paranoid. But it is nothing more than the spawn of these night reveries – recollection of wrenched partings, unfinished goodbyes, handshakes offered and refused (by myself as much as by others), faces never seen again that pass before my eyes, mute, on parade to their death and to my own.

The amusement of this deepest held conviction – my refusal to give trust easily and the rightness of this refusal – is that I am thought in so many things to be trusting to a fault, to be unconniving, unshrewd, essentially benign in my attitude to the matter-of-fact transactions of everyday life. I believe the superintendent of my building when he promises to examine the fuse box in my apartment; I trust my publisher if he says he will advertise my book; I am only too willing to accept the judgment of some book reviewer that my prose is besotted with German usages. Should I go on with the mundanity of my belief? I believe everything in which I cannot imagine that there is purpose or intelligence to deceit. The lies that follow in the train of such persuasion derive from the fact that my judgment of benignity rests upon the unshaken conviction that human beings ought to have better things to do than lie about their obligations to the real. If they superintend, publish, review, what point is there to obfuscation, to misrepresentation, to untruth?

It baffles me – more than exasperates me – that the superintendent never comes, that I am obliged to search him out and, after pleading and cajolement, take him by the hand and lead him to my fuse box, or that I am compelled to change publishers or to reprimand the critic when I check his attack and find it undeserved.

The great mysteries are the only ones that should call forth human lies, since those mysteries drive us before themselves like chaffed grain, beaten and husked. Why do we lie for other than great deceptions, great misconceptions, great errors? Those alone I can understand, even admire, for they solace the hard way that human beings must take. For them it is better that their lights be lit by others. If not, they would travel in the dark. The great religious lies are not simple lies, designed and ordered to extract some gain from their perversity, but are rather provender for those who cannot supply for themselves, who require the connivance of others, the solidarities of community that they persevere. They are righteous lies. They assert an absolute truth with dire consequences for disbelief, whereas what they afford intelligent persons is a rarefaction of the question, a formulation which sets the juices of the imagination, the warmth of the heart, the rumblings of the mind to movement beyond their habitual confinement.

I will always prefer a lie which drives me forward towards the light than a truth so simple I feel compelled to blink in dumb assent.

I write all the time.

Writing is one reason at least that I've lost interest in events. Events, such as they are, now seem flat and insubstantial, when set beside the pages of a growing manuscript. Does it really matter that I have lunched and dined with philosophers and poets, that my lover is one of the marvelous instrumentalists of his generation, that I receive invitations constantly to teach and lecture? Such a repertoire is invariant. It goes on every day, eating with friends, with a lover, answering correspondence from petitioning faculties and friends. But my manuscript – growing like an unweeded garden – is something very different. Into that enterprise I pour my real life.

What does it mean then for a critic to write in *The American Scholar* that my "philosophy suffers from a surfeit of elegance"?

Those were his words, tossed like a bitter herb into an otherwise edible but unexciting salad of interpretation. I couldn't believe it. It mattered less to me that he got the argument wrong, that he mistook the progression of my mind – its slow movement from subject to subject over the years of my work ("an authentic morphology," he noted) – as somehow compelled by inner necessity rather than by the compulsion of historical events, but to accuse my style (and therefore my mind) of simple elegance struck me as rank philistinism.

The truth is that I understood from where he came: he was a mired academic who dragged his typewriter from the mud each time he was compelled to write. Clearly, he hated writing. Writing was for him the opposite of thought. He could think well (he seemed to be urging and the prose of his last book confirmed my suspicion) if he didn't have to set himself down in formal argument. Give him the pause, the repetition, a finger to lips, the pulled-ear of meditation, give him solecisms, pleonasms, and reformulations, and his students would applaud him as the personification of living thought ("thinking on one's feet" it is called), although my struggle to get it right is all mere elegance.

Jacob must have struggled with the angel the way I did battle with English. My victory was always by nightfall. I won a word, an expression, a new way of tempering the steel of ideas. And not only at the beginning, in the early days when I was trying to move beyond English simplisms to the formulations of complex sentences and the flow of argument.

At the beginning my English was adequate to journalism. I began with a curious fact, an odd occurrence, a riveting quotation, and proceeded from there to turn a simple point. It was possible in short-distance journalism, where fifteen hundred words was all I got. I matched the complexity of the issue to the brevity of my space. I managed by recognizing early that the principal difficulty of German syntax had no analogue in English. The endless tension of the relative clause, where qualifying modulation ran breathlessly between subject and verb, could never make good English. English could flow and eddy, dispensing with punctuation if one wanted a breathing prose, or else strapped with rules like a chastity belt, compelling the suppression of language lust. English thrived on the motility of things, while German registered shades and tonalities of complex ideas so subtly nuanced that one suspected only the ears of dogs could catch them. And I – German by childhood and indenture and American by exile and election – was pressed to bring their respective strengths to some kind of reconciliation. How I struggled! If Jacob bore the scar of his victory, so did my prose.

I, who had to master a new language in my adulthood, who suffered torment every time I had to write for my fortnightly (but did nonetheless week after week because I had to earn a living) and, in the course of the doing, forged for myself the weapon of a style, I was to be punished for fluency, for elegance even.

Son of a bitch!


*Abominations* is out.

The reaction has been astonishing, lifted by the requirements of my notoriety and the winds of enmity to a downpour of exaggerated partisanship and anger.

What have I done? My publisher thought the time had come to gather me up. I went through scores of essays written over the years and found that they broke unevenly into analytical crotchets and peeves (some twenty-two) and a later volume of *Celebrations* (about fifteen) to appear next year. Most are short breath essays, expressions of scourge and delight, written generally in response to single works, but others – longer and fuller investigations – are the outcroppings of my mind, the sheer edge of speculation where only mountain goats of some intrepidity (or stupidity) would dare to follow me. There's no particular need to rehearse here the contents of this book (or the one to come). Anyone reading this memoir will be able to clench a fist of either. My reason for even noting the appearance of *Abominations* is that it was greeted by a sufficient number of furious reviews – "Abominable Abominations" or "A Plague on Both Houses" or "Off with Their Heads" – as to suggest that all along I have been at odds with received opinion. It doesn't puzzle me, this apparent dislocation. Quite the contrary! I have understood that if you do what I do, being out of step, unsynchronized, is unavoidable. But what is it that I've done?

The German expression is *selbstdenken*, which I freely and frequently adapt from Lessing who was, like myself, very often out of step. But I suppose what it really means is that I have always worked from the inside out. It could not be otherwise. Freedom is such a monstrous undertaking – a true monster (that is, almost grotesque and still supernally human) – that anyone who stakes the whole of her spirit upon the project of being free is destined to terrify.

Quite simply: I know I terrify. I want to hold back. I so want to restrain myself, to be moderate, to be tender and loving. And I can't quite manage it. At the very least I blurt out what I really think. I point the moral. I become enraged. It isn't for show that I do this. I am actually a poor performer; the angrier I become, the more my language rushes, the more incontinent and imprudent my speech. So, obviously, I am not scored highly for tact. I have too little wit to bring it off. I have nothing in me that enables me to mock. Instead, I scorn. I strive for irony, the grace note of clever times; instead, my foot ends planted on the neck. I go with a short sword for the heart. It's too serious a business to be merely deft. When I want to kill, I want to kill. And when it's all done – whether my subject is abominated or celebrated – I have left behind a bloody trail.

Luncheon yesterday with an American novelist whom I met after a talk at the University of Rochester. He was their resident writer. (American literature is a diamond solitaire – every university keeps one stone in its vault.) He was terribly intelligent. I had read only one story of his, which I thought splendid, but my judgment of contemporary fiction is worthless. I don't know how it's made, so I can't estimate its value.

The conversation was agreeable, gossip mostly (which I enjoy, but to which I had hardly a morsel to contribute).

My novelist friend began to extol Solzhenitsyn's *First Circle*. I discerned a note of envy.

"You seem, my friend – the way you're speaking – to envy Solzhenitsyn his years in the Gulag. Is it that you'd like to be persecuted?"

He was rushing on, detailing the pressure he felt in Solzhenitsyn's prose. I had interrupted; he fell silent. "Does it sound that way? Envying him?"

"Yes. I thought so."

"Perhaps I do."

"But what does persecution add to the power of language?"

"The certainty of its power. If it weren't powerful, who would bother to repress it?"

"Do you think American novelists are powerless? No. Let me put it another way. Do you think the American word is powerless? Or that the power of the word is improved if the speaker is cast as an enemy of society?"

"I am saying that, aren't I?"

"And, tell me, what kind of persecution would you like?"

He temporized. He felt the line was baited with poison, but he was still tempted to swallow it. "Oh, I don't know. Denunciation, attack, interrogation, arrest."

"In other words, abuse without pain." He reddened. He had swallowed the bait. "But don't you know the old order is over? It isn't done without pain anymore. Suppression of books? Denunciation? Even arrest and interrogation? Child's play. Unexceptionable in the Soviet Union. Done all the time, every day. But persecution, my friend, that's something different. Its purpose is to drive you to death. Not necessarily to kill you – shoot you, gas you. That's not for poets and writers. No. No. The real purpose is to drive you beyond your wits, to drive you beyond health and sanity. To force you to *agree* to die. If you give in, they bury you quietly or return you to society cured of speech. You envy *that*?"

The other side of the argument, the undisclosed side, is no less interesting. What my novelist friend was also saying was that he wrote for an American constituency that didn't give a damn. That was another problem. But that was always true in America. It hasn't changed over the years. But it also hasn't prevented this country from producing masterpieces.


Summer is coming again.

I no longer want to go to the Vineyard. Packing myself up is always a trial – selecting summer clothes, deciding whether I will swim this year, settling upon walking shoes, contemplating sneakers at my age. During recent years I cut back on my time there. True, I maintained a lively interest in American politics, but could hardly bring myself to attend political gatherings. I couldn't bear any longer the aging frontiersmen of American liberalism. I knew them all, but they realized they had nothing to say to me, although they had everything to learn if you could only get them to sit still. So I keep my stay up there to three weeks. I take a cottage for a month and leave when I'm wrung dry. I get bored out of my mind. I really have nothing in common with most of the summer regulars and at seventy I wouldn't be much good at tennis.

Simon usually comes up for part of my vacation. For several weeks we enjoy ourselves, walking the beach, taking drives, but when excessive sociality begins to wear us down, we return to the mainland and go into hiding. Whenever that happens, I know the time has come to flee back to the City. The very idea of having to flee from one's vacation!

This summer, I doubt I will go away. I'll stay in the apartment and turn on the air conditioner. I turn off the telephone in the City when I go to the Vineyard. This year, I'll stay in the City and turn off the telephone. The operator says unfailingly that my line is temporarily disconnected. (I have checked on this.) Callers assume that I'm still at the Vineyard. In fact, I am in New York, on my bed, consuming cold milk and iced chocolate cookies; I read incredibly long books, wonderful books, books of such scale and monumentality that only by reading them prone, in bed with cookies and milk, the air conditioner whirring in my cocoon of silence, is it possible. I read Braudel's history of the Mediterranean in three days, four books by Elias Canetti (with note-taking) in five, and Proust in ten days. I savored Proust and I read slowly as I knew this reading would have to do for eternity. That realization almost prevented me from rereading it. I had begun to do things for the last time.

Someone has rung my bell. It is summer. The phone is off. No one but Simon knows I'm here, but someone has rung my bell.

▼          ▼          ▼

A telegram was delivered from the German Consulate in New York.

I have been invited by the Free University of Berlin to accept an award of the University, to be installed as an honorary doctor, to be fêted by its faculties and students, to be received by Berlin's Mayor, and toured through its institutions. I am to be made, it seems, an honorary German.

The award I am asked to accept bears the legend "in recognition of life achievement in the human sciences." It is named after Alexander and Wilhelm von Humboldt, two Berliners I knew well from Henriette's reading circle. How life comes full circle, seeking Paradise through the back door.

Wilhelm von Humboldt wrote once to his wife Caroline (for whom Jews were anathema) that "Alexander and I, while still children, were regarded as the bulwark of Judaism." An astonishing statement in itself, don't you think? Caroline, however, accounted that childish affection as the single fault she could discover in her estimable husband. For her part, she would have had the Jews destroyed by denying them access to a living and conscripting all their sons into the army. The Humboldts are taken as friends of the Jews. They argued for our emancipation; they lobbied mightily to set us free. And they were joined by many of the most celebrated German humanist intellectuals. Only a hundred and fifty years ago. A bit more, but not much. They were opposed, of course, by no less mighty minds. Why list our friends and enemies? They are frequently indistinguishable.

I read the telegram over and over. I would have wished for any award but the Humboldt Prize from Berlin and on Berlin's behalf. Even old Martens, who somehow never left Berlin, would have been startled and uncertain. There is really no one to ask for help.

The following week I received further telegrams from the

Consulate urging me to decide, but each time I replied with excuses and begged for more time. It was not something into which I could be pressured. The Consul mentioned a bursary of 50,000 DM which accompanied the Prize. I replied, "That's nice."

My God, we live in improper times. I don't know how it's managed. It seems to me such a madness that these people should want to bestow upon me the benefice of their humanism. But then again, from another point of view, correctly estimating the bourgeois ground of both their cruelty and their honor, it is all of a seamless piece. They move in a dream from which they have yet to awake: for them their worst is aberration and ill fortune; their best, genius. There's no explaining. What I must do is keep my grip upon silence.


A metallic sky, burned white by a September heat, buffed and burnished by a hazed and dying sun, covered Berlin when the plane arrived from Frankfurt.

I had thought to go to my hotel and rest. I knew they would find me soon enough. But I had not anticipated a press conference. I did not think my coming that important to them. But when I left the plane cameras began to snap and voices, calling to me in German, directed my movements.

The press conference was held in a small room at the airport. It was attended by the Minister of Culture and the Rector of the University. I was asked how it felt to be back in Germany. I replied that I had no impressions. And feelings, if not impressions? Numb, I answered. And then my history. Briefly. I kept close to the facts. My German was colorless and without passion. I wanted to disappoint the journalists. I succeeded. My picture, with the briefest of captions, was all that appeared in the newspapers the following morning.

I was received by the Mayor of Berlin. He asked me where I had lived in Berlin. In my parents' home in Charlottenburg. Does the house still stand? It didn't. I was relieved. And my own little apartment after I left home was now in East Berlin. Did I wish to see East Berlin? No. I did not. Was I pleased to be in Berlin? I stripped pleasure from my reply.

I maintained throughout, every minute, alertness and the most intense curiosity. I noticed everything. I was looking for clues, details, tiny details. I wanted to take the bus, but I was not permitted. I could not escape limousines and deputations. I was taken everywhere by car.

The celebration of my investiture with the Humboldt Prize and my honorary doctorate took place on Thursday evening. It was an immense audience, overflowing the auditorium of the University. The speech of the University Rector was filled with factual narration of the power of my books, linking their learning and their "restless pursuit of truth" (as he put it) to the courageous forthrightness of the Humboldts, on whose historic shades the original medal would have been bestowed.

I had written something very short, terribly short. They wanted to print my remarks in a special commemorative pamphlet. I am certain my remarks were too short. I doubt the pamphlet will appear.

I rose from my velvet-backed gold-gilded chair and moved towards the dais. I bowed my head slightly; the ribbon was placed over my head, the gold medallion lodged between my breasts. My single sheet of paper – neatly written on both sides – was unfolded. The actual text is of no significance. I spoke of the gratuitousness of prizes, their inability to effect a profound connection between their historical assumptions and the present occasion of their bestowal. (It was at best an artful way of disclaiming affection for the von Humboldts.) I passed on to the commonplace notion of the weightiness of history, its burden, its heaviness, the presumption of its conferred responsibility, and I commented that I thought our history not heavy but light. I defended this unconventional view of the weight of history by reference to the idea of historical gravity (my own text again): if history were truly heavy, I suggested, its gravity would have forbidden my presence – both my survival and my selection. It may well be the case, I speculated, that history's lightness, its ability to slip through the mesh of memory, its refusal to be settled and pinned, is the ultimate grace forgetfulness bestows upon us. I reversed all categories, you see; I refused the pious solemnities of my life's disciplines. And I praised the grace of forgetfulness. What I celebrated by this reversal was the delicacy and fragility of the human. We are so easily slain, I continued, so very easy to kill. And not alone perishable in the flesh, but in the mind and in the spirit. I concluded: "What we remember is so little, so terribly little of what we have had to endure. True for the living. True also for the dead. Some will think us cursed for forgetfulness. I think us blessed."

I do not know if my sadness moved the audience. I do not know for certain, but I was struck by the comparative absence of applause. The immense audience rose after my speech. Some nodded towards me. Older people in the front row applauded politely; their faces appeared grey in the dim light. The younger people, mostly students at the University, were generally silent. At last my words had received silence. Stunned with incomprehension? I don't think so. Not this time.


The following day I took the limousine to Sachsenhausen, passing by necessity through East Berlin. (The driver was over sixty and seemed grim as we approached.) The house where my parents had lived their married life was gone, but the house where they died remained. I visited their blockhouse and walked

through the neatly planted memorial garden. A representative
of the Jewish community of Berlin had accompanied me. I hardly
spoke with him. I could not understand why he lived in Berlin.
Germany should be Jew-free. But Herr Katzenbogen helped me
say Kaddish for my parents and uncle Salomon. I was struck
again, as I had been many, many years before, that the commemorative prayer for the dead was an adulation of the immense
holiness of God, never mentioning the dead for whose dying it
is spoken.

The weight of history, shifted from our shoulders, shatters
and breaks as it falls. What remains is the lightness of man and
the immensity of God.

When I returned to New York, I gave away the prize money.
The medallion, bearing the busts of the Humboldt brothers, I
hung around the neck of a plaster cast of Marcus Aurelius
Martens had saved many years earlier from the basement of the
Institute where it was about to be thrown away. "A late eighteenth-century plaster copy without value," the Institute's cu-
rator had said. Martens replied: "True, but still Marcus Aurelius,"
wrapping it carefully in brown paper.

So much seems completed now. So many whorls of time doubling
and redoubling, returning to view, recapitulating themselves,
asserting their presence with finality of form.

Each day I work on my books, but now I no longer bother
myself with finishing them. If *The Descent into Consciousness*,
a book I began shortly after the discovery of my text, remains
unfinished, no matter.

I arise in the morning, grateful for the day, and I drink my
coffee, reading slowly until noon; in the afternoons I write,

foregoing the typewriter for I have no further need of speed.
In the evenings, my friend Simon – he is himself, *mirabile*,
nearly seventy – takes me to a concert and we sit quietly
over supper, or I go out to dinner with friends and delight as
they argue over names I do not know (new names, fresh voices,
young texts that have not weathered). I allow no one to accompany me home, but I don't mind if someone sees me to
a taxicab.

As far as I have come from the home of my parents, I am still
tied to their memory.

Big history is only the vast construction that has grown from
simple beginnings, enraged in my parents' house. And isn't it
always so? If we tell the truth to ourselves, what we plan, vast
and encompassing as it may seem, reduces itself to the modest
filaments of our beginnings. What is given there – however
shallow its impression – remains throughout a lifetime, and what
is absent from the original impression remains absent for most
of us throughout our lives. It is such a sadness to understand
this mystery of beginnings – all that struggle, all that energy of
fight directed against such lightweight opposition, inflated by
the disproportions of childhood to monumental scale. And even
at the last, after seventy years of battle, when the lines are
drawn, the child goes to seek the grave of her murdered parents,
a grave at which, had it stood in pompous rigidity in a proper
burial ground, would have been disdained; but nameless and
unknown, set down in a mythic spot of earth, judged by the
weightless memory of us all, I feel compelled to say a prayer I
had hardly – until then – knew I knew and loved. In the end,
am I drawn to them and to this prayer, to their memory and the
memory of the God they and I had hardly heard, by a bonding
of myself to some fragile Jewish past? I cannot say for sure.

Now, however, having stood upon the earth that echoed their last footsteps, I find myself recovering something within me to link to something within them that was unknown to them and to me: the fatalities and destinies that are called Jew.

You will note that throughout these pages I have taken stands of rage against fragments of both the hatred and the hated, detailing my disgust with Gentile attention and Jewish servility. In those passages I was young and embattled, drawing fierce distinctions, sustaining the shifting ground of my right to be individual and alone. I do not reject those passages, nor lay upon them the gnarled hand of late-won wisdom. The integrity that I seek for myself is not linear. I have no wish to be all of a narrative piece that stretches from birth to death, but rather to be whole at each moment – whole child, whole woman, whole old woman before her death. I want each moment intact before what I am then, but not for all time and not forever, beginning to end. Such wholeness is the fabrication of interpreters who must make of me a unitary integer in order to enhance their role as my discoverer. The curse of biography!

For me, it is all different now. I can take new stands and still not be apart from myself. I never gave myself over to my people and I have not been a good daughter of Israel. I did not grow up to a right marriage and to children. I am not known throughout the world for my acts of charity and my good deeds. Have I then failed the Jews as well? I believe not. I have loved very few people and I have trusted fewer still, but I have given everything I knew to give – in my ignorance of so many things – to be in step with who I took myself to be, a woman who tried always to be in truth. It would follow from this that I have been a pain in the neck so often, but with all that abrasiveness I have never had to accuse myself of lying. Others have thought I lied. Perhaps I did, but it was a lie so well contrived it did not hook my conscience in swallowing it. Others have thought me insensitive, harsh even, and I could not begin to explain myself to them without unravelling everything I am.

So I have not been a loyal Jew, but then I have been loyal to nothing but what I took to be my own right way. Could I have had it otherwise, since the case I made was not argued from private grounds but from the authorization of public texts and universal documents of the race? I have given no consistent pleasure to my natal people and I am not regularly claimed by them among its outstanding children. From time to time I am rehabilitated, my arguments being set alongside traditional proof texts I hardly knew. And then, rehabilitated at last, I am once again reviled and cast out. It should be this way – my Jewish people always nervously sifting through credentials, sifting through themselves. Better this way – endlessly examining their sources than being suddenly born again and dying no less inexorably, with *nothing* bequeathed to historical memory.

I am delighted it is understood I have no place, no earth of my own, though I do not deny to those who need an earth their right to claim it. It is only that I remain who I was born, a pariah out of Charlottenburg, a person who carves out territory in the sky and ties her soul with cords braided of the wind and stars and almost forgotten texts.


My life in the mind is almost done.

So much winter, withdrawn to an interior hearth where even though fires burned continuously I was surrounded by chill. The cold stays without, shut doors and sealed windows bar its entry, but the otherness of that outside world and the solipsism of interior warmth make for small comfort. My life in the mind has not been all joy. Would that I had chosen long ago to stand the cold, to risk snow, to try my foot on icy paths, daring even to slip into a visible crevasse, rather than staying within, loyal to my own fire. But such a life of active enterprise is a wholly different way. All my significant decisions (my acts of will as I have called them) – exile, rejection, my womanish vanity, my habits of mind, all the event and equipment of my life – have been the consequence of election and free choice, all intelligent making and delight. Not that I would now – at the dawning end – have had it otherwise. The only freedom I regard now (at the dawning end) is to accept what has been. Along the way I might have imagined (as I did ferociously, supporting the projects of my fantasy with arguments of philosophy) that all was free, that intelligence, will, judgment – the educated faculties of our cunning – were free, since I had stripped from them their traces of inevitability.

But now, as the crepuscular days slide slowly toward what is inevitable and never free, I have come to say of what has been, I embrace all of you. So much for necessity. So much for freedom.

These last words I have dictated to my friend Simon who sits at my bedside until I fall asleep.

I entered the hospital suddenly. My doctor had followed the course of my X-rays, deciding this morning that the time had come for surgery. Only now has my tumor shown itself. There is no certainty I will survive much longer. He assures me that he has caught it early, but I remember those earlier infections and congestions. I have no knowledge of these things, although I question specialists of other disciplines with the same sceptical energy as I question experts of my own. But it must be. The doctor showed me the shadow, diligently tracing its minuscule dimension on the enlargement. I acceded. Simon came to the apartment and we packed together. He was terribly grim. I was ridiculously calm. With terror I am calm, going about everything with exaggerated care. The manuscript of the memoirs, the biography of Henriette Herz, my other papers are arranged for Cynthia who takes the task of my executor.

Whether I survive or not, I have come to a fuller age than many of my generation. It's not so terrible to die in one's seventies. What more would I have before me than to continue in the same way? Most others, excepting Simon, are growing tired of my steadfastness.

Simon, dearest beloved, forgive me my obstinacy. And should I die now, don't remember me better than I am. As I am is all I tried to be; it's quite enough, I think, for memory.

## AN ADMIRABLE WOMAN
▾

was set by NK Graphics, Keene, New Hampshire, in Bodoni Book, a face named after Giambattista Bodoni (1740–1813), the son of a Piedmontese printer. After gaining renown and experience as superintendent of the Press of Propaganda in Rome, Bodoni became head of the ducal printing house of Parma in 1768. A great innovator in type design, his faces are known for their openness and delicacy.

The display is set in Weiss Initials.

The book was printed and bound by Haddon Craftsmen, Scranton, Pennsylvania. The paper is Warren's #66 Antique.

Book design by Janis Capone.